23 Cold Cases

Also by Patrick C. Walsh

The Mac Maguire detective mysteries

The Body in the Boot

The Dead Squirrel

The Weeping Women

The Blackness

Two Dogs

The Match of the Day Murders

The Chancer

The Tiger's Back

The Eight Bench Walk

Stories of the supernatural

13 Ghosts of Winter

The Black Vaults Experiment

All available in Amazon Books

Patrick C. Walsh

23 Cold Cases

The fifth 'Mac' Maguire mystery

Garden City Ink

A Garden City Ink ebook
www.gardencityink.com

First published in Great Britain in 2017
All rights reserved
Copyright © 2017, 2020 Patrick C. Walsh

A CIP record for this title is available from the British Library

ISBN 9781985129771

Cover art © Seamus McGuire 2017
Garden City Ink Design

"The secret of being miserable is to have leisure to bother about whether you are happy or not. The cure for it is occupation."
George Bernard Shaw

For the one and only Walter Spencer

Two weeks before

He was suddenly awake and the dream was still freshly imprinted on his mind. He sat up and looked at the other side of the bed. There was no-one there and, for once, he was grateful for that.

He stood up, opened the curtains and looked out of his hotel window. Skyscrapers surrounded him and for a few seconds he had no idea where he was. He saw a huge Ferris wheel and he thought he must be in London but, if he was, he had no idea what he was doing there. Then he remembered. He was in Singapore, yes of course, they were shooting the car chase scenes tomorrow.

He looked down at his hands and expected to see blood on them, her blood. His hands were spotlessly clean but he knew the blood was there anyway. He hadn't thought about her for quite a while so why now?

In the dream he had been with her. She had been so beautiful and so real, so real that he still had the smell of her body in his nostrils.

Even after all these years he realised that he still loved her and the pain he felt was almost physical.

Why now though? he thought.

He had a sort of premonition. It was all going to come back to haunt him somehow but he found that he didn't care.

Perhaps it would be a relief.

Chapter One

Each tiny crack in the ceiling was becoming familiar now. Mac had a pile of books within reaching distance, books he'd promised himself that he'd read when he had the chance but he made no move towards them.

He sighed at the realisation that he was bored rigid and he knew that he needed something more than books to take his mind off his current predicament. In something close to desperation, he picked up his phone and called Detective Superintendent Dan Carter to ask for a favour.

The predicament in question was an enforced six week stretch of bed rest after Mac had sustained some damage to his back in what the tabloid press had dubbed 'The Girl in the Cellar' case.

'It's just soft tissue damage,' his doctor had told him but, whatever it was, it hurt like hell.

His daughter had bought books for him to read and she'd also suggested that he might want to start writing his memoirs. However, he found that, even with the best will in the world, he just wasn't interested. In order to push back the pain, he had to be doing something, something real.

The 'favour' arrived an hour or so after his call. A uniformed policeman delivered a memory stick with the complete files of twenty-three cold cases going back some fifteen years. He gratefully plugged it into his laptop. After a few minutes he began to get absorbed in the files and the pain started to tune out a little.

Eventually he made the mistake of moving and red-hot spears of pain radiated out from his lower back. He couldn't stop himself from letting out a loud grunt. A second later the door opened and his new nurse hurried in.

'Are you alright, Mr. Maguire?' she asked with some concern.

He had to wait a few seconds before he could speak.

'You know that's the really strange thing about pain?' he eventually gasped. 'I've lived with it for years now yet it always comes as a surprise. God you were quick! Were you waiting outside the door or something?'

His nurse nodded.

'I didn't want to interrupt you. I had a peek in the door a while back and, you seemed so interested in what you were doing, that I thought you were best left alone for a while.'

Mac looked at her closely. She was in her fifties and had a kind face, a face that Mac had immediately warmed to. She had jet black hair with no traces of grey and she was wearing a bright blue sari with a lighter blue scarf around her neck. She wore sandals that were decorated with bright stones that glinted when she walked. Nurse Amrit had worked with his daughter Bridget when she was training to become a doctor and she had come highly recommended. This was another reason why Mac thought that they would get on.

'Nurse Amrit, please sit down and talk to me for a bit,' he said waving towards the armchair.

'Oh, please just call me Amrit. After all, I'm not a nurse anymore.'

'And please call me Mac. When anyone calls me Mr. Maguire I still look around for my dad. Okay, as this is our first day together, I was just wondering if there was anything that you wanted to know about me?'

She thought for a moment and then smiled.

'Bridget told me that you're a private detective these days. What's it really like?'

'I take it that you're a fan then?'

'Oh yes, I watch all the shows on TV,' she said excitedly.

'They run around a lot on the TV, don't they?' Mac said with a frown. 'Well, I'm not exactly up for much of that these days so I'd guess it would be quite different. Then again, I've only worked on a handful of cases so far and most of those were helping the police. So, if I'm being honest, I'm not really sure what being a private detective is like yet.'

'Not as exciting as on the TV then,' she said looking a little crestfallen.

'No probably not. For me it's more about thinking your way through a case than physical action but I find it exciting enough, especially when you begin to sense that you're on the right track and things start falling into place. That's always quite exhilarating. I guess that it wouldn't make for good TV though.'

'From what I read in the papers your last case was exciting enough though. You saving that poor girl from hanging herself and all.'

'A little too exciting as you can see,' Mac said with a frown. 'Anyway, it wasn't just me who saved her. I never liked all that 'hero' nonsense in the press, in reality it's always a team effort.'

'What was it like?' Amrit asked with wide eyes. 'You know when you saved her?'

Mac thought back to those excruciating few minutes when his already crippled back had to bear the weight of a whole other person. Before he went unconscious, the pain had been the worst he'd ever experienced. Then he woke up in the hospital to find that it was still there, sharp-toothed and waiting to greet him.

While he lay there and, as the hours and days inched by, it had slowly dawned on him that, for all the doctors and their fine words, for all the drugs and flashing machines they had in that bright shiny hospital, they really couldn't do much to help him. At the end of the day it was just him and the pain and that was the thought that scared him the most. He knew that he'd

4

never be able to go through anything like that again. He could only comfort himself that, if it did ever happen again, he had the solution tucked away at the back of his sock drawer.

'Desperate,' he said tersely as he tried to push the dark thoughts back.

Amrit had the feeling that she'd overstepped the mark. She got up to go. Mac looked up at the movement and managed a smile.

'I'm sorry, don't go. I was in a bit of a dark place just now, that's all.'

Amrit sat back down.

'No, that's okay. It's me who should be saying sorry. Life's not really like the TV at all, is it?'

'No, no it isn't.'

Amrit decided to change the subject.

'Do you mind me asking what you're working on now? As a policeman brought it then I take it that its crime related?'

'Yes, it's definitely crime related,' Mac replied. 'I must admit that, although it's only my first day at home, I was already more than a bit fed up. I've got plenty to read as you can see but I did enough of that in hospital and it didn't work all that well anyway.'

'Work? What do you mean?'

'I need something that I can lose myself in other-wise...well, otherwise I really don't think I'm going to be able to cope.'

'Oh, I see,' Amrit said with a smile. 'You're talking about pain management, aren't you?'

'Spot on,' Mac said returning her smile. 'Anyway, I rang the head of the local Police Major Crime Unit and asked if there was anything I could help with and luckily for me there was. He's sent over a load of cold cases for me to have a look at.'

'Cold cases? Yes, I've heard that phrase on the TV.'

'They're just old cases that haven't been solved yet. We never close most cases as such, we just park them. Although sometimes that turns out to be pretty much the same thing.'

'And these cold cases will help you?' Amrit asked. 'With the pain I mean.'

'Oh, most definitely. If all I have to do is to stare at the ceiling it'll only magnify the pain. Work is the best painkiller.'

'Yes, I know. Did Bridget tell you that I used to work in a pain clinic? I always found that the patients who managed their pain the best were the ones who kept themselves busy. Tell me have you tried acupuncture yet?'

'Acupuncture? No, I haven't,' Mac said his face clearly showed his scepticism. 'I always thought that having someone stick needles in you would be painful enough by itself. I can't see how that would help at all.'

'You should try it though. One big advantage of acupuncture is that there are no side effects like you get with a lot of pain medication. It doesn't work for everyone but, for those it does help, it can really make a real difference.'

'I'll think about it,' Mac said firmly parking the question. 'Do you mind if I ask you something?'

She shrugged.

'No, go ahead.'

'Where are you from originally?'

Mac could sense that her defences had gone up.

'Why would you want to know that?' she asked.

'I'm just curious.'

She thought for a moment and then gave him the benefit of the doubt.

'Okay, I was born in India and I came to this country when I was two years old.'

'I was one when I came here,' Mac said.

'Really, you're an immigrant like me?' she asked with a surprised look on her face. 'Where did you come from originally then?'

'From Ireland. My mum and dad came over in the early sixties when there was lots of work here in the car factories. There was nothing in Ireland at the time.'

'Yes, your accent, it's from the Midlands, isn't it?'

'Yes, it's from Birmingham. Although I've lived here in Letchworth for well over twenty-five years, it doesn't seem to have had much effect on my vowels,' he said with a wry smile.

'I like the accent. It sounds unpretentious and honest,' Amrit said.

'I must admit that moving here was the best thing I ever did though. My wife loved it here too. What about you?'

'Oh, I love it here too. I was brought up in Letchworth and when I go and visit relatives in places like Luton or Watford, I always feel a bit sorry for them. I mean Letchworth is such a lovely place, isn't it?'

'It is but, like most other places, it can have its dark side too,' Mac said.

Amrit looked at her watch.

'Anyway, it's nearly twelve thirty now. What would you like for lunch? Bridget's made sure that you've got lots of food in the fridge.'

'I don't know. What are you having?' Mac asked.

'Me? I'm okay, I brought my own,' Amrit replied.

'And what's that then?' he persisted.

'Just some Tarka Dal and rotis, that's all.'

'Tarka Dal and rotis?' Mac said his mouth already salivating.

'Do you like Sikh food?' Amrit asked with some surprise.

'No,' Mac replied. 'I love it. Is there enough for two?'

'Of course,' she replied with a wide smile. 'I was fairly sure that you wouldn't want any but I did a little more just in case. I'll get it started then.'

Chapter Two

'I take it that you're finished then?' Amrit asked as she looked at his empty plate and a bowl wiped clean.

'That was wonderful,' Mac replied with real sincerity. 'Can you bring some more tomorrow?'

'Yes of course, no problem. So tell me, how are your cold cases coming along?'

'I've skim read a few and they should definitely keep me busy for quite a while but I've only looked at the one case in any depth so far. To be honest, I'm not sure what I make of it yet. Are you busy right now?'

'No, of course not,' Amrit replied. 'I'm here for anything you need.'

'Well, what I need right now is someone to bounce things off,' Mac said.

'Bounce things off?' she asked with a puzzled expression.

'Yes, I always find it easier to talk through the cases with someone else. I often get ideas that way.'

'You want to talk through your cold cases with me?' she asked looking surprised.

'Yes, why not?'

'Well, I'm not in the police or anything.'

'But you are a nurse and I'd guess you've had to keep lots of things confidential that you've come across in your working life?' Mac asked.

'Of course. Why would you even ask?' she said looking slightly affronted.

'So, just a few more things for you to keep confidential then.'

She thought on this for a few moments and then gave Mac a quizzical look.

'So, you're really going to discuss your cases with me?'

'Yes, really.'

'Oh goody!' she said with an excited smile. 'Just let me sit down and get comfortable.'

'Okay, the first case. Alex Paterson was a forty-five year old male, a refuse collection driver who lived in an ex-council house just off Shephall Way in Stevenage. He was single at the time having split up with his partner of fifteen years some five years before. There were no children and the break-up was fairly amicable or so it says here.'

'Do you doubt that it was amicable then?' Amrit asked.

'I've always found it best to. I've come across very few partings of the way where there hasn't been at least some resentment on one side. Unfortunately, his ex-partner had a really good alibi. She was two thousand miles away at the time, sunbathing on a Mediterranean beach.'

'So, how was he killed then?' Amrit asked. 'Was it a gun, a knife or poison?'

'No, none of those. He was run over.'

Amrit gave Mac a puzzled look.

'He was just run over?'

'Yes.'

'Well, couldn't it have been as accident then?'

'Not according to the investigators,' Mac replied. 'They were pretty sure that it was murder. From what they'd learned, Mr. Paterson's life ran pretty much like clockwork. He started work early in the morning and finished early in the afternoon. After that he would shower and change and go to his local pub where he'd drink more than he probably should. Even so, he always left the pub no later than nine as he had to get up early the next morning and he always took the same route home. It was a walk of around seven or eight minutes which took him across one main road. So, regular as clockwork, at just after nine in the evening he crossed the main road using the same pedestrian crossing. On this particular occasion three witnesses saw a car driving in his direction but rather than slowing down it speeded up. Mr. Paterson was on the crossing when the car swerved across the carriageway and hit him square on at over fifty miles an hour. The car didn't stop.'

'So, it definitely looks like murder then?' Amrit asked.

'Yes, but if it was murder the big problem is the motive. The investigators never found any credible reason why someone might want to kill that particular dustman. As he was a driver he rarely came into contact with his customers and he seemed to be well liked at his local pub. I've checked his run but it was nothing out of the ordinary.'

'What do you mean 'his run'?' Amrit asked.

'You know, the areas that he picked up rubbish from,' Mac replied.

'Why would that be important?'

'I suppose it's because of a case we had some years ago where another dustman was murdered.'

'Can you tell me about it?' Amrit asked with an expectant smile.

'Sure, why not?' Mac replied. 'We've got plenty of time, six weeks of it in fact. I won't divulge the victim's real name so just treat this as a story that I'm telling you.'

Amrit sat back and waited with anticipation for the story to be told.

'I suppose it was around seven or eight years ago now when the body of a man was found in an alleyway that ran along the back of one of the big hotels in Central London. A member of the hotel kitchen staff had gone out for a cigarette when he noticed the body. It had been dumped on top of a pile of black plastic refuse bags and, seemingly, no attempt had been made to hide it. The hotel called us immediately. It was the body of a man in his late thirties. He was muscular and had lots of tattoos. We identified him by the contents of his wallet which also contained a debit card, a credit card and eighty pounds in cash so robbery as a motive seemed unlikely. Forensics concluded that it was murder. It wasn't a hard call really as he had four bullets in him, two in the heart and two in the head.'

'Oh, it was a contract killing then?' Amrit asked her eyes widening.

Mac smiled.

'Yes, that's more or less what we thought too. To me it looked as if whoever had done it was almost trying to advertise the fact. Placing the body where it was sure to be found fairly quickly, and the professional manner of the killing, made it seem like it was some sort of warning. But who was the warning meant for and why? We wouldn't have been surprised if the tattooed man turned out to be a minor gangster of some sort but we were all a bit flummoxed when it turned out that he was a dustman. We investigated his immediate family and friends first and found nothing, not even the faintest motive for murder. They were all from the Paddington area and, while some were a bit shady, they didn't look like the type of people who would be up for using guns. Anyway, Mr. Binman, not his real name of course, seemed to be generally well liked and liberal with his money. Eventually, we had to look elsewhere and it was the money that gave us our first clue. There was just too much of it. Some of it was in his bank but, when we searched his house, we found over twenty-five thousand pounds in notes hidden under the mattress.'

'Under the mattress? It's not exactly the last place you'd look is it?' Amrit commented.

'Well, I guess his wife wasn't the brightest as she seemed as surprised as we were when we found it. Anyway, we felt that, if we could find out where the money came from, then it might get us a bit closer to identifying a motive for the murder. We decided to look at his job next and we interviewed all of the bin crew he worked with except for one who had gone missing. They all seemed as baffled as we were as to why anyone would want to kill their driver. As they all seemed quite genuine then our next job was to find the missing member of the bin crew. He wasn't at home so we had to spread our net a bit wider and we eventually found him at his younger sister's house. He was hiding under the bed.'

'He was under the bed! Really?' Amrit asked in some disbelief.

'Yes, it sounds daft I know but, sometimes, people are just daft. Anyway, we questioned the missing member of the bin crew and discovered what it had all been about. Mr. Binman and he had been running a little scam for some years. Part of their round covered one of the most expensive parts of London, an area where only the very richest lived, and that's how they made their money. They sold what they collected.'

'They sold rubbish?' Amrit asked her face crinkling in puzzlement.

'Yes, literally,' Mac replied. 'It's really amazing what you can learn from a person's rubbish bin. It's often one of the first things we look at if we want to know more about a person. It's not only food that gets thrown away although that can tell you a lot by itself.'

'How?' Amrit asked.

'Well, for a start it can usually tell you how many people are in the house, their ages and where they're from.'

Amrit gave it some thought.

'Yes, I guess that the number of people might be easy to guess. Then the remains of burgers and chips and takeaway cartons might hint at their age and, if it's a particular type of food, then that might tell you where the people are from.'

'That's right and besides that private papers, draft contracts, letters, even financial ones believe it or not, can all make it into the rubbish. People also regularly throw out clothes labels, receipts and tickets stubs so you can even tell what they've bought and where they've been.'

'Ah I see! They were selling the rubbish to newspaper reporters,' Amrit said excitedly.

'For the most part yes,' Mac replied, 'but recently they'd taken on a new contract as it were. They had no idea who they were dealing with but the money was really good and so they took it. They were given an address but neither of them had any idea who lived there. They just took the rubbish and placed it in a certain bin in an alley in Central London and that was that.'

'Was this the same alley that Mr. Binman was found dead in?'

Mac smiled.

'Got it in one. Yes, Mr. Binman had been delivering the rubbish when he ran into someone he wasn't expecting.'

'Who was it?' Amrit asked excitedly.

'It took us quite a while to find out. The house was owned by a company registered in Panama but we put a couple of people from the Fraud Squad onto it and they managed to follow the paper trail to a shell company owned by a well-known Middle Eastern arms dealer.'

Mac went quiet for a moment.

'So, what happened then?' Amrit eventually prompted him.

'Oh, I'm sorry. I was just thinking. What happened? Nothing happened.'

'Nothing?' Amrit asked with a disappointed look.

'Unfortunately, we don't get to solve every case but, in this instance, we weren't given a chance to. Only a day or so after we'd identified the arms dealer my boss had a visitation from the men in suits and we were taken off the case.'

'Men in suits?'

'Yes, it's what we used to call them years ago; SIS, MI6, the intelligence services or whatever it is they call themselves nowadays. Anyway, after they had a word with my boss that was that, case closed.'

'So, you never got to find out what really happened?' Amrit asked.

'Well, I'm afraid that curiosity got the better of me and I did a little quiet digging around on the side anyway,' Mac replied. 'I found that Mr. Binman had, in actual fact, been employed by a tabloid newspaper to pass on the rubbish of a certain film star who was very hot news at the time. However, he made a big mistake. Unfortunately for Mr. Binman he was a bit dyslexic and he wrote the address down wrong. He reversed the house number and ended up stealing the rubbish from a house at the other end of the street instead. A simple mistake to make perhaps but it turned out to be a fatal one in his case.'

'That's a good story but it doesn't really help us with Mr. Paterson's case, does it?' Amrit asked.

Mac smiled at the 'us'.

'No, it doesn't.'

'So, what do you think?'

'If you want my honest opinion, I think there's still an outside chance that it might be an accident,' Mac said.

'Really? How could that be though?' Amrit asked once again looking puzzled.

'Well, there was a case that one of my colleagues from the traffic division told me about some years ago that might be relevant. A lady in her seventies somehow managed to have eight separate collisions with parked cars as she drove home one night. When she was finally stopped, she said it had happened because it was dark and she wasn't used to driving in the dark. However, when they examined her, they discovered that she'd been wearing her reading glasses by mistake. She was basically as blind as a bat.'

'But, in this case, wouldn't the driver have noticed the impact when they hit Mr. Paterson?'

'Not necessarily. In the case I just told you about, she thought that she was just hitting the kerb and that was good she said as she knew it was keeping her on the right side of the road. Perhaps in Mr. Paterson's case that driver also thought they'd hit the kerb. Even if they'd looked in their rear-view mirror, they probably wouldn't have seen anything as he'd have been on the floor.'

'That's bizarre,' Amrit said.

'Yes, life is sometimes and, if this was the case, we've got zero chance of ever finding the truth. Anyway, it seems as likely an explanation as murder as far as I can see.'

'But what about the car speeding up and crossing over to the other side of the road? How could that have been an accident?'

'Perhaps the driver dropped something and, in bending over, he moved the wheel and accidentally stepped harder on the accelerator,' Mac replied.

'But how likely would that be?' Amrit asked looking somewhat unconvinced.

'Something similar happened on a motorway near London a few years ago. It caused a fatality and several serious injuries.'

'What did they drop?'

'A packet of mints,' Mac replied.

'Now that really is bizarre,' Amrit said with a shake of her head.

Mac couldn't help noticing that Amrit looked a bit disappointed.

'Maybe the next case might be a bit more yielding to our detective skills.'

'What is it?' Amrit asked suddenly looking a little more animated.

'It's the case of a university lecturer who disappeared in Cambridge in very suspicious circumstances. The police suspected murder but a body was never found.'

'A bit like Morse then?' she asked with a smile.

'Yes, but that was Oxford, wasn't it? And it wasn't real.'

'I'll leave you to it then,' Amrit said. 'Just shout if you need anything.'

Chapter Three

Mac read on and quickly became so engrossed in the case that even the thought of pain didn't cross his mind for well over two hours. He'd finished reading and was deep in thought when he heard a tentative knock on the door.

'You don't have to knock, just come in.'

'I was just wondering if you were alright. You've been so quiet. Would you like a cup of tea?' Nurse Amrit asked.

'Oh yes, and please have one yourself and join me. This case has some interesting points to it.'

She gave him a big smile.

'It's as good as the telly this. I'll be right back.'

She came back with a cup for her and a spill-proof plastic beaker for Mac. She saw him scowl at it as she handed it to him. She made a mental note.

When she was seated comfortably, Mac explained the circumstances of the case as she sipped her tea.

'Mr. Rupert Quarry-Parker was a Professor of Sociology at one of the big universities in Cambridge. He was forty-two years old at the time that he disappeared. He was married with two children, both of who were away at university. One went to Edinburgh and the other to Glasgow which might tell us something.'

'That they liked Scotland perhaps?' Amrit tentatively ventured.

'Well, maybe but there could be another reason why they picked places to study at that were so far away from Cambridge. I'm thinking that all might not have been well at home and, being so far away, it gives you a good excuse for not going home very often, doesn't it?' Mac said. 'Anyway, Mr Quarry-Parker…God that's a bit of a mouthful, isn't it? Let's call him Mr. QP instead. So, Mr. QP went out one evening just over nine years ago to visit a student he was mentoring, a Mr. Daniel Guilden, and he never came back. Mr. Guilden had a room in a shared house in one of the cheaper districts of Cambridge, one that's also a high crime area. He'd been having some personal problems and was thinking about leaving his course. Mr. QP made the appointment himself but then he never turned up.'

Mac made a note on the computer.

'What are you writing?' Amrit asked.

'Just making notes as I go. I suppose I'm always a little suspicious when there isn't a body. So, why did the investigators think that he'd been murdered? On the same evening he disappeared, he took the maximum amount out of his account using an ATM not far from where Mr. Guilden lived. CCTV footage showed Mr. QP at the ATM with a hooded figure behind him. It looked like the figure could have been holding something against Mr. QP's back, most likely a knife they thought. Then Mr. QP's wallet was discovered a couple of days later in the cistern of a toilet at a nearby pub, a well-known thieves' den apparently. Of course, all his bank cards and his money were gone. Mr. QP's car, an Audi, was then involved in a car chase the evening after he disappeared. The police eventually used stingers to stop it and they found a large consignment of cannabis in the back. The driver admitted stealing the car the night before from a road close to where Daniel Guilden lived. So, it looks as if Mr. QP had actually made it to within a few hundred yards of where Mr. Guilden lived. The theory was that, after getting out of his car, someone accosted him at knife point and marched him to the nearest ATM. They had no evidence for what happened after that until they found his shoe.'

'His shoe?' Amrit asked.

'Yes, it was found by the side of the rail tracks underneath a bridge by a maintenance worker. The bridge was no more than two hundred yards away from the ATM machine.'

'How did they know that it was his?'

'DNA,' Mac replied. 'The railway worker who found it said he wouldn't have bothered handing it in except for the fact that he'd heard about the lecturer's disappearance. That, plus the fact that the shoe was brand new and from a well-known designer label. They found that Mr. QP had bought them just two days before. The question I'm asking myself is why he'd want to wear such an expensive pair of shoes in that neighbourhood? It's like asking to be mugged.'

Mac was silent for a while.

'Sorry, where was I?' he asked.

'Shoes,' Amrit prompted.

'Yes. Anyway, the theory was that Mr. QP had been killed by his assailant who dragged his body to the railway bridge and dumped it over the wall and on to the tracks. This theory was supported by the fact that traces of Mr. QP's blood were found on the brick work of the bridge as were some of his hairs. The investigators thought that his assailant may have gotten lucky and that the body landed up in one of the numerous freight trucks that go underneath the bridge day and night. So, if they were right, he could have ended up anywhere and, if it was a coal truck, there's a chance that it went straight into an industrial furnace somewhere and so his body and all the evidence would have been destroyed. They searched all along the tracks but they found nothing else.'

'It sounds straight forward enough to me,' Amrit said.

'Perhaps, but perhaps not. The insurance is the thing that bugging me.'

'Oh, did he get himself insured just before he disappeared?' she asked excitedly.

'No, exactly the opposite, he let it lapse. He'd kept it up for over fifteen years and then he let it lapse a couple of months before he vanished.'

Mac went silent again.

'Can you hand me my phone?' he eventually asked. 'I'm going to call someone who might just be able to give us the answer.'

'How?' Amrit asked as she passed him the phone.

'Well, technology has moved on a bit since the time Mr. QP disappeared. Now let's see.'

Mac called a number.

'Martin, how are you?'

'I'm fine but how are you doing, Mac? I heard that you've been ordered to rest for a while.'

'That's true enough but I'm helping Dan with some cold cases to keep the boredom at bay. Can you do me a favour? Do you know of any way that you can use facial recognition on social sites such as Facebook? I'm sure I read something about an app that could do this quite recently.'

'Why yes, funnily enough I was talking about this to someone only yesterday. There's a newish Google app that's really good. I've already used it on one case.'

'Well, this will make two then,' Mac said. 'If I send you a photo over can you see what you can find?'

'Of course, no problem.'

Mac said his goodbyes and put down the phone. Seeing Amrit's puzzled expression he thought he'd better explain.

'Martin's a policeman but he's a computer specialist too and he's really good at what he does. I'm going to email him a picture of Mr. Quarry-Parker and see if he can find him on social media.'

'You think that he's still alive then?' Amrit asked looking puzzled.

'Yes, that's exactly what I think.'

Mac busied himself sending the email off and then thought that he'd probably be in for quite a long wait. He got a reply just over an hour later. The email from Martin contained a single URL. He clicked on it. He was smiling when Amrit came into the room.

'Have you found something?' she asked excitedly.

'Here,' Mac said moving the laptop so she could see.

'That's not him though, is it?' she said peering at the screen.

'No, that's the newly appointed Professor of Sociology at UCLA Daniel Guilden and there, behind him, is his life partner Roger Stanton.'

Amrit's face showed her surprise.

'That's him! That's Mr. QP, he's alive!'

'Yes, alive and well and living in California. He's done well to keep himself off social media all this time but I suppose this was one occasion that he just couldn't turn down.'

'So, what are you going to do?' Amrit asked with wide eyes. 'What are you going to charge him with?'

Mac was thoughtful for a while.

'Nothing, I should think.'

'Nothing?' Amrit asked her face dropping.

'If he'd defrauded the insurance company then that would be another thing but, apart from wasting police time which we'll never get back anyway, who would gain from him being charged? His wife's re-married as he's been officially pronounced dead and, as she started going out with her current husband only weeks after Mr. QP disappeared, then perhaps there wasn't that much of a marriage left anyway. I'd bet that his children know that he's alive anyway. He's built a new life in America now so who would be served by destroying it all?'

It was Amrit's turn to be thoughtful.

'Justice perhaps?'

Mac shook his head.

'And what's that exactly? In my time I've heard a lot of talk about the concept of justice and I've often found that the definitions totally contradict one another. My old boss taught me to be pragmatic, to identify exactly who had been injured, what the injury was and what would be gained by charging someone. I've found it as good a guide as anything else I've come across. In this case it could be argued that the only injured party at this moment in time would be the police whose time had been wasted. So, in order to serve the cause of justice, would you destroy the lives of Mr. QP and his partner as well as upset the rest of his family while actually wasting even more police time and taxpayers' money by bringing it all to court? Does that make any sense to you?'

'I hadn't thought about it like that,' Amrit replied. 'Of course, you're right. So, what are you going to do?'

'I'll forward all the information to my boss Dan Carter and let him decide. However, I'd be amazed if he takes any action other than categorising the case as closed and leaving it at that. He'll be happy anyway, a case closed is a case off his books and a win as far as he's concerned.'

'But I'm still a bit puzzled. Why couldn't he have just left his wife and told her the truth?' Amrit asked.

'That's a good question. Why do people do anything? Perhaps he honestly loved his wife in his own way and would sooner have her think him dead than know that he'd abandoned her for another lover and a man at that. As a gay man he'd probably been living a lie for most of his married life and it can be hard to admit that to someone you love.'

'Okay, I can see that but what about the clues? How could they be so sure that the wallet and the shoe would be found?' she asked.

'Well, the wallet's a bit of a no brainer. Most publicans I know who've run pubs in dodgy areas regularly check the cisterns. They're usually more worried that people might have drugs or weapons stashed in there. However, we're dealing with a couple of very intelligent men here and I'd bet that there might have been a few more clues scattered around, perhaps quite subtle ones. These were just the ones the investigators found.'

Amrit sighed and looked at the photo again on the computer. She smiled.

'Actually, I'm glad that no action will be taken. They look very happy, don't they?'

'Yes, they do,' Mac said. 'Okay, on to the next one.'

A short while later, Mac was so engrossed that he didn't hear the front door open. Amrit popped her head around the door.

'Bridget's back now, so I'll be off.'

'Thanks, Amrit. I'll see you tomorrow then.'

'I'm looking forward to it. Part two of the series as it were. See you Mr…sorry, see you Mac.'

He could hear voices in the hallway but couldn't make out what was being said. A minute later Bridget opened the door.

'Hi dad, I believe that you've had a busy day then?'

'I have. I've almost enjoyed it to be honest.'

'So, after all the books I bought, you've still managed to cadge some cold cases from Dan Carter,' she said with a mock serious expression.

'Well, I'll still have plenty of time to read I suppose but these cases are really interesting. You don't mind, do you?'

'Mind? No, I'm very grateful to Dan and, if I'm honest, I wish I'd thought of that myself. I know you like reading but, even when I bought them, I had my doubts as to whether they'd keep your mind off things. So, how's it going?'

'I've already solved one,' Mac said with a smile.

'Really?'

'Yes, really. Well, Martin Selby did in actual fact but all the same we've closed a case.'

'You know there's something that I've always wondered about you,' Bridget said.

'What's that?'

'Ever since I was young, I've been puzzled at how my quiet, gentle dad could not only work full-time solving the most violent crimes while rubbing shoulders with murderers but enjoy doing it too.'

Mac took off his glasses and gave it some thought.

'It's the puzzle, I think. I used to do a lot of crosswords when I was younger, you know the hard ones from the broadsheet papers, but I found real life a much harder puzzle to crack. There's something about people and the incredibly weird things they do that's endlessly fascinating if I'm honest. As for all the gore and the bad stuff, I'm grateful that I've always been able to keep that at arm's length, you know, in my head.'

'I'm just glad to see that you're doing okay,' Bridget said. 'Anyway, I'd better get us some tea. I've got the makings for a pasta dish unless you'd like to celebrate your first day at home with some fish and chips?'

Mac's eyes lit up.

'Oh, fish and chips please!'

'Okay, and after that we can have a few games of backgammon if you want,' Bridget suggested.

'That sounds great. Tim said that he'd drop around later but we should still have plenty of time for a game. Prepare yourself for a thorough thrashing though.'

'In your dreams,' Bridget said with a smile as she left.

Chapter Four

Mac was glad when a crack of light appeared around the edges of the curtains. He'd had a bad night and had dozed more than he'd slept. Every time he felt himself slipping into a deep sleep, the pain jumped up and reminded him that it was still there. The night was always the worst time for pain. The only resource you have to fight it is what's between your ears. Mac had tried thinking about the cold cases and, while it did take his mind off the pain for a while, it didn't exactly help him sleep either.

He lay looking at the light slowly getting stronger and thinking until the door opened a crack.

'Are you awake, dad?' a little voice whispered.

'Yes, you can come in Bridget, I'm awake,' he replied with some relief as he turned his bedside light on.

He was quite glad to have his thoughts interrupted. Lying there, he'd started ruminating about the weeks that lay ahead and how he'd cope. It hadn't exactly cheered him up.

'Did you get any sleep?' Bridget asked with some concern.

'A little perhaps,' he said keeping his reply intentionally vague.

His daughter gave him a sad look and then kissed his forehead.

'It'll pass, dad.'

'I know. I'll be okay, don't you worry,' he said managing a faint smile.

She looked at her watch and said, 'I'm sorry but I'll have to go in a few minutes. Amrit will be here in half an hour or so. Is there anything you need?'

'The loo unfortunately and some orange juice would be nice.'

'I'll get the wheelchair.'

Bridget had tried to persuade him to use a urine bottle and a bedpan but Mac had drawn a line. She knew better than to argue when he was like that and so she had to watch her father wince with pain as he sat up before sliding himself into the wheelchair. Luckily, the bathroom was a good size so it was easy to manoeuvre the wheelchair into place. She'd also ordered a high toilet seat so her father wouldn't have to sit so far down. It had metal handles on each side so he could use his arms to pull himself on and off. When she'd first set it up, she saw him scowl at it but he said nothing and used it anyway.

She closed the door and went into the kitchen and poured some orange juice into a spill proof beaker. As she came back, she could hear him grunting with pain as he got himself back into the wheelchair. She wished that he wouldn't be so obstinate and would do as he was told. She wished to God that she could take some of his pain on herself, she wished...a tear ran down her cheek.

'I'm ready,' he shouted.

She quickly wiped her cheek and smiled as she wheeled him back to his bedroom. After much huffing and puffing and grunting she got him comfortable and handed him his orange juice.

'Do you want me to set up your laptop?' she asked glancing at her watch again.

'No, you'd better get going or you'll miss your train. Amrit can do it when she gets here. Have a good day, love.'

'You too, dad.'

He heard the front door close and listened to the silence for a while. He started thinking about the last case he'd read and how sad human beings can be. Lost in his thoughts he was surprised when he heard the front door open. A few seconds later his bedroom door opened and revealed a smiling Amrit in a purple sari.

'Ah, there you are, Mac.'

'And where else would I be?' he said with a scowl.

'Oh, feeling a bit down today are we? Well, perhaps some breakfast might help. What would you like?'

'A fry up might be nice but I daresay it'll be muesli or whatever healthy birdseed Bridget's got in.'

'Well, while you're inactive it would be good if you watched your weight,' she said.

'Okay, birdseed it is, I suppose,' he said grumpily.

'Well, that's a real pity when I've just bought these,' she replied producing a plastic pack of bacon and a carton of eggs from a carrier bag.

'Thanks, Amrit. You're a godsend,' he said giving her a broad smile.

'Now that's more like it. Shall I set up your laptop while I cook your breakfast?'

Mac read the case again while the seductive smell of bacon frying gently wafted in from the kitchen. It concerned the brutal murder of a seventeen year old girl, a so-called 'honour killing' the investigators concluded, although Mac could never see the slightest shred of honour in the senseless slaying of a young girl.

Twelve years ago, the body of seventeen year old Asma Rafiq was found on a walkway in Stevenage by a cyclist on his way to work. She'd been stabbed eight times. A student on his way to school had arrived on the scene shortly afterwards and had tried to perform CPR on the girl while the cyclist phoned for an ambulance. They arrived less than five minutes later but, despite the young man's and the paramedics' best efforts, she was declared dead fifteen minutes after she'd been found.

The cyclist, a Mr. Harry Jeavis, was on his way to work at one of the high-tech factories on Gunnels Wood when he came across the body. He stated that he'd glimpsed a young man in a hoodie run past him just a few seconds before, indeed he'd almost run into his bike. He had a dark track suit on and yellow trainers that were stained with blotches of some dark red substance. He realised after he found Asma that the stains must have been blood. Unfortunately, he couldn't give a more detailed description beyond that.

The seventeen year old student, Lawrence Taylor, had come from the other direction on his way to school. He hadn't seen the hooded man. He'd been taught how to do CPR at school where he was sixth former studying for his A levels. He knew Asma by sight, as they both went to the same school, but he said he didn't know much about her beyond that.

The investigators seemed to have concentrated on Asma's family as an honour killing seemed the most likely motive. The family consisted of her father, Mr. Mohammed Rafiq, her mother Fatima, her elder brother Youssef and a younger sister Farzana.

The family were all very close-lipped and said that they'd been together all day. They searched the house but found no blood-stained clothing or yellow trainers. Never the less, they still considered Youssef to be the most likely suspect. He was the same height and build as the hoodie and he might have had a motive if he'd found out that Asma was seeing a boy. However, they spoke to all her friends and found no evidence of any attachment. The investigators noted that one of Asma's aunts mentioned that a marriage had been arranged to a friend of her uncle's in Pakistan. They were never able to establish how Asma felt about it. Perhaps she'd refused which would have been motive enough for murder in some families.

They were even more certain that the murderer was Youssef when his family reported him missing a day or so later. They said that some of his clothes, his wallet and his passport had also disappeared. From what he could glean from reading between the lines, the investigators felt at first that it was most likely that he'd done a runner back to Pakistan and probably with the help of his family. However, some of his friends had reported that he had been talking about travelling to Afghanistan to join Bin Laden and fight for the Islamic cause. His family confirmed that this might be a possibility.

They were absolutely certain it was Youssef after they searched the Rafiq house again and found a large steel sling-bladed knife hidden under a loose floor board in his bedroom. It had Youssef's fingerprints all over it and traces of his sister's blood too. They also found some computer print-offs in his sock drawer containing detailed information about a terrorist group in Afghanistan.

The last entry in the case file was a note dated just over a year later. It stated that a suicide bomber, who had blown himself and several members of the Afghan security forces up, had been identified as Youssef Rafiq, a young Pakistani man from Britain.

Mac's thoughts were interrupted by the arrival of his breakfast which he polished off in a few minutes.

'Hungry, were we?' Amrit asked as she took his plate and cutlery away.

'I'll say. That really hit the spot. Would you be ready for a chat now?'

'Is this about the latest case?' she asked excitedly. 'I'll only be two ticks.'

She came back with a cup of tea and a large travel mug that had a handle on one side.

'I know you like your coffee,' she said. 'I hope I've not made it too strong.'

Mac took a sip, it was perfect.

'Did you buy this?' Mac said holding up the travel mug.

'Well, I could see you didn't like that plastic beaker. It made you feel like a little child, didn't it?'

Mac looked at his nurse with renewed respect.

'Perhaps you should have been the detective.'

'Anyway, a travel mug's a bit more grown up, isn't it?'

'It is,' Mac agreed with a smile as he took another sip.

Amrit smiled, seated herself and waited the next instalment in anticipation.

As Mac related the details of the case, he could see Amrit becoming more and more uneasy.

'Is this bothering you?' he eventually asked.

'No, it's making me angry. These men who kill women always talk about honour but they have none. It's all about control really. They're scared that their women will realise that they're stronger than they know and where would the men be then?'

'They've had these killings in the Sikh community too, haven't they?' Mac asked.

Amrit nodded sadly.

'Unfortunately, we've got our share of stupid men too.'

'Do you have a daughter?'

Amrit smiled, 'Oh yes, she's twenty now and away at university. We're very proud of her. But, personally, I'll never understand some of the mothers in these cases. They cover up and sometimes even help the men to kill their daughters. If any man said that they'd harm a hair on my daughter's head then I'd tear his heart out.'

Amrit's fierce expression convinced Mac totally.

'What about your husband? How does he feel about your daughter being at university?'

'Who Prem? Oh, he was so made up when she got her offer,' Amrit said with a smile. 'He misses her though. He bought her a car so that she could come back home more often.'

'I know how he feels,' Mac said remembering how desolate he'd felt when he'd had to leave Bridget and her luggage behind at the student accommodation block. 'What does your husband do?'

'He's a doctor, no I should say he's a consultant,' she replied with eyebrows raised. 'It's strange, you know he was so proud when he stopped being Mr. Prem Singh and became Dr. Prem Singh. Now he's become a consultant, he's even prouder that he's no longer called 'doctor' and has gone back to being called 'mister' again.'

'I take it that he's a specialist then?' Mac asked.

'Yes, he's an orthopaedic surgeon at Addenbrooke's in Cambridge. He does backs too you know,' she said meaningfully.

Mac let that one slide. He'd had so many medical people poke him about only for it to end up with them telling him the numerous reasons why they couldn't help him. He'd given up any hope of things getting better.

'Anyway, I might as well get on to the next one. This one's a bit of a dead end.' Mac suddenly thought of what he'd said. 'Sorry, I could have phrased that better.'

'I know what you mean though. If it was the brother then he's dead too. Sad though, isn't it? A family killing each other like that.'

Mac glanced up at Amrit and slowly nodded.

'Anyway, why wasn't the case closed out if they knew who did it?' Amrit asked.

'Well, no-one's been convicted in a court of law yet but I'd guess it's mostly down to the fact that we can't be certain that the Youssef Rafiq who died in Afghanistan is the same man as the suspect. If he wasn't then he might try to come back one day. Okay, on to the next one,' Mac said.

'I'll leave you to it then,' Amrit said. 'Oh, is it okay if I clean your kitchen cupboards? They're a bit dirty and there's a lot of out of date food in there too.'

'Well, I'm not sure if I'm honest,' Mac said feeling slightly ashamed. It had never occurred to him that the cupboards might need cleaning. 'I mean you're employed as a nurse not as a cleaner.'

'Oh, forget about that, I'm not a nurse anymore and I really don't mind. I'm like you, I'm happiest when I'm being kept busy.'

'Well, if you're sure…' Mac said still uncertain.

'I'll get on with it then,' she said with a smile. 'Shout if you need anything.'

Mac made a mental note to talk to Bridget about it.

Chapter Five

Case number four didn't look any more promising than the previous one had. However, he'd managed to read it all before Amrit's head poked around the door.

'Are you ready for some lunch?' she asked.

'Is it that time already?' he asked with some surprise.

'It is. I've got some Chicken Tikka, rotis and salad. How does that sound?'

'Heavenly,' Mac replied with total sincerity. 'Why don't you eat in here with me? There's a tray in the kitchen and we could talk about the case while we eat.'

'Okay,' Amrit said with a smile.

While he waited for his lunch, he thought over the case he'd just read. Mac was roused from his thoughts by a divine smell that was coming in his direction. He started salivating. Amrit helped him sit up a bit and then handed him the tray. She came back with her lunch a few minutes later.

'Oh, this is wonderful!' Mac said as he let the spices roll around his mouth. 'I love tikka.'

Amrit smiled and then said with anticipation, 'So what's the new case then?'

'I was just thinking before you came in about the role sheer chance plays in some crimes. I mean people who have it in them to be murderers will murder but they always need a victim, don't they? A lot of the time who that victim turns out to be is just luck or bad luck I suppose for them, just being in the wrong place at the wrong time.'

'Is that what happened in this case?'

Mac took another bite of tikka and paused while he savoured it.

'It looks like it. Here's what happened, a twenty-five year old woman called Terri Maynard was last seen driving home from a friend's house one winter evening around six years ago. The friend's house was in Royston and Terri was driving back down the A1198 towards Papworth Everard where she lived. Terri was a receptionist at the sleep clinic at Papworth Hospital where she'd worked for the previous four years.'

'Oh yes, I know someone who works there,' Amrit interrupted.

Mac paused and made a mental note before carrying on.

'Anyway, she had a boyfriend who she'd been living with for two years. He was a nurse and he worked at the hospital too. He became concerned when she didn't arrive home and phoned the friend that Terri had been visiting. She confirmed that she'd left some hours before. As Terri was driving their jointly owned car, he got a friend of his to drive him down the route that she would normally have taken home. Their car was quite old so he thought that she'd probably just broken down. They found the car parked in front of a disused entrance into the Bassingbourn Army Barracks but there was no sign of Terri. They shouted for her and looked around the immediate vicinity but found nothing.'

'I've got a bad feeling about this. Poor Terri,' Amrit said.

'Yes, poor Terri indeed. They called the police who conducted a search and they found Terri's body in the undergrowth about twenty yards away from the car. She'd been sexually assaulted and her throat had been cut. The police tested the car and found that it had genuinely broken down. Terri must have just managed to get the car off the road and into the entrance to the barracks. Unfortunately, the phone signal was quite weak in that particular spot so she may not have been able to get a call out. They surmised that someone must have stopped and offered to help her and then that someone overpowered her and raped her.'

'Cutting her throat though,' Amrit said with a grimace. 'Why do they do that?'

'Usually that happens when the rapist is holding a knife against his victim's throat to control them and they sometimes get carried away when they ejaculate. I've had a couple of murders where that's happened and both murderers said that they didn't plan to kill their victims, it just happened.'

'Bastards!' Amrit said with feeling.

'Exactly. Unfortunately, the evidence in this case was pretty thin, there were no traffic cameras on that route and very little traffic at that time of night. Even so, someone must have driven past Terri's car but, even after a televised appeal, no-one came forward. Not surprising I suppose as it's a fast road and it was night. It hadn't rained for days and the ground was hard so no tyre marks were found. However, forensics did find what they believed to be the murderer's DNA on Terri but, of course, they needed a sample to compare it to. The only thing they could say for sure was that it wasn't anyone directly related to Terri or the boyfriend. There were also some fibres and other trace evidence but again by themselves they weren't of much use.'

'So, was that it?' Amrit said with some disappointment.

'Yes, more or less. They investigated Terri herself, the boyfriend and anyone who knew her but got nowhere. They concluded that in all probability it was an opportunistic crime. Unfortunately for Terri she just broke down in the wrong place and at the wrong time. It would have been a very long walk before she came to any houses and, as she was wearing high heels, perhaps she didn't think that was an option anyway. The investigators thought that she probably tried to flag a car down. It was just her bad luck that she picked the wrong one.'

'So, another dead end then?' Amrit asked. 'If they had his DNA then why didn't they test all the men in the area? I saw a programme on the telly about a real case where they did that.'

'Yes, they did that in the Pitchfork case, the first investigation ever to use DNA testing. There were two murders in the same area so they suspected that it might be a local man. The only problem in this case was that this happened on a road. If the murderer had been driving north then he could have been heading for Cambourne, Huntingdon, Peterborough or anywhere north on the A1. If he was driving in the other direction then he could have been heading for Royston, Bishop's Stortford or even London. You'd end up having to test half the men in the country.'

'Yes, I see what you mean. So, there were no leads at all?'

'It looks that way but I'm going to go through it again just in case. By the way, who is this friend of yours that works at Papworth?' Mac asked.

'Her name's Dr. Zaynab Teymouri. She's a specialist in sleep disorders now but she was just a junior doctor when I first knew her.'

'How long has she been at Papworth?'

'Oh, it must be six or seven years now,' Amrit replied.

'Do me a favour, when you next speak to her can you ask her if she knew Terri? Also ask her if there's been any rumours going around the hospital about the murder, you never know.'

'I'll do that. It'll be nice to play the detective for real.'

Amrit stood up and put Mac's empty plates on her tray.

'Thank you Amrit. That was entirely wonderful,' Mac said.

'You're welcome. Oh well, the cupboards won't clean themselves. Give me a shout if you need anything and, of course, if you get a lead.'

Mac read it all again. He had the feeling that there was something, some little detail that he'd missed. He'd keep reading until he found it. It took him quite a while but he found it buried in a very lengthy autopsy report.

The pathologist concluded that the neck wound was consistent with a blade that wasn't sharp along its entire length. Mac looked at the photos for some time. The report also stated that there were small traces of polystyrene in the wound consistent with the type of material used in protective packaging. The pathologist in a note tucked away on page eleven added that, although she couldn't be entirely certain, she thought that a home-made box cutter might be a good candidate for the weapon. This would also explain the presence of polystyrene.

So, our man was probably a delivery man or courier of some sort, Mac thought. It pointed again to the crime being a spur of the moment thing as he'd used whatever was to hand. Was it his first time though? He was aware that men who carried out these sorts of crimes usually had a compulsion that they couldn't control. If this was his first time then it would in all likelihood happen again.

He went through the file and it looked like the investigators had done their due diligence in checking with other police authorities for any similar crimes. They'd found nothing. Perhaps Terri was the murderer's first victim and, if that was the case, then he could have done it again in the six years since.

Given the paucity of leads Mac felt that this was probably the only way that he was going to make any headway with the case.

Mac phoned Martin and explained the situation.

'Well, I can check for any murders using a similar weapon and MO but, if it's just an assault for instance, then I'm not sure that we'll find it on the national databases,' Martin replied.

'Okay, well check for any similar murders and call me back,' Mac replied.

He didn't hold out much hope so, when Martin rang back, he wasn't too disappointed.

'So, there's nothing then,' Mac said. 'Okay, so what if our man had assaulted someone but it didn't come off for some reason? I take it that we're back to ringing around all the police forces for information like we did on the Natasha Barker case?' Mac asked hoping he wasn't going to be right.

'That's pretty much the case I'm afraid. I'm sorry Mac I'd like to help but at the moment I'm...'

'No problem, Martin. The case isn't a priority and it's not as though I'm short of time at the moment. However, I would be grateful if you could send me all the phone numbers that I'll need to call.'

'Sure thing Mac, right away. Best of luck.'

Mac thought he'd need it. Anyway, it would definitely keep him occupied for quite a while.

Mac had a look at the map. He decided that he'd try the eastern side of the country first. He'd go as far south as he could and then he'd go north. If he didn't get anything then he'd try the western side.

It took him almost three days to make all the calls and, although he was still waiting for some call backs, it looked like he'd drawn a blank.

Oh well, he thought, it was a long shot at best and it did pass the time.

His phone rang. He was surprised to hear a familiar voice at the other end.

'Hello, is that Mr. Maguire?'

'Mrs. Collins, how are you?' Mac replied somewhat puzzled.

'Oh, I'm fine. I'm sorry to disturb you but we needed to speak to someone and Emily thought that you might be the best person.'

Mrs. Collins ran a retirement home, mostly for elderly people with dementia. He'd questioned her and Emily, who was one of the 'guests' as they liked to call them, during the Natasha Barker case. He smiled when he thought of Emily, in her seventies and learning computer programming. There was certainly no hint of dementia there.

'Well, I'm afraid that I'm stuck in bed for a while, quite a while perhaps...'

'Yes, I know but I could pop around to your house if that would be alright.'

'Yes, of course if I can be of any help. Can I ask what this is about?

There was a moment's silence.

'It's about a murder Mr. Maguire and we think we might have some information.'

Chapter Six

To say that Mac was intrigued would be putting it mildly. A half an hour later the doorbell rang and Amrit ushered a clearly agitated Mrs. Collins into his room. She'd looked familiar when Mac had first met her as she'd reminded him of his old primary head teacher, well upholstered and with a sure air of authority. However, today she looked a little flustered.

'Please sit down, Mrs. Collins,' Mac said.

'Would you like a cup of tea?' Amrit offered.

'Oh yes please,' Mrs. Collins replied her gratitude evident. 'Mr. Maguire, I'm really sorry to trouble you when you're like this…'

'Oh, it's no trouble, no trouble at all. It's actually quite nice to have a visitor. It can get really boring being stuck in here.'

'How are you? I read all about the case in the paper, you were so brave,' she said with some sympathy.

'Oh, I wasn't that brave, believe me. I'm afraid that the papers make more of things than they should. Anyway, I'm okay, just stuck in this bed for another few weeks. Well, just another five weeks or so actually,' Mac said with a sigh. 'Anyway, how can I help?'

They were interrupted by Amrit who brought in a cup of tea and the travel mug.

'Aren't you having one too?' Mac asked.

'Well yes but…' Amrit tried to reply.

'No buts, bring it in here. You might as well hear this too. It'll just save me having to tell you later.'

Amrit smiled.

'Okay, I'll go and get a chair.'

'Amrit's my nurse but she's also helping me with some enquiries,' Mac explained. Seeing a suspicious look on Mrs. Collin's face he quickly added, 'Oh not in that way. I mean she's helping me with some old cases that I'm reviewing for the police.'

Once Amrit was seated Mac said, 'You said you had some information about a murder...'

Mrs. Collins thought for a moment before answering.

'Yes well, I don't know. It's a bit difficult that's why we decided to talk to you first rather than the police. It's probably nothing but....'

'Tell me.'

'As you know, apart from a few like Emily, most of our guests have dementia of one sort or another. With some it's permanent while for others it can come and go. Well, around two months ago a new guest arrived, a Miss Cassandra Bardolph. She's only fifty-four but she's had severe dementia for a couple of years now. I always find it sad when it strikes people that early in life. Anyway, I could see from the medical records that she'd been sent to all the best hospitals for treatment, even to one in the US, but there was obviously nothing they could do. So, she came to us in more or less a vegetative state. For over six weeks she said nothing and then she started talking, saying the same thing over and over again.'

'What did she say?' Mac asked.

'Here, you can see for yourself.'

She pulled out a tablet, turned it on and selected a video. She handed the tablet to Mac.

'I take it that we've got Emily to thank for this?' Mac asked.

'God yes, I wouldn't have a clue personally. I only use my tablet to read books,' Mrs. Collins replied.

Mac waved at Amrit to come over and look at the screen. He started the video off.

A woman who looked a lot younger than fifty-seven sat in a chair with a vacant expression on her face. Her eyes then started moving as though she was watching something happen in front of her. The camera moved to show that she was staring at a blank wall.

'What is it?' she said a look of concern on her face. 'There's blood on your hands, what's happened?'

She then stopped as though listening intently.

'You killed her? Oh my God, she's dead and you're saying it's your fault? Tell me exactly what happened, every detail.'

Again, she listened.

'We need to get you away. They'll be looking for you and you could be in danger. Don't worry, I know just what to do.'

She then seemed to relax and fall asleep in the chair. The video ended there.

'That's all she ever says. She just keeps on repeating those few sentences,' Mrs. Collins explained, 'like it's on a loop or something. What do you think?'

'I take it that you've tried to get more information from her?'

'Of course, but, other than what you've seen on the video, she's totally unresponsive and doesn't even seem to know we're there.'

Mac gave it some thought.

'Well, as luck would have it, I'm looking at some old cases at the moment. Perhaps hers might be one of them, if she's from the area that is. If you can send me whatever information you can about her then I'll look into it.'

'I'm afraid that I won't be able to give you anything other than her name, her birth date and where she used to live.'

'Why? Data privacy issues?' Mac asked.

'Well, yes that would apply but, if I'm being honest, it's because that's all I know about her. Her fees are paid by a firm of London solicitors and, while I've tried to get more information about her from them, they'd tell me absolutely nothing.'

'What did you want to know about her?'

'What her job was, what hobbies she had, whether there were any old photos we could have, that type of thing,' Mrs. Collins replied. 'We can sometimes stimulate memories in dementia sufferers by reminding them of their former lives but, to be honest, Miss Bardolph is probably a bit too far gone for that anyway.'

'Okay then, send me what you've got and I'll see what I can do.'

Mrs. Collins visibly relaxed.

'Oh, thank you Mr. Maguire, it will be a weight off my mind.'

Mac gave her his email address. After she'd gone, he thought about what she said. He was interrupted by Amrit collecting his mug.

'Can you find out much from just a name, birth date and address?' she asked.

'You'd be amazed at what information you can get just from going to a few government departments. Besides any criminal convictions we should be able to quite easily find out about her family, siblings and so on, what her income was, who she banked with, where she worked, any major bouts of sickness, what car she drove and so on. Once you've got that then you can really start digging and begin building a picture of the suspect. Not that she's really a suspect yet, I suppose.'

'It's a bit frightening that, isn't it?' Amrit said with a frown.

Mac looked up.

'What, the amount of information that's held on us?'

Amrit nodded.

'God that's the very least of it. I'm not really into all the high-tech stuff but, believe me, if you've pressed a key of a computer or posted a message on social media somebody, somewhere in the government will know about it. However, they're rarely willing to share this

44

information with the police so we'll start off with what we've got and see where it takes us.'

'It's still a bit of a challenge though, isn't it?' Amrit said. 'Building up a picture of a person from just a name and address?'

Mac smiled broadly.

'Yes, it'll be a challenge alright but that's just what I need right now. It should keep me going for quite a while I hope.'

The first thing Mac did was ring Martin Selby. He was happy to make the initial enquiries with the relevant government departments. Mac made a mental note to send him a bottle of something to show his appreciation.

In the meantime, Mac skim read the rest of the cold cases so he'd have them all in his head when the information arrived.

He was interrupted in this by his friend Tim. It was a more than welcome interruption though. Tim had been calling around most nights for a chat but he'd come early today as he was off at four the next morning on a buying trip that would take him away for a few days. Mac told him about what he was working on.

'It's good that you've got something to keep your mind going,' Tim said. 'Do you think that there's any-thing in it though?'

'As Mrs. Collins said it could be something or nothing but, if I'm honest, it's more likely to be nothing. If I was investigating this officially then I'd have to make a decision on whether to expend resources following it up and, based on the low probability of success, it would inevitably have been parked. However, the only resource involved here is my time and, as I've got quite a lot of that, I'm going to give it my best shot.'

Before he left Tim brought him up to speed with all that had been going on at the Magnets. Mac found that he was really missing his sessions at the Magnets with

Tim. He heard Tim closing the front door as he left and he knew he'd miss his friend's visits even more.

Chapter Seven

The day after, while he waited for Martin to send him whatever information he could about the mysterious Miss Bardolph, Mac tried to whittle down the cases to only those that might be relevant. The murder had to be that of a woman and blood must have been spilt.

He ended up with just six cases.

There was the murder and rape of Terri Maynard. That was one he'd love to solve as he was sure that whoever killed Terri would inevitably kill again.

The second cold case was that of twenty year old Marie Callaghan. She'd disappeared just over three years ago after leaving a night club in Hertford. Her body was found by walkers two days later in a forested area some two miles or so from the town centre. Her skull had been split open by a rock so there would have been blood enough. She hadn't been sexually assaulted but the investigators still thought that rape was the probable motive. They figured that she'd put up more of a fight than the assailant had planned for and so he'd killed her with whatever there was to hand. After a search they found the rock but no prints. It looked like whoever killed her was wearing gloves. There were partial tyre prints but these proved inconclusive as they were from a popular brand of budget tyres. That was about it for evidence. No CCTV from the club or from the area around it and no-one saw Marie get into a car or saw a car in the vicinity of the woods. It looked as if the investigators had followed up every lead that came their way, no matter how faint it might have been, but they still came up with nothing.

Mac's heart sank as he closed the file. He had a feeling that Marie's case was one of those that, through bad luck as much as anything else, would never get solved. Somewhere out there was a man walking around who should be behind bars. He could only pray that the murderer was living in constant fear that he might feel a hand on his shoulder or get a knock on his door early one morning. Indeed, he could remember a couple of men who had admitted that they'd actually been relieved when they'd been arrested. Waiting for the other shoe to drop can be an exhausting business.

The third cold case was that of thirty-seven year old Agniezka Coleman who had been murdered some seven years before. She was originally from Kracow, Poland and her maiden name was Malinowska. She had been married to a Mr. John Coleman for eleven years and, on the surface at least, the marriage seemed a happy one. At the time of her death she'd been a care worker in an old people's home in Baldock. Mr. and Mrs. Coleman had also lived in Baldock where he worked as a supervisor at a local supermarket.

She'd finished her shift at nine o'clock one evening in March and left work to walk home. She walked along the same route that she always took. Her husband arrived home after finishing his shift at eleven to find that she wasn't there. He tried to phone her on her mobile but he got no response. He walked back towards the old people's home and found his wife's body in an entryway that ran between a low block of flats and a house. She was dead having been stabbed several times.

The investigators quickly ruled out robbery as her purse and credit cards were still in her bag. They also ruled out her husband as a suspect once the time of death had been firmly established as being just after nine. John Coleman had been working with his team at the supermarket at that time and his colleague's testimony, backed up by the supermarket's CCTV footage, meant that every minute between nine and eleven o'clock had been more or less accounted for. It couldn't have been him.

Nevertheless, the investigators searched Coleman's house but couldn't find anything that pointed to the husband or anyone else. They then concentrated on the old people's home but again found nothing of use. They even went as far as to travel to Poland to interview Agniezka's family but again found nothing, no family feuds, no disagreements, indeed, from what Mac read, the family seemed quite close. They never found the knife that was used or any forensic traces other than some stray fibres that could have come from anywhere. The investigators had absolutely no leads and, reading between the lines, he could sense their frustration.

An old case popped into Mac's head and he immediately wondered if it might be of some relevance.

Amrit came in with a welcome mug of coffee. Mac gestured to her to sit down while he went through the two cases.

'Pity about young Marie, isn't it?' she said. 'You'd think someone would have seen her, wouldn't you?'

'It happens sometimes, just bad luck really.'

'And what about this poor Agniezka? It doesn't look like that case is ever going to be solved either,' she said a little gloomily.

'Well, I've had some thoughts about that one. It reminded me of a similarly frustrating case we had a while ago, one that was finally resolved by a piece of luck as much as anything.'

'Just let me get comfortable,' Amrit said a smile as she plumped a cushion and placed it behind her back.

'Okay? Right then, one May Day Bank Holiday evening a man was found dead in Hyde Park. His body was found on a park bench and the cause of death was massive blunt force trauma to the head. In other words, he'd been bludgeoned to death with a blunt instrument of some sort. Most probably a baseball bat, the forensics people guessed. We never found any witnesses and no-one saw a man with a baseball bat in the park around the time of the murder.'

'Well, Hyde Park of all places! You'd have thought that someone would have seen something,' Amrit interrupted.

'Well, the bench was somewhat hidden behind some bushes and there weren't all that many people around as it had been quite unseasonably cold that day. Anyway, what weapon a person chooses when they set out to kill someone can tell you a lot in itself. Using something like a baseball bat is quite visceral and would normally involve some personal hatred on the part of the murderer. Although, having said that, I've known some instances where such attacks were used to send a message of some sort, usually to a rival criminal gang.

Anyway, we investigated every aspect of the dead man's life and we couldn't find even the slightest reason why anyone would want him dead. He seemed to have been quite a mild, self-effacing type of man and we were stumped as to why anyone would not only want to kill him but kill him in that particular manner. So, in desperation we started interviewing everyone again just in case we'd missed something.

Six days after the murder we spoke to some members of the park staff including one who hadn't been interviewed previously as he'd been on holiday. He said that he'd been surprised when he'd seen the photo of the dead man because another man usually sat in that particular bench every Monday evening. He supposed that it being a holiday must have meant a change in the man's routine.

Well, we were there the evening afterwards and we caught the murderer as he was about to attack a man sitting on the bench. He'd circled around behind the bench and then pulled a baseball bat from one of those tubular cardboard poster tubes. He was about to raise it when he suddenly found himself surrounded by armed police. The man on the bench was, of course, one of my team. Once we caught him the full story came out.

The murderer was in the process of getting divorced by his wife but he was still insanely jealous about her. Although she'd taken out a court order against any contact with him, he'd started stalking her anyway. That's how he found out that she was seeing someone. The park bench was regularly used as a meeting place and his wife's lover would sit there while he waited for her to finish work. He'd been watching the lover for a couple of weeks but, unluckily for the dead man, when the murderer made his move, he was so wrapped up in his plans that he forgot that it was a bank holiday. So, in the end, it was quite simply a case of mistaken identity. Someone being in the wrong place at the wrong time. I'm wondering if this case could be one too?'

'And would knowing that help?' Amrit asked.

'It could. The one advantage that I have over the policemen who originally investigated the case is time. If it was mistaken identity then something could have happened in the meantime that might confirm the theory.'

Amrit left him to it. Mac checked his tablet but there was nothing from Martin as yet.

The fourth cold case was that of Mrs. Edith Dickinson from Hemel Hempstead. She was a pensioner who had been found dead by her son some eight years before. She'd been battered around the head by a blunt instrument so again there was quite a lot of blood. The murder weapon, something smaller than a baseball bat forensics said, had never been found and the motive was assumed to be robbery as money and jewellery had been stolen. There had been a spate of pensioner burglaries in the area around the time of the murder but strangely none of the others had involved any violence.

Mrs. Dickinson had three children, the eldest Robert who found the body, and two twin daughters, Ellen and

Eloise, who also lived nearby. The time of death was established as around one in the morning. All the children were married and their partners stated that they had been asleep in bed with them at the time of the murder. The investigators checked out the family's financial situation and found that, apart from the house itself which was to be split three ways, Mrs. Dickinson left very little money behind. Her children didn't seem in be in any financial difficulties either so the investigators thought that money might not have been a motive.

Mac gave this some thought. He then made a mental note to find out if any of the siblings had gotten divorced in the time since the murder.

The fifth cold case was the most recent of the twenty-three. Some eight months ago, a twenty-three year old woman called Ashley Whyte was found dead in her flat which was situated in a 'nice' part of St. Albans. She'd been killed by multiple blows with a hatchet and her right hand had been completely severed so there would have been plenty of blood. There was no CCTV and the neighbours said that they saw and heard nothing. Mac looked at the photos again and suspected that at least some of them must be lying.

Traces of heroin were found all over the flat and a small plastic bag of the drug was found stuffed into her throat. The investigators concluded that the crime was probably drug related.

This was also due to the fact that a more or less identical crime had occurred just a few weeks before in North London, a crime that had been linked to a gang who were major drug dealers in the area. The word on the street was that the man who had been hacked to death had been a dealer working for the gang. He'd been skimming money off the top and that's why his right hand had been cut off as a warning to others.

Police had long suspected that this gang was branching out and had begun peddling crack and heroin in the Hatfield and Hemel Hempstead areas as well as in St. Albans. Ashley had been cautioned once for possessing a small quantity of cannabis when she'd been seventeen but that was it. However, the photos of the needle marks on her body testified that she'd been a recent user. The investigators obviously assumed that Ashley had also been defrauding her suppliers and that's why she'd suffered the same fate. They'd concentrated on trying to establish a link between the drugs gang and Ashley and, when they found nothing, they seemed to have just given up.

There was something about this case that didn't sit well with Mac and he decided that he was going to look at it in a bit more detail.

The last one he included was the murder of Asma Rafiq from twelve years before. Mac had hesitated as it looked highly likely to be an honour killing with the murderer now also being deceased but he put it in anyway.

Just in case.

He lay back and stared at the now all too familiar cracks in the ceiling as he thought. Of course, if Miss Bardolph had been living out of the area for any length of time, then the murder could have happened anywhere. The thought had also occurred to Mac that the murder scene might well have been from a scene in a TV drama or a book that had particularly stuck in her mind. To call it a long shot was probably being optimistic but, as he reminded himself, he didn't really have anything better to do and he was more than grateful for the distraction that it provided.

He was interrupted by lunch. He could smell it coming and he started salivating.

'What is it today?' Mac asked with an expectant smile.

'It's just some vegetable and onion pakora with some raita on the side, all home-made of course.'

'Oh, it smells heavenly,' Mac replied.

He did Amrit's cooking full justice and not a word was uttered until every last crumb had been despatched.

'Now that really was heavenly. You know I'm so glad Bridget managed to get you to look after me. I really look forward to lunch and there's not much else to look forward to being stuck in bed all day.'

Amrit gave him a look of disappointment.

'And here was me thinking that it was our little chats that you so looked forward to.'

'Oh, of course I do look forward to that...as...as well as the food,' Mac replied getting a little flustered.

'Oh, it's okay. I'm just pulling your leg,' Amrit said with a big smile as she collected Mac's plate.

'Well, talking about chats, come back as soon as you can and I'll take you through the last two cases.'

She returned in less than five minutes and made herself comfortable while she waited for Mac to start.

When he'd finished taking her through the cases Amrit was quiet for a while.

'You know, it's a real eye opener listening to these cases. I've lived in this part of the world all my life and you'd think that nothing like that could ever happen here.'

'Well, it is a low crime area but unfortunately not zero crime,' Mac said. 'Nowhere ever is.'

'Okay, so we've got a lot of different weapons; a box cutter, a rock, a blunt instrument, a hatchet and two knives. So, what's next?' Amrit asked.

'My God, I'm impressed!' Mac replied looking suitably impressed. 'You have been paying attention. Well, I've only been skim-reading the cases to get a feel for them. I'm hoping that Martin will come up with something that will point me in the right direction and then I might be able to start digging a bit deeper.'

Unfortunately, his 'digging deeper' would have to wait. A few minutes after Amrit left him, his phone informed him that he'd just received a text message. It was from Martin.

'Sorry got called onto another case so won't be able to get you info until Monday.'

Monday? Of course, it was Friday today. Mac had totally lost track of the days. Okay so the 'Bardolph case', as he was beginning to think of it, would have to wait. He had a whole weekend before he could do anything on that so what to do in the meantime? Without really thinking about it his mouse had opened the Ashley Whyte file.

What was it about this case that bugged him? It was an old enough story. A young woman falls in with the wrong crowd and gets sucked into a situation where she no longer has any control over her life. Perhaps she was trying to steal enough money from the drug gang to get away or perhaps she was just being greedy.

Still it bugged him. He knew that something wasn't right about the case and he made his mind up that he was going to find out what it was.

Chapter Eight

Mac read the file again very carefully.

Ashley Mariah Whyte was born in North London but had moved to Hertfordshire with her family when she was quite young. Her father was a doctor and, around the time of his daughter's death, he had a prosperous private clinic in London. He was a plastic surgeon who specialised in face lifts. Her mother had died a few years before and she had one sibling, a younger sister called Leah.

Ashley had graduated from Durham University with a degree in Educational Studies and she'd managed to get a two-one. Mac checked the dates and found that her mother had died while Ashley had been in the first year of her course. In those circumstances a two-one was a real achievement. It seemed to have all gone wrong for Ashley as soon as she returned home. Her father had expected her to go straight into teacher training, as that had always been her plan, but she hadn't. In fact, she hadn't seemed to have done anything in the year and a half since she'd finished her course, except get hooked on heroin of course.

Mac stopped reading and looked up at the cracks in the ceiling. He tried to imagine what it had been like for Ashley. She'd lost her mother, who she'd been very close to, yet somehow had managed to keep herself going until she'd gotten her degree. After that it seemed like she'd just given up. Perhaps it was only at that point that it had all hit her and he knew all too well how debilitating depression can be following the death of someone you were close to.

It was her father who had discovered that she had a habit. He'd visited her flat unannounced and found her unconscious after taking too much heroin. She nearly died and Mac couldn't help thinking that the overdose might not have been a mistake. Anyway, her father got her some help and paid quite a lot of money to put her into a private clinic for a month. This seemed to work and her father was convinced that she'd been clean around the time of her death. However, the photos said otherwise.

She could have been dealing for as long as a year yet she hadn't shown up anywhere on police records. He looked again at the photos of the crime scene. It seemed even more surreal than it had when he'd first looked at them.

Could that really have happened to a 'nice' girl in a 'nice' part of St. Albans?

He remembered a number of times when horrible crimes had been committed and the neighbours would always say, 'Things like that never happen here.'

He supposed what they really meant was 'rarely' rather than never. Of course, rare events do happen but Mac had learned to distrust them and to always try and look a bit deeper. So, where to start? Mac's eyes were still on Ashley's dead body and the severed right hand. He had the thought that making sure it was a genuinely drug related killing would be a good place to start.

He picked up his phone and then hesitated for some time. He finally summoned up his courage and dialled a number he knew by heart.

'Hello, West End Central Police Station, how can I help?' a young lady asked.

'I need to speak to DS Peter Harper.'

There was a slight pause.

'I'm afraid that we don't have a Detective Sergeant Harper but we do have a Detective Inspector Harper, would that be the same person?'

'Yes, yes it would.'

So, Peter had gone for that promotion at last.

'I'm afraid that DI Harper isn't available at the moment. Can I take a number?'

Mac left his number and the line went dead.

Mac had a sad moment while he thought about the life he'd left behind when he'd been forced to retire. Being a policeman had formed the warp and weft of just about every working day in his life and he found that he missed it almost as much as he did his beloved Nora. He knew it was being unfair but deep down he still felt that he had been betrayed by the force in some way, that they'd somehow let him down when he'd needed them most.

When he'd retired, he had just walked away and never looked back. Yet he'd had many good friends in the force, friendships that had been forged and tested over many years and in some difficult situations. He'd walked away from them too.

Peter had been the best of all of those friends. He'd been his sergeant for over twelve years, his right hand, almost his other self. Yet Mac hadn't seen him once since he'd retired. This hadn't been Peter's fault as Mac knew he'd called on at least two occasions. He knew this because he'd been hiding in the house when the door-bell rang. Deep in depression he hadn't been opening the door to anyone at the time. The sympathy etched in people's faces only served to remind him that his wife was dead and the reality of that was just too hard to bear.

It still was at times.

Mac was grateful to have his thoughts interrupted by the phone ringing.

'Mac, is that really you?' a familiar voice said.

'Peter, it's so good to hear your voice.'

'How are you? I've heard all about your daring exploits. I was going to call over but I wasn't sure...'

Peter never finished the sentence. Mac knew that he owed his old friend an apology.

'I'm sorry Peter, I really am. I've been in a very strange place and I think I'm only beginning to realise now how strange it's been. After Nora died, I desperately needed to work. I suppose I was using it as a crutch, it was the only way I felt I could get through it all. Then, when that was taken away, I went into a dark place for quite a while. I think I'm only coming out of it now if I'm honest.'

There was silence for a few seconds.

'I would have liked to have helped you, Mac, I really would have....'

'Peter, you weren't the only friend I pushed away. God knows there were many times when I wouldn't even see Bridget. Anyway, if I'm honest, I'm not sure anyone could have helped me. I've had to find my own way out.'

'And have you?' Peter asked.

Another silence.

'I hope so, I really do.'

'Is that what you rang about?'

'It should have been but no, there is something else. I could do with a case file if you could track it down for me.'

Mac told Peter about the Ashley Whyte case and about the related case in North London.

'Yes, I remember that one. From what I heard the gang were sending out a message, they reckoned they were being ripped off far too often. Anyway, it must have worked as there hasn't been anything like that since as far as I know.'

'Can you get me the full case file? I'd like to compare it to the St. Albans case,' Mac explained.

'No problem, in fact I'll bring it over myself if you like. You're not going anywhere in the next few hours, are you?'

Mac assured his friend that the likelihood of that being the case was exactly zero.

When Amrit came in with a mug of coffee she noticed a difference in him.

'You're looking happy, my coffee must be better than I thought.'

'No, it's not that...'

'What? Are you saying that my coffee isn't that wonderful?' she said in mock indignation.

Mac's smile went even wider. He was beginning to realise that his nurse was a bit of a leg puller.

'Your coffee is as delicious as ever, of course, but no, I was happy because an old friend is going to visit, one that I haven't seen for a long while.'

'I'm glad then, what is they say? Oh yes, if you haven't learned the meaning of friendship, you really haven't learned anything,' Amrit said.

'That's all too true. Is that a Sikh saying?'

'No Muhammad Ali. My father loved him when he was boxing and he used to quote him all the time when I was young.'

'He was a great man,' Mac said. 'He once came to Birmingham you know, not long after I left. I heard that he closed the city centre down, there were such massive crowds everywhere he went. A friend of mine saw him in the flesh and he still talks about it today as being something very special.'

'Okay, is there anything else you need before I go?' Amrit asked.

She could guess from Mac's face what he needed.

'Okay, I'll get the wheelchair. I really wish that you'd at least consider a urine bottle. It would save you a lot of pain...'

One look at Mac's face told her that this was a subject that was not up for discussion.

She'd got him back in bed and comfortable just before Bridget came in. Again, he could hear them talking in the corridor but, listen as hard as he might, he couldn't quite make out what they were saying. He heard the front door close just before Bridget came in.

'Is that right? Is Peter really coming?' she asked with a wide smile.

'Yes, he should be here in an hour or so.'

'That's great, dad. It will be really nice to see him.'

She thought it was better than great actually. It had been a source of worry to her that he'd cut himself off from his former friends in the police.

'Is he going to be here for a while?' Bridget asked.

'I hope so as he's driving all the way from London. Why?'

'Well I thought that I might go around and see Tommy for an hour,' she said.

'Tommy?' Mac asked.

'Yes, he's around at the flat. He's trying to redecorate it before...well...you know, for when I go back.'

Bridget looked a little uncomfortable as she said this but not as uncomfortable as her father felt when he realised the situation.

'God, I have been so selfish!' he said.

His daughter and her boyfriend Tommy, a detective constable, had just bought a flat nearby and were planning on moving in together. Mac had been so grateful when Bridget had volunteered to stay with him until his period of confinement was over that he hadn't considered what Tommy would be doing.

'You know I honestly never gave it a thought,' Mac said. 'So, Tommy's around at the flat which is what, some three or four hundred yards away or so, while you're stuck here every night with me. Is that right?'

She nodded.

'You could have arranged a night nurse, you know?'

'Well, yes I could have but I wanted to be here for you, dad. I know how hard it's going to be for you in getting through these next few weeks. Anyway, it was my decision and believe me I can be every bit as stubborn as you when it comes to it,' she said.

Mac knew that was only the truth. He thought for a moment.

'Okay, when Peter comes go around and tell Tommy to pack a bag and take him back here with you.'

bring ⌠ ·

Bridget looked puzzled.

'What? You mean Tommy can stay here?'

'Of course, it's the only sensible solution. If you've got to stay here then so must Tommy.'

'In my room?' Bridget eventually asked.

'Of course, he's not going to sleep on the sofa, is he? Bridget, your mum was the religious one in this house but she was also the practical one as well. Believe me she'd have said exactly the same thing too.'

'Thanks dad. I had thought of it but I just couldn't think how to ask you. I have missed him.'

'Well, luckily I like him too. Anyway, he can keep me up to date with everything that's going on down the station.'

'Ah, so there's an ulterior motive after all then,' she said with a sly smile.

Mac couldn't help smiling too. His daughter looked happy again.

He passed the time by re-reading the Whyte case again from the beginning. He was surprised when he heard the doorbell ring and he felt a sudden thrill of fear, or perhaps it was embarrassment or shame. Or most likely a mixture of all three.

He could hear Bridget say 'Peter' then she exchanged a few words with their visitor.

Mac felt quite tense as the door to his room opened. However, all his fear and misgivings dissolved the second Mac saw his old friend's face again.

'Peter,' Mac said warmly.

'Mac,' Peter replied with a wide smile.

They shook hands firmly and looked at each other. They both knew at that moment that their friendship was as alive as ever. Peter was only a little taller than

Mac but he was much more broadly built. He was an ex-Army man who had always kept himself fit while Mac had never been able to turn down the odd sausage and egg sandwich from the police canteen. He was also someone that Mac respected both professionally, as one of the best policemen he'd ever worked with, and personally as a good friend.

'So, this is what you get these days for being a hero?' Peter said with a grim smile as he sat down.

'Oh, enough of the 'hero' nonsense. We worked as a team on that case just as we used to do, a team.'

'I know but it still seems a bit harsh, doesn't it? Save a girl's life, get your photo in all the newspapers and then follow all that up with six weeks lying flat on your back. How long have you got to go before you're up and around again?'

'Another five weeks,' Mac replied. 'It feels like a prison sentence if I'm honest.'

Peter shook his head.

'You've not had the best of luck lately have you, old friend?' Peter stated with a sympathetic expression.

'No, perhaps I haven't but I'm hoping that's about to change. After all you're here.'

Peter smiled and very gently put his hand on the back of Mac's hand.

'Anyway, here's what you were after,' Peter said as he pulled a memory stick out of his pocket. 'It's a pretty slim file, no leads and no suspects I'm afraid.'

'Thanks. How's it going at the station? Are most of the old team still there?'

'Yes, we're all still there more or less. We've got a new boss now, DCS Malcolm Acton.'

From Peter's expression he could tell that he didn't think much of DCS Acton.

'I hope the team are giving him a chance. How long has he been in charge now?'

'Just over six months. I think it's fair to say that we've given him a chance but I think he managed to more or less blow it the first day he arrived.'

'Why what happened?' Mac asked wondering what he could have done that so terrible.

'Remember the stationery cupboard?'

'Oh yes, it used to be the chief's office before I came.'

'Well, I remember when you were first appointed. You looked a little green around the gills but your instincts were good. Before you came all the other chiefs used to have their own office and they kept themselves well away from the likes of us ordinary plods. The first thing you did was take over an empty desk right in the middle of the room and, when some-one asked what should we do with the office, you suggested that it might make a good stationery cupboard.'

Mac remembered that first day well. He supposed he'd wanted to make the point that, whatever you were in the team, everyone was just a part. He also had to admit that he liked being in the thick of things, really getting to know each team member's strengths and weaknesses, as well as keeping up with what was going on in the investigation in real time.

'Anyway, DCS Acton had it cleared out and had a plaque engraved and attached to the door. The plaque reads 'DCS Malcolm Acton – Knock and wait'. Knock and bloody wait. That didn't go down too well with the team I'm afraid and things have gone downhill further since then.'

Before Peter could explain further Bridget stuck her head around the door.

'I'm just off to see Tommy,' she said. 'Just in case I'm not back before you go Peter, I'll say goodbye and thanks for calling around. I know how much it means to dad. Take care.'

'You too, Bridget.'

As they heard the front door close Peter said, 'My God she's all grown up, isn't she? Makes me feel old.'

'Tell me about it. There was a time when I used to tell her what to do, it's definitely the other way around now. Anyway, I want you to tell me everything that's been going on since I left and a bit more about this DCS Acton too...'

Chapter Nine

The next morning Mac awoke to daylight and had the wonderful feeling that he might have actually slept for a few hours. He looked over at his clock and saw that it had just gone eight o'clock. He'd been awake in the night for a while but he must have had at least five hours sleep which was good.

He lay there with a smile on his face as he replayed his old friend's visit in his head. He'd been brought fully up to date with everything that had been going on at the station since he'd left and Peter had gone away with Mac's promise to visit as soon as he was mobile again. It was a promise that Mac was determined to keep.

He felt uncomfortable and tried to re-adjust his position. As he moved a flash of pain ran down his left leg. He hadn't been aware of making a noise but he must have as Tommy's head appeared around the door a few seconds later.

'Are you okay Mac?' he asked with some concern.

'As I'll ever be, I suppose. It's okay, come in and sit down.'

Tommy was dressed in a loose-fitting T shirt and track suit bottoms. From the sleepy look on his face Mac guessed that he'd just got up.

'No lie-in today?' Mac asked.

'No, I'm not all that great at lie-ins to be honest. I thought I'd let Bridget sleep on for a bit while I started breakfast, she was really tired last night. Oh, and thanks Mac, it's kind of you to let me stay.'

'Tommy, it's not being kind at all. I'm sorry, I just didn't think when Bridget volunteered to stay with me. I was just glad she'd be around and I selfishly agreed. Anyway, I believe that you're redecorating the flat?'

'Well, I haven't gotten too far to be honest. I've had a few late nights at work and with Bridget not being there,' Tommy said with a shrug.

'I'll give you the number of a decorator that one of my neighbours used a few months ago. He's supposed to be good. Tell him what you want and then get him to send me the bill. It'll be a nice surprise for Bridget when she goes back.'

'Really Mac, you don't have to...'

'Oh, but I do. I was planning on doing something for you both when you got the flat anyway but the case was gaining momentum at the time and it went right out of my head. I want to Tommy, so long as it's okay with you that is?'

Tommy smiled as he said, 'Well, it's more than okay with me. Over the past week or so I've discovered that DIY isn't exactly one of my strengths. Well, if I'm honest, I'm just rubbish at it.'

'Yes, me too,' Mac admitted. 'Well, I suppose there's more to life than being able to wield a paint brush effectively.'

'Although I have to admit that I'm a little bit better with a frying pan. Fancy a bacon sandwich?' Tommy asked.

Mac's smile was answer enough. Tommy returned fifteen minutes later with a tray on which were two coffees and two bacon sandwiches. Tommy handed Mac a plate and his travel mug.

'Someone left a note in the kitchen saying to use the travel mug for your drinks,' Tommy explained.

'My nurse,' Mac replied. 'She's very thorough.'

While they ate, Mac had Tommy bring him up to date with everything that was going on with the Major Crime Unit.

'So, Jo and Gerry are still an item then?' Mac asked.

Mac had been surprised when he'd heard the news. His colleagues Jo Thibonais and Gerry Dugdale had met each other for the first time during the Natasha Barker case. The last time Mac had seen them together they hadn't seemed to getting on all that well. In fact, they gave all the appearance of pretty much hating each other.

'Not only that but I've heard that wedding bells might be in the air,' Tommy said.

Mac shook his head in wonder while inwardly saying a little prayer wishing them luck.

'So, what are you working on at the moment?'

'Well, we're all working really hard on the 'Priory Park Strangling' as the press have called it. I've been partnering Martina but, as she's on a course for the next week or so, I'm not quite sure what I'll be doing on Monday.'

'Tell me a bit about the case,' Mac asked.

He was curious. All he knew about it was what he'd read in the papers.

'Okay, just over a week ago the body of a man in his early twenties was found in Priory Lake by the members of a sailing class. Forensics said that the body had been in the water for some time and had come to the surface due to gases caused by decomposition. It had been fairly windy that day and forensics think that the wind pushed the body up onto the bank of a small island in the centre of the lake where it was spotted by a group of dinghy sailors. They called the local police in. At first, they thought that it was just someone who'd gotten drunk, fallen in the lake and drowned. Apparently, it's happened there before. However, the autopsy stated that the cause of death was asphyxiation, whoever he was he'd been strangled.'

'You haven't identified him yet then?' Mac asked.

Tommy shook his head.

'They managed to get two partial fingerprints and, so far at least, they don't match anything we've got on our records. He had no identifying marks and dental records haven't come up with anything as yet. They've identified some fragments of cloth as possibly belonging to a black track suit. The cloth, however, is fairly generic and the track suit could have been bought anywhere.'

'Any underwear?' Mac asked.

'Underwear? No, they didn't find any traces of underwear.'

'An old copper years ago used to say 'No underwear then its murder' on the premise that any self-respecting suicide would always put underwear on. He had a point though.'

'Well yes, I suppose that makes sense but, in this case, they said that it was possible that he was wearing underwear but, being quite thin material, it wouldn't have lasted long in the water.'

'So, you're stuck then,' Mac said.

'Yes, it looks like it and it's frustrating the hell out of Dan Carter. Jo reckons that there's a direct correlation between how grumpy Dan gets and how well the case is going. The 'grumpometer' she calls it.'

'He just cares that's all.'

'Yes, I know. Anyway, we're doing all we can to establish an identity but until we do...' Tommy said with shrug by way of a full stop.

'Yes, I've had some cases like that. Once we were able to identify the body, we generally solved the case fairly quickly. It was usually more than obvious who the murderer was once you knew who the victim was. Unfortunately, there were more than a few cases where we couldn't get any identification at all. I must admit I personally found that really galling, in part I think because it made me feel absolutely helpless, and that's not a feeling I enjoy. I'd guess that's why Dan's so grumpy.'

'So, what's the answer?' Tommy asked.

'Just keep going. You have to put the work in whatever happens. When things are looking a bit hopeless, I always try to convince myself that the answer will be just around the next corner, the next person you interview, the next evidence report or the next phone call you take. And sometimes it is. Then there are other times when you know you've reached a point in a case where there's no other option than to give up,' Mac said with a sombre expression. 'I always hated having to do that.'

In the short silence that followed neither heard the door opening.

'Talking shop, are we?' Bridget asked with a smile.

'Guilty as charged,' Mac quickly replied.

'Bacon sandwich and coffee?' Tommy asked as he stood up.

'Please,' she replied giving him a grateful glance.

She sat down in the seat that Tommy had vacated.

'Did you get any sleep?'

'Yes, I did actually,' Mac replied, 'and I feel all the better for it too.'

She put her hand over Mac's and gave it a squeeze.

'Thanks, dad.'

'For what exactly? It's me who should be thanking you. Anyway, what exciting plans have you got for the weekend?'

'Well, we desperately need some shopping doing today but apart from that nothing. For once we both have a weekend off together too, can you believe that?' Bridget replied.

'Well, don't spend it all with me. Can't you get someone in while you and Tommy have a night out?'

'Not this late and, anyway, I don't want just anyone looking after you.'

Mac gave this some thought.

'Look, Tim's back tomorrow afternoon. I'll give him a ring and see if he'll sit with me for a few hours so you and Tommy can at least have one evening out.'

'Oh dad, that would be great! I've been dying to try that new Italian restaurant in town. I've heard it's really good.'

It took Mac quite a while to persuade his daughter to take Tommy with her to do the shopping. He said that he'd be okay by himself for an hour or two. She made him comfortable before she went but she still didn't look totally convinced as she shut the door behind her. She made sure his phone was switched on and within reach before she left.

In truth Mac was dying to see what was on the memory stick that Peter had brought him. He fired up his laptop and had a look. He was so wrapped up in it that he was more than surprised to hear the front door opening. He thought that Bridget must have forgotten something.

'Sorry we've been so long,' Bridget said. 'Have you been okay?'

'Yes, in fact the time's flown by. I've been looking at a file that Peter brought me last night.'

'Good. Do you fancy a coffee?'

He did.

Tommy arrived with Mac's coffee a few minutes later and he brought one for himself too.

'Bridget says that you're working on an old case. Are you getting anywhere with it?'

'Yes, sit down and I'll tell you all about it if you like.'

Mac took him through an outline of the case as it stood.

'So, what do you think?' Mac asked.

Tommy looked uncertain.

'Well, it all seems plausible enough but St. Alban's? I don't know, have they ever had anything like that happen there before?'

'Not quite and that got me thinking. I know that there has to be a first time for everything but I still had some doubts. So, I asked one of my old colleagues from

71

London if he could get me a copy of the case file for the original gang murder in North London. It makes for interesting reading.'

Mac showed Tommy the photos from the original murder scene.

'God that's pretty gruesome, isn't it?' Tommy exclaimed as he looked at the laptop.

'Well, I suppose that was the whole point of the murder, it was supposed to send a message out to anyone who was thinking of robbing the gang. Now, have a look at scene from the St. Albans case.'

'Equally gruesome but I can see one major difference straight away, the hand,' Tommy said pointing to the screen.

'There are a few others but yes that's the main one. According to the case file Peter gave me, after chopping off his hand, the gang had used some stiff wire to fold down all the fingers except for the middle finger which they left straight. They then placed the hand on his chest.'

'The Americans call it 'flipping the bird',' Tommy explained.

'Really? I've only ever heard the words 'Up yours' used with that particular gesture. Anyway, it's supposed to be a thing with this gang. Apparently, one of the punishments they mete out for more minor offences is to break the middle finger on each hand with hammer. Then, if someone transgresses again, they snip them off with a pair of chain cutters.'

'Nice people!' Tommy said with a grimace.

'Yes, but if it's such a trademark of theirs why didn't they wire back Ashley Whyte's fingers?'

Tommy gave it some thought.

'Well, if I had to guess I'd say that the wiring back of the fingers and the severed hand being placed on the chest were details that weren't released to the press.'

Mac smiled.

'Go on.'

'So, I'd guess that this might be a copycat crime, someone dressing it up to make it look like a gang killing.'

'That's exactly what I've been thinking but what's puzzling me is why didn't the investigators spot it?' Mac said with a puzzled expression. 'It seems from what I've read that they only pursued the drug gang theory.'

'Who led the investigation?'

'A DCI Joseph Ibbotson working out of Hatfield.'

Tommy shook his head.

'No, I haven't come across him before. If it's Hatfield then Jo might know him. I think that she worked there for a while on relief. Shall I get her to give you a ring on Monday?'

'Yes, please do. I was going to try and call him on Monday myself but I'll wait until I speak to Jo,' Mac said. 'A bit of background knowledge never hurts.'

Chapter Ten

Apart from the fact that he was stuck in bed, the weekend went reasonably well. He liked having Tommy around but the thing he enjoyed most was seeing Bridget being a little more relaxed. She not only had Tommy's company but his help in looking after Mac.

They both enjoyed their night out at the restaurant but Mac made Tommy promise not to say anything to Bridget about getting the flat redecorated. He wanted to save it for a surprise. Meanwhile, Mac had really enjoyed his night in with Tim. He'd managed to pack a lot into his furniture buying trip and his tales, somewhat embellished no doubt, took some time to tell. A few cold cans of Mac's favourite beer helped the storytelling along nicely.

Even so, Mac was glad when Monday morning arrived so he could get on with the Whyte case. Tommy had promised to get Jo to call as early as she could. However, Mac was still surprised when his phone rang just before eight thirty.

'Mac, how are you?' Jo asked. Without waiting for a response she continued. 'Tommy says you need some information?'

'Yes, I was just wondering if you'd come across a DCI Joseph Ibbotson before?'

Jo was silent for a moment.

'Yes, unfortunately,' she replied with no enthusiasm in her voice whatsoever.

'Why unfortunately?'

'Well, I'll try and put this as delicately as I can. He's a racist bastard.'

Mac thought this might explain a lot.

'Really? Tell me.'

'Well, in the old days I used to get a lot of it, the constant innuendo, the so-called jokes, taking the piss out of my accent, oh and the total lack of promotion, you know little things like that. It's better now but I think it might be safe to say that Joe was one of the old school, a bloody dinosaur if you ask me. The best thing he ever did was retire.'

'When did he do that?' Mac asked.

'Late last year I think it was.'

So, the Whyte case might have been his last one.

'He was lazy as well as being racist from what I heard,' Jo added.

'Do you know anything about a DS Grimsson?' Mac asked.

DS Grimsson had signed off a lot of the documents in the file. It had stuck in Mac's head as it was an unusual name.

'Yes, I met her a few times, strange looking woman. She seemed okay. You could tell that she didn't like working with Joe. I could see a look of disgust on her face whenever he thought he was being at most hilarious.'

'Jo thanks, you've been very helpful indeed.'

'Have I? Anyway, I hope that you get better soon Mac. I'm not going to say why but if you're not up and about by the end of July you'll have to come to the church on a stretcher.'

'So, it's really going to happen then? Don't worry Jo, I wouldn't miss that for the world and give my best to Gerry.'

Mac was thoughtful for a while after the call. Then he rang the station and got DS Kate Grimsson's mobile number.

'Hello, DS Grimsson.'

Her voice was light and almost musical.

'I'm Mac Maguire and I'm helping out the MCU with some cases...'

'Oh yes of course, a pleasure to speak to you DCS Maguire. I heard that you were giving us a hand. How can I help?'

'I'm unfortunately a bit tied down today but I'd like to speak to you about the Ashley Whyte case. Could you pop over and see me sometime? I'm in Letchworth.'

'You're looking into the Whyte case?' she asked.

'Yes, DS Dan Carter's asked me to have another look at the case, along with a few others.'

There was a slight pause.

'If you give me your address, I can be with you in around forty-five minutes.'

Mac did just that. She was obviously surprised that someone was looking into the case and, from what little he could tell from her voice, it didn't seem to have been unwelcome news to her.

Amrit came in with his breakfast.

'I heard that you were on the phone so I waited a few minutes,' she explained as she placed the tray on his lap.

There was a beaker full of orange juice, his travel mug from which the rich aroma of coffee wafted and a bowlful of muesli.

'So, the bird seed at last,' Mac stated with a frown.

'Well, you have been having quite a lot of fatty foods recently. Bridget said that we should be a bit relaxed about what you ate for the first week as that would be the hardest time for you but you need to be careful not to put too much weight on. It won't help your back much when you get mobile again.'

Mac sighed. He knew that Amrit's logic was totally unassailable.

'Actually, I love muesli,' he said with a forced smile.

'That's the spirit,' Amrit replied.

He found that it actually wasn't that bad, not that Mac would ever admit that to his nurse or his daughter.

Kate Grimsson made it in less than forty minutes. Amrit ushered her into Mac's bedroom. She didn't seem at all surprised to see Mac in bed.

As she sat down Mac looked her over. She was a little older than her voice had suggested, around thirty perhaps. Her flame red shoulder length hair was immediately striking and perhaps even more so as her skin was quite pale in colour. Her features were symmetrical and quite delicate. She wore a charcoal grey trouser suit that was softened by a very feminine pink lace blouse. If Mac had been challenged to guess her profession then being a police detective might have been quite low on his list.

'DCS Maguire, it's nice to meet you. I heard that you were indisposed after the Barker case,' she said.

Mac was more than intrigued by her use of the word 'indisposed'. It wasn't a word that you heard used that often nowadays.

'Yes, I've just under five weeks still to go,' Mac said a little glumly. 'It's nice to meet you too, Sergeant Grimsson.'

'Oh, please call me Kate.'

'And you can call me Mac, if that's okay. Thanks for coming to see me so soon. Before we start, do you mind if I ask you about your surname? It's quite unusual.'

She smiled at the question.

'It's Icelandic, my father comes from a place called Kopavogur.'

'Shouldn't you strictly be called Grimsdottir then?'

'Very good Mr…sorry, Mac. Not that many people here know about Icelandic surnames. However, my father's name is Einar Grimsson so strictly I should be called Kate Einarsdottir. However, as my father had permanently settled here, he found it simpler to just use his surname.'

'Thanks Kate. Anyway, as you're aware I asked you here because of the Whyte case…'

She interrupted, 'I'll bet you want to ask about the hand and why the fingers weren't wired back.'

'Yes, exactly.'

Mac decided to let Kate do all the talking. He could see that she had something on her mind.

'Well, I said exactly the same thing but I'm afraid that my boss at the time didn't agree.'

'Did he say why?' Mac asked.

She looked up at the ceiling.

'Yes, he said something along the lines of 'Well, she's black so it must be drugs' if I remember right. Except he didn't use the word black if you know what I mean.'

Mac could see the uneasiness in his visitor's face.

'Why didn't you report him?' Mac asked bluntly.

'Who, Joe? I suppose I should of, he certainly gave me enough ammunition,' Kate replied. 'Then again he seemed to be well connected in the local force and he was retiring anyway...'

She looked at Mac who said nothing. He wanted her to carry on. He was sure that there was something else. She looked down at the floor and her shoulders slumped.

'The real reason is that I just didn't feel strong enough at the time. I'd just moved to the Hertfordshire force from Essex as I was going through quite a messy divorce and I wasn't exactly brimming with confidence at the time. To be honest no-one else seemed to be rushing to report him either.'

Mac could see that she would have been in a tough position. She was new to the station and it would have been hard enough reporting a senior officer anyway without having the added complications of an ongoing divorce.

'Okay, we are where we are,' Mac said. 'Was there anything else about the case that you disagreed with?'

'Just about everything, I think. Every time I made a suggestion it got steamrollered, so I stopped making any.'

'So, tell me what you think happened to Ashley Whyte?'

'I think that drugs might have been involved in some way, as she was a user, but I think that the hatchet attack was a ruse, someone trying to make us think that it was related to the North London gang murder. Besides the hand there were other differences. The assailant was left-handed in the Whyte case while the assailant in the North London murder was right-handed. There were defence wounds on both Ashley's arms and that implies that it was likely to have been a lone attacker. In the North London murder, there were no defence wounds meaning that the victim was obviously restrained while the killing blows were struck. That would imply that there were at least two and, perhaps more likely, three assailants. Most importantly pictures of the North London killing appeared on a social media site seconds later but there was total silence online after Ashley Whyte's murder.'

Mac was silent for a moment.

'I hadn't been aware of that last fact which is very suggestive in itself,' he said. 'Why go to all the bother of killing someone for stealing from you if you're not going to advertise the fact?'

'Obviously the photos weren't up for long before they got taken down,' Kate said, 'but they were up long enough so that anyone who followed the gang would get the point.'

Mac thought about what he'd just learned. Anyone from the gang or even someone following them on social media would have known about their calling card, the severed hand wired up. The police hadn't released this fact to the press so he could only conclude that it was indeed a ruse. Of course, the press could have found this out for themselves but he guessed that the routine murder of a drug dealer wasn't felt to be interesting enough for their readers.

'What are you planning on doing?' Kate asked.

'I'm going to advise that the case be re-opened,' Mac replied. 'I'll have to pass it back to Dan Carter's team even though they're currently up their eyes trying to identify a water-logged corpse in Bedford.'

'Can I have a go at it for a few days first, sir? I've not got much on at the moment.'

Mac had a feeling that she might say that. Her heart was in the right place and she obviously wanted to try and make amends for her ex-boss's shortcomings and possibly her own.

'I'm sorry but that's not my decision. However, I'll put a word in for you. I think that it might be useful to have someone involved who knows the case well.'

She stood up and shook Mac's hand.

'Thank you DCS...sorry Mac. You've got my number.'

After Kate left Mac found himself thinking about her, although not in any sort of romantic way. Certain people he met intrigued him for some reason as though they were an interesting puzzle in themselves. Kate Grimsson was definitely one of those.

He got his phone and called Dan Carter.

'Hello Mac, I hope things are going better with your cold cases that the one I'm working on.'

'Still getting nowhere?' Mac asked.

'Nowhere is exactly where we are. My God, you'd think in this day and age that people couldn't just disappear without someone noticing. Anyway, enough of my whingeing. How can I help?'

'I'd like you to re-open the Ashley Whyte case,' Mac said.

There was a moment's silence while Dan tried to recollect the details.

'She was that girl who was murdered with a hatchet in St. Albans, wasn't she? Drug gang or so they thought.'

'Yes, that's right.'

'So, what have you got?' Dan asked.

Mac took him through the facts of the case and then told him what he'd learned from Kate Grimsson.

'Bloody hell! It seems like this DCI Ibbotson's made a right bloody mess of it and, unfortunately, it's our mess now. What do you suggest?'

'DS Grimsson knows the case well and she says she hasn't much on at the moment. So, I was wondering if you could get her on a temporary attachment and have her work with one of the team. I'd think of having a team of two to kick off with, so it wouldn't impact on your current caseload too much and, if they uncover anything, then you can always think about putting more resources in then.'

'Well, I suppose that makes sense especially as the case has been parked for a while anyway. Okay, I'll see what I can do. Will you be okay to liaise with whoever I put on it?' Dan asked.

'Oh yes, absolutely. I'd really like to know how this case works out.'

'Okay leave it with me then. I'll call around later and let you know what the arrangements are going to be.'

Dan called around less than two hours later.

'So, how's it going?' Dan asked.

Mac thought that he looked a bit grumpy, which was normal for Dan, but he also looked a bit worn out too.

'As well as it can be, I suppose in the circumstances,' Mac replied. 'Oh, and can I say thanks again for the cases. I'd have gone totally doolally by now without them.'

'God Mac, it should be me who's thanking you. You've already solved one and, knowing you, I wouldn't bet that you won't crack this Whyte case too.'

'So, you're re-opening the case then?' Mac said with a grin.

'Yes, I am,' Dan said. 'I've arranged for DS Grimsson to join us for a while and she's going to team up with Tommy for a while as Martina's away on a course. I'll get them to liaise directly with you. Just let me know if there's any progress in the case.'

'That's great, I'll see if I can get together with both of them later today and get the ball rolling. By the way, how's the Priory Park case coming along?'

'It isn't, which is the other reason I came to see you if I'm honest,' Dan replied. 'I've had the team scurrying around doing all the usual things but, for all their work, we've come up with absolutely nothing.'

'So, I take it that you now think it's time to try some of the unusual things?' Mac asked.

'To be honest I'll try anything just now but all we've got is the corpse and that's not yielded anything of use so far. I was thinking about facial reconstruction. Have you had any experience of that?'

'Yes, I've used it in two cases where we came up against the same brick wall that you have.'

'How did it work out?' Dan said as he leant forward.

'Well, the first time we tried it we got nowhere but the professor did warn us that it wasn't fool proof.'

'The professor?'

'Yes, Professor Catherine Watkins. She works out of the Medical School at Manchester University,' Mac explained.

'So, you said that it didn't work the first time but what about the second?'

'We got a positive ID within two days and had the murderer behind bars twenty-four hours later.'

'So why did it work for one and not the other?' Dan asked.

'Any number of factors really. The Professor said that, although she can get the face looking reasonably like it would have done in life, things like skin or hair colour are a bit of a guess. Then there are other things such as

82

wrinkles, moles and scars. Apparently, you only have to get a few things wrong for a face to become more or less unrecognisable.'

'It sounds like it might be worth a shot though,' Dan said looking a little more cheerful.

'Oh definitely, I think you'll find it a really interesting process too.'

Mac smiled at seeing Dan leaving a bit happier. He would have phoned Tommy straight away but Amrit insisted that he should eat his lunch first. Mac relented on learning that it was Lamb Tikka. He repaid Amrit by giving her lunch his full and undivided attention.

'You know, I keep thinking that your lunches just can't get any better and then they do. That was fantastic,' Mac said as Amrit took his tray away.

'Oh, it's easy to cook for someone who appreciates food the way you do,' Amrit replied with a smile. 'Do you need anything else?'

'No, I'm okay for now. By the way I'm hoping to have a couple of visitors a bit later on. Dan Carter's agreed to re-open the Ashley Whyte case.'

'Really?' Amrit said with wide eyes. 'You will let me know what happens though? I'm only halfway through the series as it were and I'm dying to know how it all ends.'

Mac smiled at Amrit's insistence.

'Don't worry, I'll keep you fully informed,' Mac said reassuringly.

Mac arranged to meet Kate at four. He then rang Tommy and asked him to come a half an hour earlier. He arrived at three thirty on the dot and Mac brought him up to speed with the details of the case before Kate Grimsson arrived.

Amrit ushered Kate into Mac's bedroom and then returned with an extra chair.

'Does anyone want coffee?' Amrit asked.

'Oh yes, please,' Mac replied.

Kate and Tommy smiled and nodded.

'So, introductions first. Kate this is DC Tommy Nugent and he'll be working with you on the case. Tommy's part of the Major Crime Unit team and I've worked with him on a few cases now. By the way, not that it will have any bearing on the case but just so that you know, Tommy is also my daughter's boyfriend. Tommy, this is DS Kate Grimsson from Hatfield who worked on the original investigation. Dan's managed to get her temporarily attached to the MCU for this case. With Kate on board we can get the new investigation up and running straight away.'

Kate and Tommy shook hands and exchanged pleasantries.

'Okay, so we start tomorrow and, for now at least, it will just be the three of us,' Mac continued. 'Kate is in charge of the investigation but Dan has asked that you liaise with me if that's okay.'

'I'll be I charge?' she asked as if she was unsure that she'd heard him correctly.

'Well yes, you're the senior rank here. I'm just a civilian.'

Mac could see a fleeting look of mistrust in her face but she quickly regained her composure.

'Yes, yes of course I'll liaise with you. What does that mean exactly?' she asked.

'That's a good question. I suppose it means whatever we want it to mean. My idea was that we could get our heads together every day or so and, based on what we've learned, discuss what direction we think the investigation should take. I'm happy to give advice but it's totally up to you whether you follow it or not.'

Kate gave this some thought.

'Okay that sounds about right to me. However, I'm aware of your reputation so I think that I'll be taking your advice very seriously if that's okay.'

Mac smiled.

'Okay, so Kate where do we start?'

'I've been giving it some thought. As I said earlier, I think that the 'North London drug gang' theory is just plain wrong but drugs could have something to do with it. Ashley was a user so where was she getting it from? Was she dealing on the side? We interviewed her sister and some of her friends and they all denied any knowledge of Ashley being back on heroin. Someone must have known something though. Then there's the rehab clinic. Her father paid for her to go to a private clinic to try and get her off drugs. She started going nine months or so before she died.'

'Yes, it was called the Al-Faran Clinic, wasn't it?' Mac asked.

'Yes, that's right. She spent four weeks in the clinic initially and then she went back every couple of weeks or so as an out-patient. I'm thinking that she could have met someone there. I mean places like that are useful if you want to recruit dealers, aren't they?'

'Yes, that's a good point. If you can get them hooked again then they won't have much option but to sell to others to keep their habit up,' Mac said. 'Okay then, the clinic seems like a good place to start.'

'We also spent a lot of time looking for this 'dre man' but we were probably looking in the wrong place,' Kate said.

'Dre man? What's that?' Mac asked.

'Wasn't it in the file?' Kate asked.

Mac's puzzled expression was answer enough. Kate fished out her phone and after many taps on the screen passed it to Mac. It showed a text message or rather an image of a text message. It was from Ashley and it was dated the day she died.

'Trina worried can I stay at yours think I said wrong thing and dre man's men are coming scared A'

Mac sighed and wondered what else was missing from the files.

85

'Who's Trina?' Mac asked.

'Trina Derbyshere, she was an old friend of Ashley's. DCI Ibbotson thought that 'Dre man' was some sort of gang nickname,' Kate explained.

'Why wasn't this in the case file?' Mac said with a frown.

Kate shrugged, 'When he knew that we weren't going to solve the case in five minutes, he lost interest. As he was retiring, I honestly don't think Joe Ibbotson cared one way or the other about whether we found who killed Ashley.'

'Is there anything else I might be missing?' Mac asked still scowling.

To him all evidence was sacrosanct and not including it in a case file was a cardinal sin.

'I'll let you have my case file tomorrow. I've made sure that everything's in there,' Kate said.

'Thanks.'

'There's a Dr. Dre,' Tommy volunteered. 'He's a rapper, he used to be in NWA.'

'NWA?' Mac asked.

'They were a sort of band. Don't ask what it stands for,' Tommy warned. 'Anyway, I think that 'Dre' is short for Andre.'

'So, this 'dre man' might be a dealer, possibly called Andre. Even if he isn't involved in drugs Ashley said she was scared of him and then died a few hours later so we need to find him. Who runs the clinic?'

'A Dr. Al-Faran. She's in her forties and she's got quite a good reputation for getting people off drugs,' Kate replied. 'However, it might be slightly easier for her than for a lot of other doctors as most of her clients tend to be very rich. Apparently, she charges somewhere in the region of thirty thousand pounds for a basic course of treatment.'

'Basic? How much do the extras cost?' Mac asked.

'Well, if you need more than one stay at the clinic it can cost up to fifty thousand.'

Mac shook his head

'Well, I suppose if you've got the money and it works but it still seems a bit steep to me. Were you able to get a list of her patients before? I didn't see anything in the file, unless that's missing too.'

'No, she totally refused to give us any information about her patients,' Kate replied. 'She insisted that she'd only hand any details over if we had a court order and she said that, even if we did, she'd contest it in court. Her clients pay for 'total discretion' is how she put it.'

'For fifty grand I suppose that's the least you might expect,' Mac said. 'Did you do any surveillance on the clinic, see if you could spot any of the clients going in and out?'

'I tried but it was a waste of time. The clinic's in an old country house just outside St. Albans. There are some pictures of it in the file.'

It took Mac a while to locate them.

'I think I see what you mean,' Mac said, looking at the photos.

He was looking at a massive old Victorian house set well back behind an electronic gate with very tall hedges on either side.

'Clients arrive in a Mercedes four by four owned by the clinic and, unfortunately for us, it has black tinted windows,' Kate said. 'It always pulls up around the back of the house so you can't even get a clear shot with a long lens from anywhere outside the clinic grounds.'

Mac looked up at Kate with puzzlement.

'How in God's name would you know that?'

'We arrested a paparazzi once when we were doing observation outside the clinic one day. He was hanging out of a tree trying to take a photograph with a long lens when we saw him. He was about thirty feet up and he'd have probably killed himself if we hadn't come by.'

'Who was he after?' Mac asked.

'He was trying to get a shot of a famous actress who, it was rumoured, was staying at the clinic in between movies,' Kate said. 'However, we never found out if she was ever there or if the photographer had just gotten a bad tip.'

'Okay, I tend to agree that the clinic might be a good place to start,' Mac said, 'especially as DCI Ibbotson's investigation leaves us knowing virtually nothing about it. I'd advise that you get a court order anyway and see what happens. You never know, she might just be bluffing.'

'Okay, that's what I wanted to do in the first place,' Kate said.

'What about the father?' Mac asked. 'In his statement Dr. Mason Whyte says that he chose the clinic for Ashley based on a personal recommendation. Did we ever find out who recommended it?'

'Yes, it was through a colleague of his, a GP called Dr. Edward Rowan. He said that the clinic had achieved good results for some of his patients,' Kate replied.

'And did we interview this Dr. Rowan?'

Kate shook her head.

Mac sighed again.

'Okay then, I'd suggest that you interview the father again and also this Dr. Rowan. See if he'll divulge who these patients were. You never know, we might get lucky.'

'Okay,' Kate replied.

'You mentioned her sister and friends earlier. Do you think they might be worth interviewing again?' Mac asked.

'Definitely, I always felt that some of them knew a bit more than they were telling us,' Kate replied.

'Anyone in particular?'

'Well, the sister for one. She was definite that it wasn't a gang murder but when we asked her how she could be so certain she just clammed up. Then there's Trina Derbyshere, the friend who Ashley sent the text to. I remember her looking really uncomfortable when she was being interviewed. I think she'd be worth following up on too.'

'So, enough to be getting on with?' Mac asked.

'Yes, more than enough I should think,' Kate replied with a smile. 'So, a court order for the clinic's records and then re-interview the father, sister and Trina Derbyshere, after which we'll see if we can speak to this Dr. Rowan.'

It struck Mac that this was the first time that Kate hadn't actually looked unhappy.

'Is that okay with you, Tommy?' Kate asked.

'Absolutely and it's nice to have someone who already knows the case well,' Tommy said. 'It means that we can hit the ground running.'

'And that's exactly what we're going to do.'

Mac thought that he could see a glint of determination in Kate's eyes.

This could become quite interesting, he thought.

Chapter Eleven

Mac hardly closed his eyes that night after a bright shard of pain had pierced his lower back. It wasn't to be the only one. Every time he was close to drifting off to sleep, the pain brutally reminded him of its presence. He was in a bad way by morning, being both in pain and groggy from lack of sleep. He gave up on the idea of sleep and tried to do some work but it was hard going. He hated it when the pain started getting the upper hand. It made him feel helpless like he was drowning in it and, try as hard as he might, all he could do was just about manage to keep his head above water.

By an act of will he managed to keep it from Bridget and Tommy that morning but he couldn't hide it from his nurse.

'It's bad today, isn't it?' Amrit said. 'I can tell from your face. You've had all your medication, I take it?'

Mac nodded. He was only just about holding it together and he was afraid that if he spoke, he'd scream.

'Okay then, I know it's going to hurt but move over onto your tummy,' Amrit ordered. 'It's time for some needles.'

In desperation Mac did as he was told. He grunted loudly as the pain spiked when he rolled over.

Amrit rolled his pyjama top up and said, 'If I do it right you shouldn't feel any pain, just a little pressure as the needles go in.'

At that point Mac was beyond caring. If it hurt a bit more who cared? It would be like adding a pebble to a mountain.

Amrit had been right, he didn't feel anything as the acupuncture needles went in which surprised him. He counted them, six in all, arranged in a circle around the base of his spine.

'So, what happens now?' he managed to ask.

'People react a little differently but most say that they feel a sort of pleasant tingling at first but it will take at least ten minutes to kick in.'

Mac lay there waiting desperately for the tingling. It came on slowly and felt strangely like a breath of cool air on his lower back. He wasn't sure if the pain was any less but he definitely started to feel a little better.

Amrit smiled as she watched him slowly relax, his body no longer clenched in pain. She waited until the full twenty minutes were up before she carefully removed the needles and dabbed his back with some cotton wool in case of bleeding.

'You can go to sleep now,' she said softly.

Mac rolled onto his back and was soon fast asleep. Amrit picked up his phone and then pulled the curtains over. She was going to make sure his sleep wasn't interrupted. She looked back at him before she left the room. He looked at peace.

Mac awoke in stages. It took him an age to get his eyes focussed so that he could read the time on the clock. It was four thirty. He looked at the window and could see light at the edges of the curtains so he knew it must be four thirty in the afternoon. He saw the door soundlessly open and Amrit's head pop around.

'Ah, awake at last,' she said. 'Did you have a good sleep?'

'Yes, I think I did,' he replied.

He did a quick audit of his body and realised that the pain levels had dropped considerably.

'There must be some magic in those needles,' Mac said with a smile. 'Thanks, Amrit, really thanks.'

'My pleasure Mac. Now, Kate and Tommy rang while you were asleep and said they'd call around five thirty. Is that okay?'

'That will be fine. I could kill an orange juice though.'

'I'll get you one and I take it that a coffee and a quick bacon sandwich wouldn't be refused?'

Mac answered with the widest of smiles.

He still couldn't get over it though. One minute there he was writhing in pain and a few needles later he was sleeping like a baby. Amrit brought a tray with a plate, a glass and two cups. She sat and had a cup of coffee while she watched him eat.

'So, how does it all work then, the acupuncture?' he asked just before he took a big bite from the sandwich.

'Well, the Chinese say that inserting the needles alters the flow of Qi or life force but we think that what it really does is encourage your body to produce its own natural pain killers, something called endorphins. Although I have to admit that a lot of people are still quite sceptical about it and think that it's just the placebo affect at work.'

'I've heard about that,' Mac said. 'Didn't they give people sugar pills and found that in some instances they worked?'

'Yes, that's right but, so long as it works, do you really care?'

'God no. Anyway, it definitely did something, that was the best sleep I've had in ages. Anyway, it's nice to know that I've got something I can fall back on when it gets really bad. Just knowing that will help a lot too.'

Mac and Amrit's discussions were halted by the door bell ringing.

'That will be your colleagues. Are you ready for them?' Amrit asked.

'I am now,' Mac replied with a grin.

Amrit ushered Kate and Tommy inside and informed them that she'd just made a pot of coffee.

'Oh yes please Amrit, we haven't had anything for ages,' Tommy replied.

After they'd seated themselves Mac asked, 'Okay so what have we learned today?'

'Well, we went to see Dr. Whyte first but he didn't have anything new to add to what he'd told us before,'

Kate replied. 'We asked him why he specifically chose the Al-Faran Clinic for Ashley and he said it was desperation really. After the shock of finding her nearly dead from an overdose he asked around his colleagues to see if anyone knew of a good rehab clinic. He confirmed that it was Dr. Rowan who told him that the Al-Faran Clinic had a very good record and that every patient was treated with discretion.'

That word 'discretion' again. Then again, he supposed that if it was his daughter, he wouldn't want the world to know about it either.

'How did he react when he learned that we were re-opening the case?' Mac asked.

Kate gave it some thought.

'I don't think he was totally happy about it. I could sense that he wanted whoever had killed his daughter to be caught but I think he also feared that there'd be a cost attached. He mentioned that his business had suffered because of the murder.'

'Yes, I'll bet it did,' Mac said. 'Did you ask him about Leah?'

'Yes, and we got a pretty abrupt answer,' Kate said. 'He said that he had nothing to do with her any more. She was living in one of his houses but, apart from that, he didn't support her in any way.'

Mac wondered what had happened to cause such a rift between father and daughter.

'Okay, so what about this Dr. Rowan then?'

'We managed to get a few minutes with him in between his appointments,' Kate replied. 'He has a private practice in the centre of the town, quite from what we could see. He confirmed that he'd recommended the clinic to Dr. Whyte. He said that he'd had three of his patients attend the clinic, all for cocaine addiction, and he felt that it had done them a lot of good even though he admitted a little later that one of them had recently gone back on drugs.'

'Back on cocaine?' Mac asked.

'No, heroin actually.'

'I don't suppose he gave you any names?' Mac asked hopefully.

Kate shook her head, 'No chance.'

'What's he like this Dr. Rowan?' Mac asked.

'Mid-forties, tall, thin, very well-dressed, likes to look down his nose at people. He seemed to know what he was doing though,' Kate replied.

'Kate had us wait outside for a while to see what type of people went in,' Tommy said. 'From what we saw I'd safely say that his patients had money to burn.'

Mac glanced over at Kate. That's exactly what he'd have done. They were interrupted by the arrival of coffee.

'I'll be off now Mac, if that's okay,' Amrit said.

'That's fine. I'll see you tomorrow and don't forget your needles just in case.'

'I won't,' Amrit said as she waved goodbye to Kate and Tommy.

'Sorry, where were we?' Mac asked.

'Dr. Rowan but there's not much more to say about him. Next, we went to see Leah Whyte,' Kate said. 'Her father gave us her number. I think it would be safe to say that she didn't look happy to see us.'

'Why was that?' Mac asked.

Kate shrugged and glanced over at Tommy.

'I agree with Kate that Leah didn't exactly look thrilled that the case was being re-opened,' Tommy said. 'She avoided eye contact and, for the most part, just gave us 'yes/no' answers.'

'I'd like to dig a bit deeper there,' Kate said.

Again, that glint of determination in her eye.

'Agreed. That comment from her father about Ashley being the stronger one implied that Leah was weak in some way. It might be worthwhile seeing if you can find out what he meant by that,' Mac said.

'Will do. We also tried to find Trina Derbyshere but she's not at her last known address. We asked Leah but she just shrugged her shoulders and said that Trina had disappeared, apparently none of her friends know where she's gone,' Kate said. 'We should also have the court order early tomorrow so we'll call on Dr. Al-Faran as soon as it comes.'

'That should be an interesting experience,' Mac said. 'Have we got all of Trina Derbyshere's information in the file?'

'Perhaps not the one you've got but it's all on here,' Kate said as she gave him a memory stick.

Mac took it with gratitude. He'd found that working with an incomplete case file was more than annoying.

'Thanks, I'll see if Martin Selby can dig up anything on her, you never know.'

'So, we've got Leah Whyte to follow up on and Dr. Al-Faran to visit tomorrow. Is there anything else that we should be doing?' Kate asked.

'There was another of Ashley's friends who gave a statement, Adeline Smyth-Stortford. What did you think of her?' Mac asked.

Kate had to think.

'Oh yes, Adeline said that she and Ashley went to school together but she also said that she hadn't seen much of Ashley since she'd come back from university. Why are you interested in her?'

'This, I found it this morning when I couldn't sleep. I Googled every name I could find in the file,' Mac said as he turned the laptop around so Kate and Tommy could see the screen.

It was an article from the BBC News website dated a few months before Ashley's murder –

Reality television presenter Naomi Cadogan today admitted that the leaked stories about her having been in a rehab clinic for the past few weeks were true. She said that she had gone into a spiral of depression after breaking up with her actor boyfriend Adam Westerley. She said that the rest had done her good and that she was now looking forward to the next series of 'Dancing Dates in the Jungle'. She thanked her family and especially her cousin Adeline Smyth-Stortford for helping her through this difficult period.'

Next to the article there was a photo of the TV presenter hugging a young woman.

Kate smiled.

'Yes, that's definitely Adeline alright. So, now we probably know who at least one of Dr. Al-Faran's patients was,' she said.

'Well, I'd guess that Miss Smyth-Stortford might have known about the Al-Faran clinic through Ashley. Who knows, perhaps she even went there herself. Do you think it's worth following up?' Mac asked.

'Absolutely,' Kate replied. 'Although thinking back, Miss Smyth-Stortford seemed to very careful with what she said when we interviewed her. She absolutely denied any knowledge of Ashley's drug taking but I thought that she was protesting a bit much, if you know what I mean. Anyway, another interview wouldn't do any harm.'

'So, in the meantime I'll go through the case file again and I'll let you know if Martin comes up with anything,' Mac said. 'Shall we meet up same time tomorrow then?'

Tommy dropped Kate back at the train station. Five minutes later he was back.

'I might as well go and get dinner started,' Tommy said. 'It'll take a while to cook.'

'What are you doing tonight?' Mac asked with an expectant smile.

'Linguine with chicken and olives in a tomato sauce. I like to do the sauce for at least two hours so I'd better get cracking.'

Mac was already mentally licking his lips at Tommy's description of dinner as he asked, 'Before you go tell me what you made of Kate today. Did you get on okay?'

'Yes, I think we got on really well actually. She discussed everything with me and asked me what I thought which, if I'm honest, reminded me of you. There was something else too.'

Mac was interested.

Tommy continued, 'When she's interviewing someone, she's not just listening to what they say, she also pays a lot of attention to what they're doing, you know their body language. You do that too.'

'So, you're looking forward to working with her?'

'Yes I am. I think it'll be interesting.'

Mac could only agree.

'By the way what was all that about needles? Tommy asked. 'Is Amrit giving you pain killing injections or something?'

'No, acupuncture. I must admit that it was a long shot as far as I was concerned but it seemed to have done me some good.'

'If it works don't knock it,' Tommy said with a smile.

'Exactly my feelings too.'

He let Tommy get on with the dinner while he re-loaded the case file. He couldn't help noticing that the new file was nearly ten percent bigger than the old one. He'd have to read it all again to make sure that he up to date. He would have cursed DCI Ibbotson if it wasn't for the fact that he was looking forward to it so much.

Chapter Twelve

Mac was surprised that, after sleeping most of the day before, he slept quite well again that night and woke up just after six. The first thing he did was to fire up his laptop and send off an email to Martin asking him if he could find out anything about Trina Derbyshere. He hesitated and, before he pressed the 'send' button, he also inserted Leah Whyte's name and details.

You never know, he thought, before resuming his reading of the case file.

A while later the door opened and Bridget's face appeared.

'Oh, you're awake!' she said giving her father a bright smile. 'We're off in a minute, Tommy's driving me to the station. Is there anything I can get you before I go?'

'Just some orange juice. Amrit will be here soon and I can wait until she comes for anything else.'

Bridget returned a few minutes later with a travel mug full of cold orange juice which Mac gratefully accepted.

'You seem to be getting on well then. You and Amrit, I mean,' Bridget said.

'Oh yes, she's better than I could have hoped for. When you first said that you were getting me a nurse, I kept picturing Nurse Ratched out of 'One Flew Over the Cuckoo's Nest' in my head but thankfully Amrit's nothing like that.'

'Okay, I just thought I'd ask,' Bridget said as she stood up.

'There is something though. Do you think she might be interested in a longer-term job? Not full-time like this but perhaps a few days a week?'

Bridget sat down again.

'You know I was thinking along the same lines myself but I didn't want to you think that I was pushing her on you.'

'So, you'll ask her then?'

Bridget nodded, 'Absolutely. It would make me feel so much better knowing that you had some help.'

'Thanks love. While I've been lying here, I've realised just how useless I am around the house, how useless I am without your mother.'

Bridget reached out and held her father's hand.

'Poor Amrit's been cleaning the whole house from top to bottom when all she's supposed to be doing is looking after me,' Mac continued. 'I've realised that I'm going to need some help, even when I'm up and about, and we seem to rub along together okay.'

'I'll ask her and let you know,' Bridget said. 'I think it's a really good idea though and if Amrit can't do it we can always get someone else.'

Mac prayed that Amrit would agree. He still had that picture of Nurse Ratched in his head.

Tommy came in and said hello and goodbye in almost the same breath. He was meeting Kate at the police station and, if the court order had arrived, they were going to go straight to the clinic to see Dr. Al-Faran.

Mac wished him luck.

After he heard the front door close, he snuggled down, opened up the new case file and dove in.

Kate hadn't slept so well. She'd had a restless night plagued by dreams. Her ex-husband was in most of them which she supposed qualified them as nightmares.

Giving up on sleep she glanced over at the clock. It was nearly six. She got up and sat on the side of the bed for a few minutes thinking about the dreams. It was over four months now since they'd split up and she'd gotten the decree nisi just a few days ago. She guessed that was why she'd started dreaming about him again.

In all the dreams he was with another woman, doing things. She could never see the woman's face or exactly what they were doing but she knew what they were up to. After all it was only the truth, he'd slept with just about every available woman in the station and even some of her own friends. Of course, she'd been the last to find out.

It had been so humiliating and yet Neil had admitted everything when she'd confronted him. That had surprised her. She thought he'd try to slither his way out of it like he always had before.

Of course, she'd had to ask him why but, as soon as the words had left her lips, she wished that she hadn't. She had the feeling that she wouldn't like the answer. She was right, she didn't. He'd looked straight at her and she could see real pain in his eyes.

He said, 'You don't love me Kate. You've never loved me and, the worst of it is, I don't know how to make you love me.'

As she sat on the bed staring at the beige wall of her rented flat, she had to admit that he was right. Perhaps it had been down to her after all.

She'd liked him when they first met. They'd worked together on some burglaries and he was handsome and fun to be with. Had she mistaken this for love? She realised now that she'd never felt that fierce love that you read about in books or see on the cinema screen, the love that transcended reason, the love that you'd die for. She'd always thought it was a fiction and that life wasn't really like that. She'd met someone nice and she'd decided that he'd do and that was about it.

Yet, in the end, he couldn't settle for anything less and, deep down, she knew that he was probably right.

She looked at the clock again. It was now six fifteen. She stood up and shook herself, shaking away the dreams and all thoughts of her ex-husband too. She was alone and this was the way it was going to be. It didn't frighten her as much as it had when she was younger. There are worse things than being alone.

At least that's what she told herself.

She was so glad to be in the station and away from all her sad ruminations that she had a smile on her face as she walked in.

'You're looking happy today,' Tommy said.

'Am I?' she asked in some surprise.

She quickly recovered the situation.

'It's because we're going to have a lucky day today, I can feel it,' she lied.

'I hope you're right. It would be nice to take something back to Mac this evening,' Tommy replied.

Kate looked at Tommy. He reminded her of Magnus, her younger brother. He was probably the only person in the world she was close to.

'You really like Mac, don't you?' she asked.

Tommy looked up at her and replied a little sheepishly, 'Yes, yes I do. After all he's a great investigator, isn't he?'

'I've had a look at some of the cases that he's been involved in and I couldn't disagree with you about that. There's more to it than that though, isn't there?'

She looked closely at Tommy who had the sudden feeling that he was being interrogated.

'Well, I suppose I look up to him, I'd like to be a bit like him if I was being honest,' Tommy said with a shrug of his shoulders.

'I take it that you never got on with your own father then?' Kate asked her eyes never leaving Tommy's face.

'I don't really remember him that well. He died when I was young.'

Tommy's words suddenly brought Kate back to reality and she looked away. What in God's name had she been doing?

'Can I ask you a question, Kate?'

'Sure,' she replied.

'Has anyone ever told you that you can be a bit scary sometimes?'

Kate gave him a sad smile.

'Many times, Tommy, many times.'

She put a hand on Tommy's shoulder.

'I'm sorry, I shouldn't have done that. It was none of my business.'

'Well, I'll tell you one thing,' Tommy said with a wide smile, 'if we get anyone in for questioning, I'm quite happy for you to take the lead.'

This made Kate smile too. She was grateful that he had found a way to lighten the moment.

'Thanks, Tommy.'

'No problem. Anyway, it looks like the court order has finally arrived so what do you want to do? Shall I to give the clinic a ring and arrange an appointment?'

Kate gave this some thought.

'How do you fancy surprising them and just turning up? It might make it a bit harder for them if they are hiding something.'

'Okay, that sounds like a plan to me,' Tommy replied.

'While we're on our way, I'll ring Miss Smyth-Stortford and make sure that she's going to be around later on,' Kate said.

Tommy was wondering what he'd let himself in for as he followed her towards the car park. However, one thing he was fairly certain of, he wasn't going to be bored.

After Amrit had taken away the breakfast things Mac returned to work. Even though he knew there was stuff missing from the case file, Mac was appalled when he discovered how important some of the information would have been to the original investigation. He opened up a new document in Word and started making notes as he went along. He knew that it would take ages to go through all the new material and then even more time to analyse it.

There was a lot more work ahead of him now. While he felt that he should have been cursing Joe Ibbotson for his sloppiness, he was a little surprised to find that he had a smile on his face. He knew that work was just what he needed right now.

Tommy pulled up outside the high wrought-iron gates of the Al-Faran Clinic. He wound down the window and pressed the intercom button. He'd already discussed what they should do with Kate. They'd agreed on saying as little as possible and see what happened.

'The Al-Faran Clinic, can I help?' a woman's sing-song voice asked.

Tommy showed his warrant card to the camera.

'Police, we're here to see Dr. Al-Faran.'

There was no response for a few seconds.

'Do you have an appointment?' the woman asked.

'No,' Tommy replied.

There was a much longer silence before the woman spoke again.

'Very well, Dr. Al-Faran will see you. Someone will meet you in the car park and show you the way.'

The huge iron gates swung silently open.

'Almost a shame,' Kate said. 'I was seriously thinking about your idea of turning the blue light and sirens on and waking the whole clinic up if she'd said no.'

Tommy had been joking when he said that so he glanced over to see if Kate was serious. He found that he couldn't tell.

They drove down a long single-track road that eventually swung around to the right and revealed the huge Victorian stately home that had now become the Al-Faran Clinic. Two men met them outside the house and directed them to a parking space. They waited until

Kate and Tommy got out of the car, watching their every move.

'Can I see your warrant cards please?' one of the men said.

Kate and Tommy handed them over. The man passed a device over them and handed them back.

Some sort of scanner, Kate surmised.

'Please follow me,' one of the men said tersely.

The other one waited for them to move and then fell in behind them. Kate looked at the man leading them. Like the one behind he was well over six feet, dressed in a dark grey suit, crisp white shirt and black tie. The suits were made to measure but, even so, they couldn't disguise the muscles beneath. She glanced over her shoulder. The man behind still watched their every move.

Very high-priced muscle, Kate thought.

The house was high-priced too. It was a rambling Victorian manor house in the gothic style from which fake mediaeval turrets and Elizabethan style chimneys sprouted. The ornamental stonework covered the front of the house like grey sugar icing.

They were led towards the side of the house and through a quite ordinary green door.

The tradesmen's entrance, Kate guessed.

A few yards down a dim hallway another door was open. The first man pointed at them to go in. They did. Once they were inside the man shut the door. They could both hear the sound of keys jangling and a lock being locked.

'He hasn't just locked us in, has he?' Tommy said in surprise.

He went and tried to open the door. It was locked.

'Friendly here, isn't it?' Kate observed as she looked around the room.

This didn't take her more than a few seconds. The room was small and dingy and only contained a low

104

green filing cabinet with two drawers, a generic desk and three chairs. There was no window.

'We're in quarantine,' Kate said. 'They obviously don't want us mixing with the paying guests.'

Kate pulled out the drawers of the filing cabinet. They were both empty.

'Well, I hope they remember we're here if there's a fire or...'

Tommy's words were cut short by the sound of keys and a lock unlocking. The door opened and a woman in her early forties strode in.

She wasn't tall by any means but stride in she did. She acted like she owned the place and that's probably because she did. She gestured at Kate and Tommy to sit down and then sat down herself.

'Good morning, I'm Dr. Al-Faran,' she said in a soothing contralto voice.

She sat and gazed at her visitors with a perfect poker face. Kate thought that she looked neither happy nor sad, annoyed or at peace, she just looked.

'An appointment would have been nice but as you're here,' the doctor said. 'DS Grimsson, we've met before, haven't we? You were with DCI Ibbotson if I remember correctly. How is he?'

Kate was surprised that she'd remembered her name.

'He's retired now, some months ago,' Kate replied.

'So,' Dr. Al-Faran said as she pointedly looked at her Hublot watch. 'How can I help?'

Kate looked at her for a few seconds. The doctor was of medium height but she held herself taller. Her skin looked slightly tanned and her hair, cut short, was jet black. She wore a tailored black wool blazer with black slim legged trousers.

Stella McCartney, Kate guessed.

Underneath the blazer she wore a black cashmere top. All in all, she was wearing as much as Kate earned in a month. There was obviously money to be made in the rehab business.

Kate decided on the full-frontal approach and she watched the doctor closely as she said, 'We're re-opening the Ashley Whyte case.'

She was certain, well almost certain, that the doctor flinched when she said this but, if she had, she recovered herself quickly.

'Oh dear, I've been trying to forget about that, it was such a bad business,' she said with a mournful expression.

For some reason Kate didn't buy it.

'Can I ask exactly why you're re-opening the case?' the doctor asked as she looked at her iPhone.

Did Kate detect a slight tremor in her voice? Was she looking at her phone to avoid eye contact?

'We've found some new evidence,' Kate replied blandly.

The doctor looked up.

'New evidence? Nothing to do with the clinic I hope?' she said with some concern.

Was she really just concerned about the clinic though? Kate thought.

'I'm afraid I can't say. Before I state the real reason for our visit I was wondering if is there was anything you've remembered that might be of help since we last spoke?'

The doctor shrugged and then shook her head.

'No, I've told you everything I know.'

Kate produced the court order and passed it over to the doctor. She opened it and read for a few seconds. She looked up and smiled.

'I can tell you now that I won't be complying with this,' she said passing the paper back to Kate.

'Well, we'll just have to confiscate all your IT equipment and we'll find the names of all your patients that way,' Kate said.

The doctor's smile widened.

'Try it,' she said.

The doctor's phone rang. She listened for a few seconds.

'Okay do that,' she said and put the phone down. 'That was my lawyer who is right now filing for an interim injunction against your court order. In about ten minutes you'll be able to light your cigarette with that.'

Kate thought that the doctor looked very confident and, she had to admit, she probably had grounds.

'Anyway, even if you did take all our computers away you wouldn't find what you're looking for. All our IT equipment is highly encrypted.'

'We have people who could break that encryption,' Kate said with more confidence than she felt.

'I doubt it,' the doctor replied with a smirk. 'Anyway, even if you did, you'd still find nothing. If anyone breaks our encryption all the data will be wiped, there'll be nothing left to see anyway,' she said as she pushed the court order back towards Kate.

Tommy had been watching the exchanges carefully. It was like a game of verbal tennis he thought. At the moment the doctor was slightly ahead.

'However, if you'll drop this nonsense, I'm still willing to cooperate, except for anything that might identify any of my patients that is.'

Kate picked up the court order.

'Okay, we'll be in touch,' Kate said as she stood up.

The doctor offered Kate her hand and Kate shook it limply. She'd turned to go when the doctor spoke again.

'Oh, by the way, did DCI Ibbotson ever identify that man?'

'Man, what man?' Kate replied.

'Oh, the man that Ashley saw a day or two before she left here. Didn't DCI Ibbotson tell you about that, dear?' the doctor said with a look of pretend concern.

'No, he didn't,' Kate replied through clenched teeth.

'Oh well, I suppose he had his reasons. Anyway, Ashley met this man at the back door. It's very secluded and some of our guests use it to leave and enter the clinic. We have a CCTV camera there for protection and it caught it all. I'll send it to you if you like, I'm sure it's still around somewhere.'

Game, set and match, Tommy thought.

'Please do,' Kate said as she fished a card out of her pocket and gave it to the doctor.

The doctor took the card, smiled at the two of them widely and left the room. The two men were waiting for them in the hallway and they shepherded them back to the car.

Tommy could feel the steam coming out of Kate's ears as they walked along in silence. She didn't say a word until they'd left the grounds and were back on the main road.

'God, I hate that bloody woman!' she screamed.

'Feel better?' Tommy asked.

Kate looked over at him and smiled.

'Yes, I do actually. She's very clever though, isn't she?'

'She certainly seemed to be well prepared for our visit.'

Kate fell silent. Tommy could hear the wheels in her head whirring. He waited until she'd finished thinking.

Kate was picturing the doctor in her mind, especially the moment when she said she was re-opening the case.

'At this moment I've absolutely no idea what's going on back there,' she said. 'But I'll tell you something, whatever it is, I'm going to find out.'

Tommy glanced over and saw the intensity of her look. He was suddenly glad that they were both on the same side.

Chapter Thirteen

'Was that okay?' Amrit asked as she took the lunch tray away.

'Okay? No, it wasn't,' Mac said with a smile. 'It was sublime that's the only word for it. You should open a restaurant, I'm sure that you'd get a Michelin star in no time.'

Amrit smiled. She liked a man who liked his food and even more if it was her food that he liked.

'I'll come by with a cup of tea in a while,' she said before she went out of the door.

Please God, she says yes when Bridget asks, Mac prayed before he returned to his laptop. He knew he'd miss her if she didn't. Having her around to talk to at any time of the day was a blessing and then there was the food of course.

He checked his emails first and was delighted to see one from Martin at the top of the list. He opened it up and read it carefully. He gave it some thought and then read it carefully once more.

It proved to be the most interesting thing he'd read all day.

They drove past streets full of massive well-kept Victorian detached houses, each seeming to have the latest BMW in the drive, before entering a small estate consisting of several low blocks of neglected sixties flats. They looked out of place, a little island of destitution surrounded by a sea of wealth and prosperity.

Kate wondered if the builders had gotten the post-code wrong when they'd built them.

'It's Compton House we're looking for, isn't it?' Tommy asked as he peered out of the windscreen.

'Yes, that's right. Look, there it is on the left,' Kate replied.

It looked just the same as the other blocks of flats being grey, square and stolid, six storeys high and showing its age. What was supposed to be have been a security door, one that only opened when the intercom was used, was half hanging off its hinges and was now permanently open. The lift wasn't working either.

'She's number fifty-six,' Kate said. 'I suppose that means the fifth floor.'

Tommy noticed that she didn't look all that happy at the prospect of climbing up five storeys worth of stairs. Tommy led. He took the steps two at a time and made it quickly up to the fifth floor. Kate arrived some time later and was blowing.

'God, have I gotten unfit!' she said as she leant against the wall. 'You're hardly breathing hard.'

'I run long distance, five thousand and that. I don't get that much chance nowadays but I try and keep it up as best I can.'

'Oh, keep it up Tommy, please do, otherwise you'll end up as useless as me.'

As they walked on Kate wondered what had happened to her. She was even more unfit than she'd thought, a few flights of stairs and she was done in. She used to play football for a local women's team but she stopped doing it because her new husband thought that it was a man's game and not for a little woman like her.

She decided that she'd have a look around and join a team as soon as she possibly could.

Tommy stopped outside the door to number fifty-six. It had been repainted not too long ago but that couldn't hide the fact that repairs had been made. Someone had smashed the door open and not too long ago.

'It certainly wasn't what I was expecting of someone called Adeline Smyth-Stortford,' Tommy remarked as he looked down the rubbish strewn hallway.

'Same here,' Kate replied. 'The last time I saw her she was living in a house with two garages and an indoor swimming pool. I wonder what happened to her?'

There was no bell so Tommy knocked the door.

'Who is it?' the frightened voice of a young woman asked.

'Police,' Tommy answered.

'Hold your warrant card up to the spy hole,' the young woman said.

Tommy did as he was ordered. The door snapped open and snapped shut just as quickly once they were both inside. They followed the young woman into a squalid living room that was virtually empty except for the broken sofa that she sat on and hugged herself. She wore an old tee shirt that was stained and a baggy pair of track suit bottoms. The last time Kate had seen her she'd been head to foot in the latest designer clothes.

Kate looked at Tommy and held her finger to her lips. Tommy understood that he was to let Kate do the talking.

'Adeline? Do you remember me?' Kate asked as she sat down beside her.

She glanced up at Kate, 'Yes, you're the police lady with the red hair. You were with a man before, I didn't like him.'

'What happened? How come you're living here?'

Adeline's eyes flickered around the room.

'I'm not living here. I wouldn't call it living, would you?' she replied bleakly as she looked around the dingy room.

'Possibly not, so what happened?' Kate asked.

'Daddy stopped my allowance, didn't he? I thought that the money would just be there, it always has been before. I just put my card in and there it was, as much cash as I wanted. Then one day there wasn't any cash and the bloody machine ate my card. I couldn't believe that he'd do that to me. I mean, he'd said he would loads

111

of times, but I never thought he'd actually do it,' she said as the tears started to roll down her cheeks.

'Why did he do that?' Kate asked softly as she lightly held Adeline's hand.

'My younger sister Jemima told him something. He said that it was the last straw but I thought that he was only joking again.'

'What was the something that Jemima said?' Kate gently probed.

Adeline pulled her hand away from Kate and looked down at the floor. She started rocking backwards and forwards.

'What was it, Adeline?' Kate gently insisted.

'She always was daddy's favourite so he believed her when she told him.'

'Told him what?' Kate prompted.

'She said that I'd tried to get her on drugs,' she said in a barely audible voice.

'And did you?'

Adeline glanced up at Kate and gave her a look filled with shame.

'Yes,' she whispered as the tears flowed again. 'I didn't want to but I had to, I was behind...'

'Do you mean that you owed money to the people who supplied you with drugs?' Kate asked softly.

Adeline nodded.

'Adeline, were you dealing drugs yourself?'

Adeline thought about it for a moment and then nodded again.

'We can help you,' Kate said even more softly. 'If you tell us who you're working for we can keep you safe.'

Adeline shook her head and stood up. She walked up and down the room, clearly agitated.

'I can't tell, I can't,' she said still shaking her head. 'I don't want to end up like...'

She stopped and looked at Kate knowing that she'd already said too much.

'Like Ashley you mean?' Kate said her eyes narrowing.

She stood up to and looked straight into Adeline's eyes.

'You know who killed Ashley, don't you?'

'No, no I don't, not exactly and I'm not saying anything else, you can't make me. You say that you can keep me safe but you can't, no-one can, they have people everywhere. I'm lost.'

Adeline became even more agitated and began walking up and down again, clenching and unclenching her fists and muttering to herself.

Then she suddenly stopped and went very still as she stared intently at something to her left. Kate followed her gaze. It led to an open door. The open door led to the balcony.

'Tell daddy,' Adeline said softly without turning her head.

'No, Adeline, NO!' Kate shouted.

Kate dove and tried to grab her. She almost caught her arm but she was just a fraction too late. Adeline ran through the door and she didn't stop running. She disappeared over the balcony's edge.

'Why?' Kate said to no-one.

Tommy had already gone. He raced all the way back down the stairs to the ground floor. Kate hesitated before going out on to the balcony and looking down. She saw Tommy bending over Adeline's broken body. He looked up at Kate and shook his head. She saw him make the call on his phone.

She sat down on the sofa and thought through what had happened. She was sure that it must be her fault somehow. Had she been too hard on her? And why hadn't she stood in front of the door to the balcony just in case? If only she'd made her come down to the station in the first place. There were no bloody balconies there.

Her thoughts were still whirling around in circles when Tommy arrived.

'The ambulance and the local police have arrived.'

Kate shot him a despairing look.

'Be honest Tommy, did I do something wrong?'

'No absolutely not, Kate. I can't quite believe it myself. I mean I know she was bit strung out and all but I had no idea that she was going to do that.'

Kate nodded. It made her feel better, a very little bit better.

'There'll be an enquiry of course and, after all, there was just her and two policemen present so you'll know what they'll say,' Kate said.

'Let them, tongues will always wag about something or other as my mum says,' Tommy replied. 'Anyway, we've got our job to do, we can only do it as best we can.'

'Such wisdom in one so young,' Kate said with a smile as she stood up.

He was so sweet that she kissed Tommy on the cheek. Tommy's face went red.

'I have told you that I've got a girlfriend, haven't I?' he said defensively.

'That was just a sisterly kiss because you remind me so much of my brother. If it was the other sort, you'd be in no doubt about it believe me.'

Their conversation was interrupted by the arrival of three uniformed officers. The lead officer introduced himself as Inspector Ken Ahmed.

'I believe you witnessed everything, is that correct?' he asked as his eyes flicked around the room.

Kate and Tommy nodded in unison.

'Okay then, you'll need to go back with us to the station and be formally interviewed as you were the only witnesses,' the Inspector said. 'Forensics will need the room in any case.'

Kate stood up and quickly looked around the room before she left. She spotted Adeline's phone on the sofa near where she'd been sitting.

Outside they walked by the forensics team who were busy taking pictures of Adeline's body and making measurements. A little river of blood had run down the pavement from her crushed skull and gathered in a small hollow. Kate looked down at it and saw her face reflected in it. She quickly looked away.

One of the white suited forensics team ambled over to them, 'I'm Bob Yeardley the team leader. I believe you were interviewing her when it happened, is that right?'

Kate nodded sombrely.

'We were just talking to her when she got very agitated, not for the first time while we were there. Then she stood very still and I saw her looking at the door to the balcony. By the time I realised what she was thinking of doing, she'd dashed out of the door onto the balcony and over. I tried to stop her but...' Kate shrugged helplessly.

The forensics officer looked at Tommy.

'If I'm honest Kate here was well ahead of me. I had absolutely no idea of what she was going to do until she was over the balcony. Bit of a shock really.'

'I'll bet. Well don't feel bad about it,' Bob said. 'I've been doing this for quite some time and I've learned that it's sometimes impossible to predict if someone will commit suicide or not and that for some it really is a decision of the moment. There's also a good chance that she was just waiting for an audience, for someone to see her go. That happens too. Perhaps it made her feel a bit less lonely or a bit better that someone was around when she went, I don't know.'

'Thanks,' Kate said.

Bob's words had cheered her up a little more.

They followed Inspector Ahmed's car to the local police station. The interviews took a while as the Inspector questioned them about every detail. He made it very clear that, even though they were police officers, they weren't above suspicion. They had a break and Kate and Tommy were supplied with tea and sandwiches for which both of them were grateful not having eaten since early that morning. The Inspector eventually seemed satisfied with what he'd been told.

'Would you mind if I tell her family?' Kate asked.

'Why, do you know them?' Inspector Ahmed asked.

'Well yes, I've interviewed them before so they know me and it might be better…you know,' Kate gave him a sympathetic smile.

'Very well but if they say anything that we might be interested in don't forget to let us know.'

'No problem. Oh, by the way Adeline's phone is still in the flat. Is there any chance that we could have first look at it?' Kate asked hopefully.

The Inspector looked dubious.

'It might have quite a bearing on our murder case and the sooner we can get it the better,' Kate explained.

Inspector Ahmed still looked dubious, 'Who would we have to send it to?'

Kate looked at Tommy for help.

'Oh, that would be Martin Selby at Letchworth Station. He's our computer forensics specialist. He's very good, well the best really and we'll make sure you get a full report of everything that's on the phone,' Tommy said with an innocent expression.

The Inspector looked at the two of them and shrugged.

'Okay then, I'll send it over to Letchworth as soon as forensics release it. I'll tell them that it will be going for a specialist examination and that they'll receive a full report too.'

'Yes, yes of course,' Kate said, nodding her head.

As they walked back to the car Kate said, 'Thanks Tommy.'

'What for?'

'For backing me up in there and being so persuasive about this Martin Selby. We could have been hanging around for a report on the phone for ages otherwise. Is he really that good?'

'Oh yes, I wasn't lying when I said he was the best.'

'Good, I'm glad as I'm really hoping that the phone might tell us something,' Kate said.

'So, where does Adeline's father live?' Tommy asked.

Kate gave him the address and Tommy fed it into the satnav.

'By the way, why were you so keen on being the one to tell the family?' Tommy asked as they drove.

'Because Adeline asked me to and it was the very last thing she said.'

Tommy didn't say anything. He had a feeling that there might be more to it than that.

'Anyway, they might know something but, if I'm being honest, I also want to see the look on Mr. Smyth-Stortford's face when I tell him,' Kate said.

They passed by the block of flats again on their way. It took them less than ten minutes to drive from there to Adeline's former residence. They drove down a street full of ordinary looking, though expensive, Victorian terraced houses and then turned off to the left. A sign informed them that they were entering a private road and more or less instructed the riff-raff to keep their distance. The houses were even bigger than the ones they'd seen previously and each one seemed to have at least one brand new Porsche in the drive.

'It's this one here,' Kate said remembering the house from her last visit.

Tommy stopped the car outside a house that was set back from the road. It would probably have been seen as futuristic in the thirties. It reminded Tommy of an old cinema he used to go to and it wasn't far off being as big. It had two front doors and a double garage on the side. The wide drive held a Range Rover, a red McClaren sports car and the inevitable Porsche so he wondered what they kept in the garage.

Kate went to the right of the two doors and rang the bell. A Filipino maid in her forties answered the door. She didn't look happy in her work.

'We're the police and we'd like to speak to Mr. Smyth-Stortford,' Kate said as she showed her warrant card.

'I'll see if he's in,' the maid replied grumpily and shut the door behind her.

'It might take her a while for her to find him in this place,' Tommy said.

It obviously did as she didn't return for over five minutes.

'Follow me please,' the maid said flatly once she'd shut the door behind them.

She scuttled down corridor after corridor turning left and right and then down some stairs. Kate found it quite difficult to keep up with her.

'In there,' she said with a sour look as she pointed at a door before scuttling away.

Kate was surprised as space and light and the smell of chlorine hit her. It was a full-sized indoor pool. She knew that there was one in the house but this was the first time she'd seen it. A man in his early fifties and a young woman were lying on recliners near the pool. They both had fluffy white dressing gowns on and a large drink to hand. The young woman lay on her side, she had her hand inside the man's dressing gown. She quickly withdrew it when she saw that she had company.

'Grab a seat,' the man said waving his hand towards a couple of recliners nearby.

Kate looked at him. He had an old face and young hair. He had the same smug self-satisfied expression that seemed to be the default amongst a lot of so-called self-made men like him. She knew it all too well.

'If it's all the same I'll stand,' Kate said as she showed him her warrant card.

'So, how can I help the police?' he asked.

'I'll bet it's Addie up to her tricks again,' the young woman said with a sneer.

'And you are?' Kate asked as she turned and stared at her.

She was around twenty, quite pretty with regulation blonde hair, pneumatic breasts and a pout.

'I'm Jemima,' she said.

Kate had taken her for a rich man's bit of fluff but she was in fact Adeline's younger sister. From where she'd had her hand Kate could easily guess why she was her father's favourite.

'Well you're right, this is about Adeline,' Kate said.

The man sat up and audibly groaned.

'Oh God, what's she gone and done now? If she needs money for bail or anything tell her she can go to hell. I don't want anything to do with her. I told her that when I kicked her out.'

'All she'll need from you now is the cost of a coffin. She's dead,' Kate said flatly.

She watched the two of them closely. They looked at each other and then shrugged their shoulders.

'Oh well, it was bound to happen,' Jemima said as she refilled her drink. 'A drug overdose, I take it?'

'No, it was a severe case of gravity,' Kate replied.

They both looked at her with a puzzled expression.

'She jumped from the balcony of her flat. It was five floors up,' Kate explained.

'Really,' the man said with a slightly sad expression.

Kate half expected some emotion from him at this point but he very quickly pulled himself together. Far too quickly for Kate's liking.

'Was that it?' he asked as he glanced at the door.

As far as he was concerned the audience was over. Kate guessed he was anxious to get back to what he'd been doing before they were so rudely interrupted.

'No, that is not it,' Kate said.

Tommy could hear an edge in her voice.

'I will need the both of you to come down to the station to answer some questions,' she said.

'Why? What on earth could we tell you about a silly girl chucking herself off the fifth floor that you don't already know?' he said as he passed his glass over to his daughter for a refill.

'We were there when Adeline killed herself. The reason we were there was because we're investigating a murder and we wanted to ask your daughter some questions. Unfortunately, we never got the chance but it's possible that you might know something that could help us in our enquiries.'

'Oh God, do we really have to?' he said with a scowl as Jemima handed him his drink.

'No, you don't have to,' Kate replied, 'but we feel that your testimony might be crucial to our case so, if you refuse to attend an interview, this will be noted and passed on to the Crown Prosecution Service. They'll provide us with a Witness Summons and you can then tell us what we need to know in court for everyone to hear. It's your choice.'

He actually thought about it for a few minutes before saying, 'Oh, I suppose we must all help the police, no matter how bloody inconvenient it is. Will tomorrow be okay?'

Kate gave him her card and the address of Letchworth Police Station.

'Will nine thirty be okay?' Kate asked.

'Ten thirty would be better,' he said glumly.

'Okay, we'll see you both at ten thirty tomorrow,' Kate said glad that she could finally leave.

The maid was waiting for them outside the door and Kate gratefully followed her to the door that led back out into the real world.

Chapter Fourteen

Tommy glanced over at Kate as they sat in the car. She looked angry again.

'You know, I have the distinct feeling that you don't like Mr. Smyth-Stortford much.'

Kate looked over at Tommy and managed a smile.

'You're right, I didn't.'

She glanced over at the dashboard clock. It was just gone four. She suddenly felt very tired.

'Any chance that we could call it a day?' she asked. 'I'll ring Mac and tell him that we're on our way.'

'Yes, sure,' Tommy replied. 'It's been a bit of a strange day all round, hasn't it?'

After Kate had spoken to Mac there was silence in the car for some minutes until they eventually got caught in the inevitable traffic jam on the motorway. Tommy was happy to leave Kate to her thoughts but it was she who spoke first.

'You're absolutely right though, I didn't like Mr. Smyth-Stortford,' she said.

'Well, he didn't strike me as being the likeable type anyway,' Tommy replied.

'No, it wasn't that, he reminded me of someone.'

'Who?' Tommy asked beginning to get intrigued.

'My father.'

Tommy could feel the anger emanating from her like a force field. She turned her head to look out of the window on her side and said nothing for the rest of the journey.

Amrit opened the door and the welcome smell of coffee hit them.

'I've just put a pot of coffee on, would you like some?' she asked brightly.

They both made it known that they would be more than grateful.

Mac was deep in thought when they opened the door and seemed a little surprised to see them.

'Oh, here already!' he glanced over at his clock. 'God is it really gone five? Sorry, I was miles away, Martin sent me something and it's given me some food for thought. Anyway, had an exciting day?' Mac asked with a smile.

Mac saw Kate and Tommy give each other a look. It was quite obvious that something serious had happened.

'What is it?' Mac asked his smile suddenly gone.

Kate told him everything that had happened at Adeline's flat.

'Poor girl, she must have felt as though there was absolutely no hope to do something like that,' Mac said with a sad expression.

Kate couldn't help noticing that Mac had expressed more emotion about a girl he'd never met than her own father had.

'There was nothing you could have done,' Mac said looking straight at Kate.

'I know but...'

'No buts. Just ask yourself whether you even had the wildest notion that she might have done something like that before she actually did it. Did you?'

Kate thought for a moment and shook her head.

'It's happened to me a few times,' Mac continued, 'and it always comes as a total surprise and yet every time you think that you should have known somehow but, of course, there's no way that you could have.'

Kate slowly nodded as a feeling of relief flooded through her. She was more than grateful for Mac's words.

'So, what happened at the clinic?' he asked.

Kate told him about the interview with Dr. Al-Faran and about the unknown stranger who had visited Ashley while she was at the clinic.

'You think that the doctor's hiding something, don't you?' Mac asked.

'Yes, I do. I'm not sure what it is though. I'd like to do a bit more digging if that's alright,' Kate replied.

'Kate, don't forget that you're running this investigation so you can do what you like but, if it's any help, I agree. Adeline had a connection to the clinic too, didn't she? Anyway, it certainly won't hurt to see what else we can find and the CCTV footage might be helpful too if we can identify who it was that visited Ashley. You did well, the both of you.'

Kate gave Mac a faint smile. He thought she looked quite down.

'Now, while you were out and about, I've received some very interesting emails from Martin and I've done a bit of digging. Firstly Trina Derbyshere, he's managed to trace her through passport control. It looks like she's done a runner. She left the country just over six months ago, so not long after Ashley was murdered. Before that she was working for a PR company in London. I rang the company and they were still quite annoyed with her as she didn't tell them that she was leaving, she just didn't turn up one day. I also contacted the company she was leasing her flat from and it was the same story there, so it looks like she left in a hurry. All we know is that she's in Canada somewhere, probably the east coast as she flew into Toronto. I've contacted someone in the Canadian police and asked them if they could help us to find her. However, it might also be worth interviewing any family members in case they have any relations in Canada.'

'Sure,' Kate replied, 'if I remember right her mother's still around, at least she was six or seven months ago.'

'Good, I'd be very interested to know why Miss Derbyshere felt that she needed to leave the country in such a rush. Who knows, maybe she was dealing drugs too and she thought that it was a better alternative than the one Adeline found. I also asked Martin to see what he could find out about Leah Whyte and that proved even more interesting. Apparently, she started training as a nurse just over eighteen months ago at a hospital in North London but she quit the course six months later. I spoke to someone at the hospital and they told me that she'd started off well and was top of the class for a while. However, during the last month, she missed a lot of lectures and turned up several times obviously under the influence of drugs. Since then she hasn't worked and she's not drawing benefits either. By coincidence the hospital is right next to the patch that the drugs gang operate out of.'

'Now that does sound interesting,' Kate said. 'Her father said he wasn't giving her any money so what's she living on then?'

'Well, you might get a clue from the fact that she was arrested in London along with one of the gang members for dealing class A drugs. He got three years but she got off with a caution as she had no previous offences and the dealer swore that she didn't know what he was doing. I suppose being from a 'good' family might have helped too.'

'Do you think that we've got enough for a search warrant?' Kate asked.

'I'm not sure but it might be worth a shot especially if you highlight the link with the drugs gang. There's also something in her original statement that might help.'

'What's that?' Kate asked.

She'd been there when Leah had given her statement but she couldn't remember exactly what she'd said.

'She said that she knew nothing whatsoever about the drugs gang. We now know that was probably a lie.'

She smiled, 'I think that will do nicely Mac, thanks.'

Mac was glad to see her smile.

'Okay, so tomorrow first thing we'll need to arrange some observation at Leah's flat,' Kate said. 'I want to make sure that we know who's there when we smash her door down. Is she still living in St. Peter's Street?'

'Yes, as far as we know,' Mac replied. 'I had a look on the laptop and discovered that they're building some new flats almost opposite. They might make a good place to observe from.'

'That sounds good,' Kate said. 'I'll have a word with Dan and see if someone can take over for a couple of hours in the evening so we can get some sleep.'

'An early morning raid?' Mac asked.

'Absolutely, so long as we're sure she's there. I'll get the Support Unit lined up for four the morning after and I'll confirm it with them a couple of hours before we're scheduled to go. One of us can then go and interview Mrs. Derbyshere in the morning once we've set the observation up.'

'That sounds like a plan then,' Mac said.

'Okay, I'll give you a ring tomorrow if we learn anything,' Kate said.

'Thanks Kate. Is it okay if I have a quick word with Tommy before he drops you back?'

'Sure, I'll see you at the car Tommy,' Kate said.

Mac and Tommy watched her leave.

When she'd gone Mac said, 'Bridget rang me, she'd tried to text you but you didn't reply.'

Tommy checked his phone.

'Oh, bloody hell! I was being interviewed and I forgot I'd put it on silent,' Tommy exclaimed. 'What did she say?'

'Don't look so worried, she just asked me to let you know that she'll be back a little late tonight, around eight probably. She's had a couple of urgent cases come in.'

The look of relief on Tommy's face was evident.

'Okay, so do want me to keep you company for a while?'

'I'd sooner that you kept Kate company,' Mac replied. 'Adeline's suicide has obviously hit her hard. Take her down the pub and buy her a few drinks and talk to her. To be honest you look like you could probably do with a few yourself.'

'Well, you're right there. What about you?' Tommy asked.

'Tim's coming to keep me company in an hour or so and Amrit said that she'll wait until he comes, so I'm fine.'

'Okay then, I'll see you later.'

Tommy thought that he'd had worse orders before.

As he drove towards the station Tommy said, 'Fancy a drink? I'm buying.'

'Was that what the private discussion was about then? Buy poor Kate a drink to stop her cracking up?' Kate said with the same edge in her voice he'd heard at the Smyth-Stortford's.

Tommy gave her a surprised look, 'No, it wasn't like that at all.'

Kate immediately regretted her outburst.

'I'm sorry Tommy, I didn't mean that.'

'That's okay it's been a tough day for both of us. Mac just suggested that we should have a few drinks and talk about it, that's all. It sounded like a good idea to me.'

'It is a good idea, in fact a few drinks sounds like a very good idea indeed.'

Tommy parked the car at the police station which was luckily situated just a few minutes walk from The Magnets.

'Where's your girlfriend tonight?' Kate asked as they walked over the railway bridge.

'Working late, I'll be meeting her in the pub around eight or so.'

'Oh, so I'll get to meet Mac's daughter at last. What does she do?'

'She's a doctor, a paediatrician. She works at the Lister Hospital in Stevenage,' Tommy replied.

Kate could see that he was inordinately proud of her and, she supposed, it was something to be proud of.

'How did you two meet up?' she asked.

'It's strange but it was a murder that brought us together, well several actually. Did you ever read about the Hart-Tolliver case?'

'Yes, I did, he was kidnapping girls from the street and testing drugs on them, wasn't he?'

'That's right,' Tommy said. 'That was the first case I ever worked on with Mac. Anyway, Mac had this idea about the hibernation drug that was used on the first girl in the case and he remembered that Bridget knew a researcher at the Royal Free Hospital in London where she worked at the time. So, we went down there and I met her and basically that was that.'

Kate shot him a puzzled look but didn't say anything.

When Tommy brought the drinks back there was an awkward silence for a few seconds. Tommy decided that he needed to break the ice.

'You said that you have a brother, what does he do?' Tommy asked.

He felt that he'd asked the right question as it immediately brought a little smile to Kate's face.

'Magnus? He's in finance just like my father but, other than that, they're poles apart. Literally now as he lives in South Africa so I don't get to see much of him these days.'

'What type of finance does he work in?'

'He's thankfully not one of those who worship money,' Kate said. 'He's an expert in ethical investment, getting people to put their money into projects that actually help others. He also handles a lot of the charity money that's sent to Africa from abroad. He makes sure that it ends up in the right place and not in some politician's pocket.'

'It sounds like he's making a difference,' Tommy said.

Kate looked up at Tommy's words.

'Yes, that's exactly what he doing, although I can't help feeling that he's also trying to make amends somehow.'

'How's that?'

Kate was thoughtful for a while.

'Well, I don't suppose it will do any harm telling you, you can go on Wikipedia and find out anyway,' Kate said.

'Find out what?'

'Have you ever heard of Sjórinnbanki?' she asked.

Tommy gave it some thought.

'Yes, I'm sure I have but I don't remember why.'

'It's a bank, well it was a bank. It went bust in 2008 and a lot of people lost a lot of money. Not just in Iceland but here too.'

'Yes, I remember now. It was quite a big story at the time but what I really remember is my uncle watching it on the news and getting upset about it all. He had part of his life savings in that bank and lost the lot.'

'Well, my father was a director of that bank,' Kate said with a frown. 'You'd have thought that they'd have at least thrown him in jail for a few years but no. Of course, being a director, he saw it coming and made sure that he was okay. I heard that he even made money betting that the bank would collapse. Yes, he was okay but it changed all our lives forever.'

Kate paused for a moment and Tommy made sure he kept quiet. He was really interested in hearing what she had to say.

'I'd not long left university and had started doing work experience in chambers in London. At the time I wanted to be a barrister. Well, if I'm honest, my father wanted me to be a barrister and, like everything else to do with him, I just went along with it. The bank collapse nearly ruined Iceland, it's only a small country and suddenly every person there was in debt, whether they liked it or not. It led to a depression and that hurt a lot of people too. My father's never been back to Iceland since. I'd guess that he's still afraid that they might string him up from a lamp post.'

From her expression Tommy guessed that would be a spectacle that she wouldn't mind seeing.

'We were ashamed of him, my mother most of all, but he just couldn't see it,' Kate said as she slowly shook her head. 'If Magnus and I have any goodness in us, it's because of her. My father's role in the bank collapse broke her heart and then we found out that she was ill. She just gave up Tommy, she just gave up. When my mother died, I quit my chambers and joined the police mainly because I knew it would annoy the hell out of my father. Magnus went to Africa as soon as he finished university. Neither of us has seen our father since.'

'Do you think he'll ever come back? Magnus, I mean?' Tommy asked.

'No, why should he? He's happy there, he loves what he's doing and he's a married man now. She's a local girl, a Xhosa. She was running one of the charity projects that Magnus went out to have a look at. He said the minute he saw her he understood why he'd had to come all the way to the tip of Africa. It was just to meet her.'

'Have you met her yourself?'

'Yes, I was there at the wedding,' Kate replied. 'She's a beautiful girl but it was Magnus that surprised me. He was different, he was happy and seeing him like that I cried. Not because of the wedding though, it was because at that moment I couldn't remember a time when my lovely brother had really been happy before.'

Tommy saw a single tear go down Kate's cheek. He hoped he wasn't opening any old sores for her.

'You know, you said something similar when we were walking down here, about Bridget,' Kate said as she wiped the tear away.

'What do you mean?'

'You said that, when you met Bridget for the first time, that was that. What was that?' Kate said with a puzzled look on her face.

'Well, I just knew, what exactly I don't know. I suppose I knew that I'd met someone special, someone that I wanted to know more about. No not want, I don't think I had any choice in it at all. I desperately needed to know more would be closer to the truth. I just couldn't stop thinking about her and that's not changed since the first day I met her.'

'I've never felt like that about anyone,' Kate said sadly. 'I've had lots of boyfriends and even one husband but I never felt that strongly about any of them. Why do you think that is?'

Tommy shrugged.

'Perhaps you just haven't met the right person yet, either that or you're looking in the wrong place. That's what my mum always says when I can't find something. She's usually right too.' Tommy noticed that Kate's glass was empty. 'I'll get them in.'

Kate thought about what Tommy had said and for some reason it resonated with her.

Looking in the wrong place? She felt it should mean something but she couldn't figure out why.

When Tommy returned Kate changed the subject. She felt it was being unfair to Tommy having to hear her moaning so they talked about films and music and holidays. She enjoyed talking to Tommy but she could have told the time by his face. Around eight he kept glancing out of the window at the street outside. He knew Bridget had arrived when she saw Tommy's face light up. She knew at that moment that she and the rest of the world just didn't exist for Tommy. He stood up and waved as Bridget came in the door. Kate saw Tommy's look reflected in Bridget's face too.

She thought that Bridget was really pretty and her eyes were quite a strange colour, a sort of blue-green that she hadn't seen before. Kate immediately felt awkward and surplus to requirements.

'It's nice to meet you Bridget. I'll leave and let the two of you get on with it.'

'Oh Kate, please stay and have a drink,' Bridget said.

Kate could see that Bridget was trying to be kind but in truth she suddenly felt deathly tired. She said as much to Bridget and Tommy.

'Okay then, next time,' Bridget said.

'Yes, next time.'

She stopped in the street for a few seconds and looked back through the window at them. They sat opposite each other, their hands touching, looking only at each other. She knew then that Bridget was indeed beautiful because she could see it reflected in Tommy's face.

She walked slowly towards the train station and wondered why she'd never looked at anyone like that. Was there something missing in her or, was it just as Tommy said, that she just hadn't met the right person yet? She thought about this as she sat on the empty train and looked out of the window into the darkness.

She was going back to an empty flat where she'd be alone. She'd go to sleep alone and she'd wake up alone. She decided that she'd had enough of it.

If the right person really was out there, she wished that they'd hurry up.

Chapter Fifteen

Mac had a bad night and was awake well before it was light. He decided to fire up his laptop and do some work to take his mind off his discomfort. He didn't look at the screen however as his mind raced off in a different direction.

Here he had a girl with a very well-off father who had gone through a bad time and then someone had got her hooked on heroin. Mac had a feeling that if he could find out who had supplied Ashley with heroin in the first place then it might go a long way towards solving the case.

Was it, Adeline? Yet another girl with a well-off father? She admitted that she was dealing so it could have been her. After all, if she had tried to get her own sister hooked, she wouldn't stop at a mere friend. Talking of sisters could it have been Leah who he knew had been taking drugs a matter of months before and who now seemed to be living on fresh air? Or perhaps it was the mysterious stranger at the clinic.

Oh well, he'd just have to wait until he had more information and the CCTV footage from the clinic might help too. In the meantime, he was going to go over everything in the file one more time.

Kate was glad to be back in the station and amongst other people. Tommy was already there. He was in deep conversation with a young man who had black rimmed spectacles and his hair sticking up in spikes.

Tommy noticed her arrive and waved at her to come over.

'This is Martin, our computer specialist,' Tommy said. 'This is Kate Grimsson who's running the Whyte case.'

They shook hands. Martin looked so young that he made her feel middle-aged somehow.

'Martin's been showing me something, something that might really help us.'

'Yes, this is a fairly new camera I bought when I went snowboarding a few months ago. It's really cool, I used it as a helmet cam when I was going down the slopes. It can take still shots or video and it all works by remote control,' Martin said with a proud smile.

Kate looked at it. It was far smaller than she'd have thought.

'So how can this help us?' she asked wondering if this was just a case of boys and their toys.

'Well, you've got some observation to do, haven't you?' Martin asked.

Kate nodded.

'Well, all you need to do is place this gizmo somewhere where it has a clear view and then leave it,' Martin said. 'I've done a bit of re-programming so that you can now watch the stream live on your computer or phone and it will also securely upload it to the cloud in real time so you'll have it all on record.'

Kate looked at it with a bit more respect.

'What about the battery, how long does it last?' she asked.

'Yes, that's normally the weak point, however, I've put together an auxiliary battery pack that will kick in when the inbuilt battery goes flat. That should last for around thirty-six hours or so all told,' Martin replied.

Kate gave this some thought. It would certainly save quite a bit of time if they didn't have to be there and could rely on the camera to do the observing for them.

'Okay, I'm sold,' Kate said. 'We'll take it.'

'There's just one drawback,' Tommy said.

'What's that?' Kate asked.

'If we break it then it's ours,' Tommy replied.

'Sorry but it cost me quite a bit,' Martin said. 'I've been trying to get Dan to buy one of these for weeks now. To be honest I was hoping that, if you guys could tell him how successful it was for you, then maybe he'll remember that when he next works out his budget.'

'Don't worry, we'll look after it,' Kate said. She then turned to Tommy. 'Don't forget that we have the Smyth-Stortford's coming in at ten thirty. I just hope that they're on time.'

They were fifteen minutes late and for all that they might not have bothered. Tommy could see the frustration on Kate's face as they walked towards the car park.

'What a waste of our time that was,' Kate said. 'They've obviously been coached. I'd bet that, if we'd asked them if the moon was made out of green cheese, then they would deny having any knowledge of the matter. For God's sake, Adeline was his daughter and yet all he could say was 'I don't know what she got up to, I just paid for it.' Smug bastard!'

Tommy decided to say nothing for a while and let Kate simmer down a bit.

They drove in silence towards Leah's flat, Kate holding Martin's camera on her lap. She made a conscious effort to calm herself down and started reading the wording on the box that held Martin's camera as she held it on her lap.

'It's really small this, isn't it?' she said as she opened the box and peeked inside.

'Small but powerful,' Tommy replied. 'Martin showed us his holiday movies a while back and I was really impressed at its resolution. I remembered him saying then that it would be a great piece of kit for observation duties.'

'Well, I'm all for technology especially when it means I don't have to sit in a car for hours looking at a closed door and getting bored stiff,' Kate said. 'Plus, there's always the chance that you might get noticed. That happened to me once. The suspect came past us from behind, saw us and then turned and knocked on the window. He said that, if we wanted to talk to him, we only had to ask. Really embarrassing that was.'

The site manager at the building works was more than helpful. The flats at the front were more or less finished so they were able to put the camera on the windowsill of the flat directly opposite Leah's house knowing that it wouldn't be disturbed. They turned the cardboard box on its side and placed the camera inside it so its outline wouldn't look so conspicuous. Tommy went outside and checked, he said that you couldn't really see the camera unless you went right up to the window.

Tommy got his laptop out and went through the routine exactly as Martin had instructed. It was a lot simpler than Tommy had thought it would be.

'Here look at this!' Tommy said.

Kate looked at a picture of Leah's front door. It was as though she was standing three or four yards away. The camera zoomed out and then in again.

'This is quite fun,' Tommy said.

'Come on, the day's wearing on. Let's go and see Mrs. Derbyshere and leave Martin's gizmo to work its magic,' Kate said anxious to get on with it.

Trina's mother lived in an expensive looking block of retirement flats not far from the centre of St. Albans. They had to first get past the concierge, a stern looking woman in her fifties who took her job very seriously. She examined both Kate's and Tommy's warrant cards in detail before using the phone to check with Mrs. Derbyshere. She eventually admitted them but with some obvious reluctance. Kate noticed that she followed them at a distance to make sure they didn't go anywhere they shouldn't.

Mrs. Derbyshere, on the other hand, seemed pleased to see them and invited them into her flat with a smile. She was younger that Kate had expected, in her mid-fifties at most, but she obviously had problems walking as she used two sticks to get back to her armchair.

'Bloody hips dear,' she said noticing Kate's looks. 'Had the replacements done but they didn't take so here I am stuck in God's waiting room. Grim, isn't it?'

She didn't look grim though. She said it with a smile and Kate couldn't see any self-pity in her face.

She managed to seat herself in an armchair with some difficulty before she said, 'So how can I help the police? I'd bet my sticks that it's about my Trina, isn't it?'

Kate and Tommy sat down on a little two-seater sofa.

'Yes, it is. I'd be interested in knowing how you guessed that,' Kate asked.

'Do you have any children?'

Kate shook her head.

'Well, I've got three and the eldest two just took life in their stride. They did well at school and at university, got good jobs and married well. They're happy, at least I hope they are, but it's hard to tell sometimes, isn't it? Anyway, I thought I had this mother thing cracked until Trina came along. She was not expected, I was over thirty at the time and happy with my regulation two children. God knows I love her but she was hard work from the start. Ask her to do one thing and she'd do the exact opposite. So, what's she done now?'

'Nothing as far as we know. We just wanted to talk to her about a friend of hers,' Kate said.

She could see a dark cloud pass over Mrs. Derbyshere's face.

'Is this about poor Ashley Whyte? What a bloody awful business that was. It really upset Trina, I think that's why she just upped sticks and left the country. The first I knew about it was when I got a postcard from the airport.'

'We believe that she's in Canada at the moment and we need to track her down. We just need to talk to her.

Do you have any relatives in Canada or family friends?' Kate asked.

'Oh no dear, I always thought of Canada as being a bit cold and draughty personally. Is that where you think she is?'

'You mean you don't know where she is yourself?'

Mrs. Derbyshere shook her head.

'As I said I got a postcard and that was it really.'

'Have you still got it?' Kate asked.

'Yes, it's behind the clock with some letters. You don't mind getting it yourself, do you?'

'No of course not,' Kate replied.

There were six or seven letters and only a couple of postcards. Kate looked at the postmark, it was sent on the same day that she didn't turn up for work. It simply said –

'*Sorry mum but I have to go. I don't think I'll be coming back but you've got Lydia and Jonny to look after you and we'd only fight anyway. I've made a right mess of things as usual, all my love T*'

'So, she's not been in touch since this postcard, no phone calls, no text messages, no emails?' Kate asked.

'No nothing at all, not a word,' she replied with a shrug and a smile.

'Was Trina a drug user?'

'God no! She had her faults but no, thank God that wasn't one of them.'

'Did she ever talk about Ashley?' Kate asked.

'She used to before, well before Ashley went on drugs. Yes, I knew about that and Trina was very upset. She said that Ashley had been at such a low point that she was easy prey.'

'Did she ever say who it was that gave Ashley the drugs in the first place?'

'No, she didn't, she stopped telling me things around that time. She started looking worried which, if you knew my Trina, was very unlike her.'

138

'Have you made any effort to track Trina down, to find out where she's gone?' Kate asked.

'Trina will do what she does, she always has and she's big enough to look after herself. She'll contact me when she's ready to,' she said with certainty.

As they walked towards the car Tommy asked, 'Did you believe her when she said she didn't know where Trina is?'

'Not a word,' Kate replied. 'She was far too relaxed about it all, as if she couldn't care less about Trina. I didn't buy it.'

'Why not?'

'The photos.'

Tommy had a think but couldn't remember any photos.

'Sorry what photos?'

'There was a group of framed family photos on a chest of drawers,' Kate replied. 'They were there so that they'd be easily visible when she sat in her armchair and they were of all of her three children. Trina's photo was the one in the middle. I had a quick look at it as I went out and there were quite a lot of finger marks on the glass and, as she lives alone, I figured that they had to be hers. None of the other photos had finger marks so it was just Trina's photo that she picks up and looks at. I think that she's very much attached to her daughter and probably missing her.'

Tommy was both impressed and a bit miffed that he hadn't noticed the photos.

'I'd be willing to bet that she's in touch with Trina by some means or other and that she knows at least something about why her daughter had to leave so quickly,' Kate continued.

'What next then?' Tommy asked.

'I've no idea if I'm being honest. I thought that we'd be spending the rest of the day sitting in a car looking at Leah Whyte's front door. Any ideas?'

'Did you believe her when she said that Trina had no relations in Canada?'

'I'm not sure.'

'So, remind me, how did Trina get to know Ashley?' Tommy asked.

'They were at university together but I think that they were friends before that.'

'School friends perhaps?'

'No, Ashley knew Adeline from school but I'm fairly certain from what I remember that Trina and Adeline didn't know each other that well. Now what was it?' Kate asked herself. 'Yes, that's right they were in the Scouts together. What are you thinking?'

'Well, if we believe Mrs. Derbyshere about having no relatives in Canada, and after all that would be something we could easily check, I was wondering if perhaps Trina might have a friend there.'

'So, someone she might have known in university or the Scouts perhaps?' Kate said. 'Let's see if we can narrow it down a bit.'

She went back into the retirement home and walked straight past the concierge who jumped up and followed them. As they came to Mrs. Derbyshere's door Kate turned and looked at the concierge.

'Have you got a pass key?' Kate asked.

The concierge nodded.

'Well, let us in then, I don't want her coming to the door again with her hips,' Kate ordered.

She unlocked the door and held it open for them. Mrs. Derbyshere was on the phone. She put it down quickly when she saw Kate and Tommy. She had an expression on her face that was both guilty and defiant.

'Saying hello to Trina?' Kate asked. 'How's her little scouting friend in Canada then?' she said taking a chance.

'You knew?' Mrs. Derbyshere said in surprise.

'You lied to us, didn't you?'

140

'Yes, yes I did and I don't care. You won't get a word out of me,' Mrs. Derbyshere said resolutely.

'We don't need to. You've just told us what we need to know. Thanks.'

Kate was smiling when she left.

'Good thinking, Tommy,' she said as they walked back to the car.

'Were you expecting to catch her on the phone? Was that why you asked the concierge to open the door?'

She looked at Tommy and, for a second, considered taking all the credit but only for a second.

'No, I was honestly worried about her hips. We were just lucky really but we need every bit of luck we can get.'

Kate took her phone out and saw that she had a message.

'The CCTV footage has arrived.'

They sat in the car and looked at it. They saw Ashley come out of what looked like the front door of a house. She waited for some time until a man approached her. They hugged and then started talking. They talked for about fifteen minutes then hugged again and the man walked off. Ashley went back into the house again and the video ended.

'We don't get a good look at the man, do we?' Tommy said.

'The camera's high up and it doesn't help that he's wearing a hoodie. It's a bit grainy too.'

'Send it to Martin, he might be able to clean it up a bit,' Tommy suggested.

She sent it by email and asked Martin to send it to Mac as soon as he'd finished processing it. She rang Mac's number. She told him that the CCTV footage should be with him soon and asked if he could find the details of the Scout troop that Ashley and Trina had attended. She was sure she'd seen them in the case file somewhere.

Mac texted her ten minutes later.

'It looks like we've got the name and address of the Scout leader. Let's go and knock on her door,' Kate said.

They pulled up outside a modest terraced house not far from the town centre. They rang the bell but got no answer. A neighbour working in her garden looked up.

'Police,' Kate said showing her warrant card. 'Do you where Mrs. Barrowclough is?'

'Oh, where she always is, the Scout hut just down the bottom of the road. I was chatting to her just a few minutes ago and she said she had to get something ready for the Beavers.'

In the Scout hut Pat Barrowclough was moving chairs that had been set out in lines from the centre of the room and stacking them in a corner.

'Oh hello,' she said with a smile when she noticed Kate and Tommy. 'Can I help you?'

The Scout leader was in her late fifties and had a long toothy face and a large nose on which a pair of high strength spectacles were perched.

Kate showed her warrant card, 'I believe that you knew Ashley Whyte and Trina Derbyshere?'

Pat's smile dropped on hearing Ashley's name. She pulled out three chairs from the stack and set them in a circle. She gestured that they should sit down.

'Yes, I knew them. I saw them grow up from little girls. They left the troop when they started studying for their A levels but they kept in touch. They were lovely girls, lovely girls,' she said with a mournful expression.

'When did you hear about Ashley?' Kate asked.

'On the news, dear, I couldn't believe it though. I was so sure that it must have been someone with the same name but then I saw her photo. I'd have never believed it, out of the three of them Ashley was usually the most sensible.'

'Three of them?' Kate said. 'Who was the third?'

'Carly, Carly MacIntosh. They all joined together and we used to have three in a tent in those days. They shared a tent on one of our trips and became inseparable afterwards.'

'Do you know how we might find Carly?' Kate asked crossing her fingers as she did so.

'Oh yes, she always keeps in touch. I think I've got one of her postcards on the board. We have a board where we ask Cub Scouts to pin any foreign postcards they might get.'

She went over a large cork board on the wall and returned with a card. The photo on the front was a night view of the CN Tower.

'So, she lives in Toronto then?' Kate asked feeling that they were making progress at last.

'Oh yes, she was born there. She was over here for seven or eight years as her father was a professor at the university. She went home just before Ashley and Trina went to university themselves.'

'I take it that you have her address?'

'Oh yes, I like to send her a letter every now and again, just to see how she is,' Pat replied.

Kate felt like punching the air. Once outside she rang Mac straight away and gave him Carly MacIntosh's address.

'Mac says that he's going to call his Canadian police contact straight away. He also said that he's managed to track down Naomi Cadogan. I was forgetting all about her,' Kate said when she'd finished the call.

'She's the TV presenter who was in the clinic for a while, isn't she?' Tommy asked.

'Yes, she's the one who thanked Adeline publicly for helping her. It's a pity that she wasn't around when Adeline needed some help herself. However, Mac told me that she's working in Los Angeles these days so maybe that's why. Mac's going to try and phone her. Anyway, it looks like we might be getting somewhere at last,' Kate said as she looked at the time on her phone.

It was already one forty five.

'Fancy a coffee and a sandwich while we figure out what to do next?' she asked.

'Good idea,' Tommy said, 'and talking of good ideas....'

Chapter Sixteen

Mac was beginning to think that the case was finally getting somewhere too. They'd found Naomi Cadogan and possibly Trina Derbyshere too. Naomi's agent told him that she'd talk to Naomi for him but it was still early in the morning where she was. Then Naomi herself had texted him a few minutes ago and said she'd ring when she had a moment.

Then there was the CCTV footage. He'd just received it from Martin and was waiting impatiently for it to download onto his computer. He clicked 'play' and noted that the clip was just over twenty minutes long.

It showed the front of a house that was on the other side of the road from the camera and it also covered a short stretch of the road that ran in front of the house too. After a minute or so the front door opened and a young woman stepped out. It was Ashley. She looked up and down the road and then stood inside the front door while she waited. Mac guessed it because it was raining as he could see drops of water falling from the leaves of a nearby tree. A few minutes later a man walked towards her. He was lean and probably young as he walked with a lithe movement. Mac never got a look at his face though as he had his hood up all through the video.

Was that by design? Mac thought. Maybe he knew about the camera and didn't want to be identified, then again maybe not. Mac reminded himself that it was raining so maybe he just didn't want to get wet.

Ashley hugged the man when they met and after that they both moved to the side of the house and talked. Towards the end of their conversation he handed her something. Mac slowed the video right down and then freeze-framed it. Even after Martin's magic the resolution wasn't that great, however, Mac was sure that the man had given Ashley something that was white and rect-angular in shape.

Drugs, Mac immediately thought.

They hugged again and the man walked away. Ashley disappeared into the front door of the house. Mac was about to stop the video when he saw it.

A car went by.

He ran the video back to the beginning. Ashley was waiting at the front door when a car went by and the man appeared a minute or so later. He slowed it down and freeze-framed it again. It looked like the same car.

So, the man had most likely driven past the camera and then parked his car and walked down to meet Ashley. That meant that the car would also be caught as he went back. He might have a lead to the mysterious stranger after all!

He played it again slowing it down as the car went past for the first time. Ashley was leaning against the door but she straightened up when she saw the car go by. He was certain now. He let the video roll on and watched the two of them hug each other. He played it back several times and decided that this was no lover's embrace but, whoever it was, he obviously had some affection for her.

He played the clips showing the car coming and going several times but couldn't quite make out the part of the number plate that was visible. It was time to contact Martin again.

'Martin, in the clip you sent me there's a car featured at around 1:18 and 19:01 into the video. Can you see if you make out the number plate? The car looks like a Vauxhall Astra to me but see what you think.'

'If I can get even a partial plate and I know what the make is then there shouldn't be a problem in tracing it,' Martin said.

'What would we do without you?' Mac said and he meant it too.

Yet another lead. Mac was beginning to get the feeling that the investigation might not be too far away from the tipping point.

'So, we get to do a bit of observation after all,' Kate said as she took a bite out of her sandwich.

'Well, maybe you do. All I can see is that great big bush,' Tommy said.

They'd been able to find the 'back door' that Dr. Al-Faran had told them about fairly easily. Tommy had looked at the map and found that there was a road that ran right along the back boundary of the clinic's grounds. Kate had freeze-framed the house that Ashley came out of on her phone to ensure that they got the right one. There were very few houses along that stretch of road so it was easy enough to find.

It wasn't so easy to hide the car though but they were lucky and found a place on the side of the road where they could pull in. They made sure that they were on the blind side of the CCTV camera which Kate could see perched on top of a high metal pole a few yards in front of her. However, while the foliage was great for hiding the car's outline, it meant that only Kate could actually see the back door. Tommy was keeping an eye on Leah's front door on his laptop.

They'd been there around twenty minutes when she saw Tommy sit up out of the corner of her eye and turned her head.

'It's Leah,' Tommy said moving the laptop so Kate could see.

She looked at the screen and just caught Leah closing the door behind her. She had a fleece and track suit bottoms on and something very odd looking on her feet. Kate looked closer.

'Would you believe it, she's wearing slippers!' Kate said as Tommy zoomed in on Leah's feet. 'Bunny rabbit slippers at that.'

147

'She's obviously not going far then,' Tommy observed as Leah disappeared from the screen.

Sure enough, three minutes later she came back holding a thin plastic carrier bag.

'I can even see what she's got in there,' Tommy said with a grin as the camera zoomed in. 'Two pints of milk, bread, butter and...yes a pack of bacon. Looks like breakfast to me.'

'Not exactly an early riser then, is she?' Kate said as Leah disappeared inside. 'Anyway, at least we know where she is.'

They then both settled back as exactly nothing happened in the next hour and a half.

Mac picked up his phone on the first ring. He quickly looked at the number, it has the US country code at the start.

'Is that Mr. Maguire?' a young woman asked.

'It is.'

'I'm Naomi Cadogan. My agent said that you're with the police and that you wanted to speak to me.'

She sounded quite nervous.

'Is this about Addie?' she asked.

'We're looking into the murder of Ashley Whyte. Did you know her?' Mac asked.

'No, I knew of her though. She and Addie were school friends but we never met.'

'How did you and Addie get on together?' Mac asked.

'Addie and I are cousins. Sorry, we were cousins. To be honest I still can't believe she's dead. Our mothers were sisters and, although I was a bit older than her, we always got on well together when we were young. I kind of lost touch with her as we got older though.'

'What about Adeline's sister?'

'Jemima?'

Mac could hear the disdain in her voice.

'Oh, she's a right piece of work,' Naomi said. 'The bitch even lied about Addie trying to get her on drugs!'

'That happened to be true,' Mac said. 'Adeline admitted it before she killed herself.'

'Oh,' Naomi said, followed by a long silence. 'I just thought it was another one of Jemima's lies. Are you looking into Addie's death too? Was it really suicide?'

'Addie killed herself in the presence of two police officers, so it was definitely suicide, but what makes you think it might not have been?'

'Just something she said before I left the country. If I'm honest I didn't know what to make of it.'

'Was this before or after her father cut her off?'

'Not long before,' Naomi replied. 'I heard about that when I'd been in my new job for a month or so. I sent her some money but I honestly thought that her father would relent once he'd felt he'd taught her a lesson.'

'What exactly did she say, can you remember?' Mac asked.

'Near enough, I think. What she said worried me at the time but I was going to the States so, I suppose I just put the best gloss on it. She said 'I'm in trouble, serious trouble and I just don't know what to do about it.' I asked her what kind of trouble but she wouldn't say. I told her that if it was that serious then she should go to the police but she just shook her head. 'Lives are at risk,' she said, 'innocent lives'. I must admit that this really worried me.'

There was short silence before Naomi continued.

'Anyway, the next second Addie was making light of it and then she told me to forget what she'd said as she was just being silly. I asked her about it again later but she just changed the subject.'

'What do you think was going on with Adeline?' Mac asked.

'I've honestly no idea. Addie was very good at hiding her feelings but I thought about it a lot and even more after I'd heard that she was dead. I think it was like looking behind the curtain and getting a glimpse of the real Addie. I think she was worried, really worried but I think she also felt that there was nothing she could do about it.'

The words 'innocent lives' kept going around Mac's head. What or who was Adeline referring to?

'Just a few more questions, I believe that you went to the Al-Faran Clinic for a while?' Mac asked.

'Yes, I was there for just under four weeks.'

'What was it like?'

'Like? Well, like a five-star jail, if you must know, but it worked so I shouldn't be knocking it, I suppose,' Naomi replied.

'What did you go there for? Was it drugs?'

'No, I've never had anything to do with drugs, they never appealed to me for some reason. It was alcohol, to be precise the best red wines that the Napa Valley can produce. After my bastard of a boyfriend dumped me, I was knocking it back by the case. I was stupidly putting everything at risk because of how that rat had treated me. Anyway, I had a lucid day and rang Addie. She suggested the clinic and I booked myself in straight away.'

'What was it like in the clinic? Did you meet any other... guests?'

Mac nearly said 'inmates' instead of 'guests' and just caught himself at the last moment.

'No, not one,' Naomi relied. 'We all had our own rooms, very spacious and luxurious, but we also had out own guards too. Very smartly dressed men with muscles who made sure you stuck to the plan.'

'The plan?'

'Before you were admitted you had to sign a treatment plan in which you basically signed your life away for the time you were there. The only people I saw were my personal therapist, a very sweet young man called Bernard, the guards and, now and again, the doctor herself.'

'Weren't you allowed outside?' Mac asked.

'Yes, but the grounds were big enough and the guards made sure that you didn't bump into anyone else.'

'What about the back door, did you ever use that?'

'Oh, you mean the house at the back of the clinic estate? Yes, I was allowed one twenty minute meeting a week while I was there. You won't believe it but I wasted the first one on my ex-boyfriend.'

'Does anyone live in the house?' Mac asked.

'Yes, I think some of the guards do.'

'Did they say what would happen if you didn't stick to the plan?'

'Oh, the doctor was quite clear on that,' Naomi replied. 'She'd basically keep all the money and you'd be shown the door, never to return.'

'That sounds a bit harsh to me,' Mac said.

'I suppose it had to be. Anyway, as I said, it worked for me. I still drink but I can control it now.'

'Is there anything else you can tell me about the clinic? Did anything unusual ever happen while you were there?' Mac asked hopefully.

'Not really if I'm being honest. What I mainly remember is being bored out of my skull, that and the feeling that I was in my own reality show.'

'What do you mean?'

'Well there were cameras everywhere,' Naomi replied, 'very discreetly tucked away of course. I'd guess that most people wouldn't even know they were there.'

'So, how did you know they were there?' Mac asked.

'Oh, I've worked on a couple of reality shows where we used disguised cameras like that. I knew what to look for.'

'So, they didn't tell you that you were being observed?'

'Not up front,' Naomi replied, 'but I did look at the fine print of the contract I'd signed and it was there in clause seventy-four or something under Medical Surveillance.'

Mac gave this some thought.

'How did Adeline know about the clinic?'

'Oh, she went there a few months before I did, cocaine. It seemed to work for her too as I didn't see her using any afterwards.'

After he put the phone down Mac thought deeply about Naomi's words. So, Adeline had gone to the clinic first to cure a cocaine habit, a habit that Naomi said had been cured. Yet it would appear that in reality she'd merely swapped it for a heroin habit instead. She'd admitted that she was dealing and that she'd been scared because she'd 'been behind' with the people who'd supplied her with drugs.

Once again Mac couldn't help feeling that this was the key. If he could find out who had supplied Ashley and Adeline with heroin then he might be closer to cracking the case.

His thoughts were interrupted by his phone. It was Martin.

'Two things Mac, I've received a phone that belonged to an Adeline Smyth-Stortford from St. Albans police. I take it that it's part of your case?'

'Oh yes, I'd be more than interested to see what it might tell us.'

'Okay, just give me a few hours and I'll see what I can get out of it. The other thing is I've traced the owner of your car. It belongs to a Mr. Joseph Whyte and here's his address.'

Mac got up Google maps and located it straight away. To his surprise it was another drug rehab clinic but it was its position that immediately interested him.

It was right in the middle of the drug gang's territory.

Chapter Seventeen

Kate was nearly falling asleep when her phone rang. She looked at the screen. It was Mac calling.

'Martin's found out who Ashley's mysterious visitor was. He's called Joseph Whyte and his address is that of a drug rehab clinic in North London.'

'Whyte with a 'Y'?' Kate asked.

'Yes, he must be a relative of some sort,' Mac said. 'Didn't Joe Ibbotson mention him at all?'

'No, it's the first I've heard of him. We'll get over there straight away. We're at the back of the Al-Faran Clinic now but there isn't anything happening.'

'Good, I've also heard from Naomi Cadogan so come back here when you're finished and we'll compare notes.'

'Will do,' Kate said.

She turned to Tommy and told him what she'd learned from Mac. He fed the address into the satnav and they were off. Both of them felt a little thrill of excitement at the thought that they might be finally making some progress.

The clinic turned out to be nothing like the one they'd just been sitting outside. An inscription carved grandly in stone just above the doors told them that they were standing before the 'Endeavour Wire Works' which turned out to be a decrepit and neglected factory building in a district of North London that was surrounded by houses that somehow managed to be even more decrepit and neglected. Kate was glad it was daylight, it felt scary enough as it was. A set of double doors with the lock protected by thick metal plates prevented them from going inside. There was a battered metal intercom with a single button. Kate pressed it.

'Yes?' a crackly woman's voice asked.

'Police, we're here to see Joseph Whyte,' Kate said.

'Hold your warrant card up,' the woman ordered.

Kate did as she was told. She couldn't see the camera but she was sure that there was one there. The door buzzed and Tommy held it open for her.

The inside was no better than the outside. Long ago someone must have painted the walls white but time had degraded it into a sickly beige. Here and there gouges in the walls showed through to the red brick-work. The space was crudely divided up by flimsy plywood partitions. A young woman was waiting for them. She was tall and slim and Kate admired her perfect Afro hairdo.

'You want Joseph?' she asked suspiciously.

'Yes, we just need some information that's all,' Kate said soothingly.

'That's what you people always say,' the young woman said making no move to go.

Kate decided to be honest.

'We'd like to talk to him about Ashley Whyte.'

'Oh,' the young woman said her face softening. 'I'll go and get him, he's in our secure facility at the moment. You can wait in there,' she said pointing to a door before she disappeared.

There was a small room on the other side of the door with three chairs, all different, and a table with a scarred surface that had a piece of cardboard wedged under one leg.

'Secure facility?' Tommy said. 'Could he be our drug dealer then?'

'He certainly could be,' Kate replied. 'He's obviously on drugs himself, what else could he be doing in here?'

They had to wait a few minutes before the door opened and a man walked in.

'I'll be okay, don't worry,' he said to someone behind him.

Kate caught a glimpse of a huge shaven headed man behind him who glared at her as the door closed.

'In my line of work, I normally have as little to do with the police as possible but you said it was about Ashley?' the man said as he sat down.

Kate looked him over. He was slim, thirty at the most and dressed in a grey T shirt and ripped jeans. He had a light beard and long dreadlocks that were held in place by a thick green, yellow and black band.

He definitely wouldn't have looked out of place selling ten pound bags on a corner, Kate thought.

'Yes, you visited Ashley when she was at the Al-Faran Clinic, didn't you?' Kate asked.

'Yes, I did,' he said. 'Before I say anything else can you tell me why you're re-opening the case now, after all this time?'

'We've obtained some new evidence and we're looking into it,' Kate said not wanting to give anything away.

The man smiled and shook his head.

'Okay, so you're not going to say. Yes, it was me that visited Ashley and I saw the CCTV camera so I'd guess that's how you tracked me down. I'm just surprised it took you so long to find me.'

'Why were you visiting Ashley?'

'She called me and said that she needed to talk to someone. I was more than happy to help.'

'Why was that?' Kate asked.

'Why would I help Ashley? Well, it's the least I could do for my niece,' he explained.

'Ashley was your niece?' Kate said in disbelief.

'Well, I know that there was only ten years or so between us but yes, I was her uncle. My mother had six boys, I'm the youngest and her father Mason is the oldest, he's twenty years older than me in fact. I suppose me and Ashley were a bit more like cousins really.'

'Do you know how Ashley got into drugs?'

'Which time, the first or the second?' he asked.

155

'Both if you can,' Kate replied.

'Well, the first time that was her loving sister Leah. Ashley and her sister were totally different. Mason loved Ashley in his own way but, unfortunately, he never had any time for Leah. To be honest most people had no time for Leah, she was spiteful and turned on everyone around her sooner or later. Even though she was supposed to be grown up, she was just a jealous little girl at heart. I'd guess that as soon as she saw a weakness in Ashley she went for the jugular. Ashley told me it was Leah who'd given her heroin. Leah had nearly killed her own sister and, if I'm honest, I think her only sadness was that her sister was still alive.'

'Who was it the second time?' Kate asked.

Joseph shook his head.

'I've no idea. I know that Ashley was keeping as far away from her sister as possible so I'd be surprised if it was her. She said that she was clean while she was at the clinic but, after she died, I had my doubts.'

'Why?'

'Here,' Joseph said as he pulled something out of his pocket.

Both Kate and Tommy, thinking of the secure facility, watched him carefully but it just turned out to be a phone.

'I took this when we met at the clinic.'

He found a photo and showed it to them. It was a selfie of him and Ashley. They were both smiling.

'So, what am I supposed to be seeing here?' Kate asked.

He enlarged the photo. Ashley had been holding the phone and part of her upper arm had also been photographed.

'Here,' Joseph said pointing to a small spot on her arm.

'What is it?' Tommy asked.

'A needle mark,' Joseph said.

'Are you sure?' Kate asked.

'Oh, I'm sure. I've seen enough of those believe me. I only noticed it when I was looking at it after I heard the news of her murder.'

Kate noticed his eyes glisten with tears. He obviously cared for his niece.

'Did you learn anything from her that might be helpful to us?' Kate asked.

He slowly shook his head.

'I knew that she was in trouble. She wanted to tell me something but, somehow, she couldn't. I have no idea what it was but I could sense that she was scared.'

'What did you give her before you left?'

'Give her?' Joseph thought for a while. 'Oh yes, it was my card. I told her to call me day or night if she needed any help but she never did.'

Kate was puzzled. Did drug dealers really have cards these days?

'Have you got a card you can give us?' she asked.

'Yes sure, I'll get someone to give you one before you go.'

'So, if you're saying that Leah gave Ashley heroin, I take it that Leah was dealing then?'

'Yes,' Joseph sighed. 'Mason thought it would do her good to do her nurse training where we all grew up and it might have worked if she hadn't met someone from the local drugs gang. He was in for knife wounds after a fight. Anyway, she fell for him, quit training and started dealing instead. She's very good at it or so I heard.'

'Yet you don't seem to think that the gang might have been responsible for Ashley's death?' Kate asked.

'They weren't, let's just say that I know some of them personally,' Joseph said as she stood up. 'I'm sorry but I've got to go now. Can I please ask that you don't call here again, I don't want certain people thinking that I'm getting too close to the police. You can call me if you want though, my number will be on the card. I really hope you catch whoever did that to Ashley.'

The huge man was waiting for him outside. They walked back together down the corridor.

'Now that was a strange conversation,' Kate said.

'Yes, I know what you mean. I've met a few drug dealers but no-one like him before,' Tommy replied.

The young woman came back and showed them out.

'Joseph said to give you this,' she said handing them a card as she held the door open. Once outside Kate stopped and looked at the card.

'My God, here!' Kate said, stifling a laugh with her hand as she handed the card to Tommy.

The card said –

The North London Wireworks Clinic, Director Dr. Joseph Whyte

'He's a doctor!' Tommy exclaimed.

'And that's his clinic! I was nearly going to say something about him being a drug dealer but I thought it was so obvious that I never did. I'm so glad,' Kate said with a smile, 'I'd have looked a right idiot. Come on, let's go and see Mac.'

Mac was engrossed in an email he'd just received when Amrit showed Kate and Tommy in.

'I'll be off now, Mac. You can let me know how the next episode turns out tomorrow,' she said leaving them alone.

'Are you and Amrit watching TV together or something?' Tommy asked.

Mac smiled, 'No, I'm keeping her up to date with what's going on with the case. She thinks it's every bit as good as the police serials on the television. Anyway, I was just reading an email from the Canadian police. It looks like Trina Derbyshere has disappeared again.'

'That was probably her mother. She must have warned her that we were looking for her,' Kate said with a frown.

'Well, the police are keeping their eyes open and we can only hope they find her. So, what have we found out today?' Mac asked.

Kate and Tommy went through their interviews with Mrs. Derbyshere, Pat Barrowclough and Dr. Joseph Whyte, leaving out the fact that they thought the doctor was a drug dealer at first. Mac went through his phone interview with Naomi Cadogan.

'So, in summary Trina Derbyshere fled to Canada at short notice but we don't know why and it looks like she might have done it again. She's obviously scared of something or someone. Ashley's uncle said that his niece was also scared but couldn't tell him why and funnily enough Adeline was pretty much the same. She did say something to Naomi about 'innocent lives being at risk' but wouldn't say any more. Ashley and Adeline were both on drugs not long after they left the clinic. Adeline got on heroin whereas her drug of choice was cocaine and Ashley actually had a needle mark on her towards the end of her stay at the clinic.'

Mac was quiet for a moment.

'For me it's all starting to point to the clinic. I'd bet that someone at the clinic is getting some of the clients hooked on drugs and then using them to sell drugs to their rich friends. Whoever it is seems to have a strong hold over them, strong enough to stop them talking even though they all seem to have been pretty desperate.'

'How would that work though?' Tommy asked.

'Easily enough, they keep all of their clients in strict quarantine from each other, all part of the 'discretion', I suppose. Naomi called it a 'five-star jail' with guards everywhere. If you had access to a client, perhaps some-one malleable who might be easy to control, then you could work on them. They'd be very vulnerable and more or less in solitary confinement so it wouldn't be too hard. If you had access that is.'

'So, who would have access?' Kate asked.

'Naomi only mentioned her personal therapist, the guards and of course Dr. Al-Faran herself.'

'My money's on the doctor,' Kate said.

'Perhaps you're right but we'll need a bit more evidence than we've got so far. Martin's working on Adeline's phone so we might learn something from that. Do you still think that Leah could tell us more?' Mac asked.

'Well, it looks as if she's involved with the drugs gang for sure so we could follow up on that but I doubt that we'll learn much more about Ashley's murder from her,' Kate replied.

'So, I take it that you're not going ahead with the raid on Leah then?' Mac asked.

'I didn't say that but yes that was what I was thinking. I don't think we can now,' she said with a sigh. 'What do you think Tommy?'

'I agree,' Tommy said. 'If we raid Leah straight after interviewing her uncle then I think that the gang will put two and two together and at the very best Doctor Whyte might end up with a few fingers missing. What shall we do about Martin's camera then?'

'I suppose we'd better not leave it there any longer than we need to in case anyone spots it. Shall we go over and get it now? You can drop me home on the way back, if you like,' Kate said.

'Okay, I'm sure Martin will be glad to get his toy back in one piece anyway,' Tommy said.

They were interrupted by Bridget's arrival. Tommy explained why he had to go out again.

'It's a pity we've got to cancel the raid,' Kate said as they drove towards St. Albans. She had the computer on her lap and she was reviewing the footage on fast forward. 'I suppose that we can always get the local police to raid her in a few weeks or so. That way the gang shouldn't be able to directly connect it to the doctor.'

'Has she had many visitors so far?' Tommy asked.

'No, I'm up to four thirty now and she's only had one so far. A man in a delivery van called about three fifteen and dropped off a sealed cardboard box. It had the company name printed on the box so it might not have been anything illegal.'

'That's not a bad way to move drugs around in bulk though, is it? I mean everyone's getting things delivered now so it wouldn't be seen as anything unusual,' Tommy said.

'Yes, that's a very good point,' Kate said. 'If you had to deliver drugs to someone how would you do it?'

'Well, I think that I'd set myself up as a seller on a legitimate site using false information and advertise real items for sale. I'd know which addresses were for real and which were for drug deliveries. So, as long as I never got them mixed up, the real items would go to real buyers and the drugs would be delivered to the dealers.'

'Yes, that would work,' Kate said. 'So maybe the delivery was for real but what was in the box wasn't. With so many deliveries being made every day there's no way you could keep track.'

They had just reached the outskirts of the town and it was getting dark. Kate was now watching Leah's front door in real time when she noticed that Leah had another visitor. A black Mercedes four by four pulled up just past her door and a young man wearing a hoodie and sunglasses got out and looked up and down the street. Kate thought that he couldn't have looked more suspicious if he tried.

'I think Leah's getting a visit from the gang. You think they'd try and blend in a bit more instead of turning up in suburbia in their four by fours and shades, wouldn't you?'

'So, she receives a box and then a visit from the gang. It sounds like something interesting might be happening,' Tommy said.

It was fully dark by the time they reached the flat. They let themselves in but didn't turn the lights on.

'Are you in a hurry to get back?' Kate asked.

'Well, I don't suppose so,' Tommy said.

'I'd just like to see what happens with our new visitor if you don't mind.'

Tommy looked at his watch.

'I could give it an hour I suppose,' he conceded. 'What are you expecting to happen?'

'I've no idea,' Kate said, 'but I wouldn't mind finding out who Leah's friend is.'

They sat at the back of the darkened room watching Leah's front door on the laptop.

After forty-five minutes Tommy said, 'By the look of it nothing's going to happen so we might as well...'

Tommy was stopped in his tracks by the sight of Leah's door being flung open by a young man dressed only in a pair of boxer shorts. He ran out into the road screaming. He expected to see a raging fire in the house behind him or a madman with an axe but there was nothing. They both ran over to the window. He stood in front of them not more than twenty yards away. He yelled at the top of his voice and Kate could see the blood vessels stand out in his neck.

'What's he got in his hand?' Kate asked.

'It's a frying pan I think,' Tommy replied with a puzzled expression.

The young man ran straight towards them, vaulting over the metal fence that marked the boundaries of the flats. Thinking that they'd been seen they both moved back from the window just before they saw him launch the frying pan at the window of the flat next door. They heard the sound of breaking glass followed by more screaming and then the sound of someone clambering up the outside of the building.

Once the sound had gone upwards, Kate and Tommy rushed outside and looked upwards. The young man

162

was already halfway up the four storied building. He seemed to be pulling himself up by his arms only in a display of tremendous strength.

'What in God's name is he doing?' Kate asked.

Tommy could only shrug. He looked around. They weren't the only ones watching the young man's progress up the building. Some of Leah's neighbours had come out of their houses and were silently watching from across the road. Once the young man had reached the roof, he pulled himself upright and then angrily shouted abuse at the people watching opposite. He started pulling tiles from the roof and then throwing them wildly in their direction.

Kate and Tommy had to move back as some of the tiles were getting a bit too close for comfort. He then stopped and looked as though he was watching something that was invisible to everyone else. He then shouted incoherently and launched himself off the roof. He was reaching out for something that only he could see, something that wasn't there.

His body did a slow turn in the air and then picked the worse possible spot to land. A gasp went up from the spectators as he landed back first on the metal fence with a loud crunch. It just about broke his body in two. It now hung down on either side of the fence like a limp piece of cloth. They could see his face. It had a look of surprise on it.

'Leah! Where's Leah?' Kate asked. 'Ring for the police and an ambulance while I go and look.'

Tommy rang and reported the incident and made a few quick calls before running after Kate into Leah's house. He had no idea what it might have looked like before because the whole house had been trashed. Furniture was tipped up on end and what was breakable was broken.

Leah was broken too. Her bloodied body lay on the floor with little white packets dotting her body like snow.

She was only wearing panties and they could both see that she'd been beaten to death with something blunt.

'The frying pan I'd guess,' Kate said with a frown. 'What in God's name happened in here?'

'Perhaps he didn't like her bacon sandwiches?' Tommy suggested giving her a mischievous look.

Kate was standing by a young woman who had been brutally beaten to death and her body strewn with packets of a substance that regularly ruins many more young lives. At that moment, standing in the middle of a chaotic murder scene, she should have been full of despair for the human condition.

Instead she laughed out loud.

Thanks Tommy, she thought, I really needed that.

Chapter Eighteen

Kate stood in front of Leah's front door and Tommy kept people well away from the young man's body while they waited for someone to turn up. The police came first.

Inspector Ken Ahmed got out of a police car and looked at the body draped over the fence and then at Tommy.

'We've got another one in the house over the road,' Tommy said.

'What happened?' the Inspector asked looking at Tommy suspiciously.

'I wish I knew.'

He told the Inspector exactly what he'd seen. The Inspector ordered one of his men to take Tommy's place.

'Show me where the other one is.'

Tommy led him over the road. The Inspector nodded at Kate as he walked inside. He surveyed the scene and then Leah's body without a change of expression.

'It looks like murder alright and so, in that case, we'll have to hand it over to the Major Crime Unit who are so efficient that they're already here. You're not on some sort of secret job creation scheme, are you?' he asked Kate and Tommy in some disbelief.

'No, we were observing this young woman, Leah Whyte, as part of the ongoing murder investigation that we told you about earlier,' Kate replied. 'We'd learned that she might have some involvement in drugs but we decided not to raid her as this might implicate the person who'd given us the information. We were on the point of removing our surveillance camera when the man who'd been visiting Leah came out in his under-wear, ran across the road screaming at the top of his voice, broke a window with a frying pan, climbed the building and then tried to fly. I've honestly never seen anything like it.'

The Inspector looked at all of the white packets strewn across the floor.

'What were they doing in here?'

'They'd received a delivery earlier today and I reckon that it was a bulk delivery of drugs. It looks like they were weighing and sealing the drugs in plastic bags ready to be sold on the street,' Kate replied.

'Look,' Tommy said pointing to a couple of syringes on the floor. 'Perhaps they tried it out on themselves first.'

'Come on, let's get back outside and leave it for the forensics team to sort out,' the Inspector advised.

It was only once she'd gotten outside that she realised there was one call she'd forgotten to make.

'Dan Carter!' she said to Tommy.

'Don't worry, I called him straight after I called these in. He's on his way. I also quickly updated Mac.'

'Thanks Tommy,' Kate said with some relief. 'I'm sorry but it's been a very strange few minutes.'

'You can say that again, I still don't quite believe it all myself yet.'

The ambulance turned up next. Someone must have told it not to rush as they heard no sirens. A couple of minutes later the forensics van turned up. Kate saw Bob Yeardley get out. He was already in his white all-in-one suit. He strolled over and looked at the man's body and then went into Leah's house. He emerged a few minutes later, gave his team some orders and then strolled back over to Kate and Tommy.

'Hello again. The Inspector said that you saw it all.'

Kate told him exactly what happened.

'That's really interesting,' Bob replied, 'something like this has happened before if I remember right. Can you do me a favour and put 'Lancashire contaminated drugs man climbs pub' into Google on one of your phones. I've got my gloves on.'

Tommy did just that. An article in a local paper from a few years before described how a batch of amphetamine pills had been contaminated causing some men who had taken the drug to become extremely aggressive and violent and, in one case, a man had climbed up onto the roof of a pub.

Tommy passed the phone to Kate.

'That looks very similar, I'd say,' Kate said. 'So, you think that the batch of drugs they received was contaminated with something?'

'Most probably,' Bob replied. 'I'd guess that it might be something like PCP judging from your description of the dead man's actions. It can cause hallucinations and, through that, some extremely violent reactions as people often think they're being attacked and so on. You'd also literally feel no pain.'

'I take it that it might be down to the lab that made the heroin not being too careful with its processes?' Kate asked.

'It happens all the time. It was probably either them not cleaning down properly between processing different drugs or more likely just getting the drugs mixed up. I'll need to get a sample to the lab as soon as possible,' Bob said. 'If that's the only contaminated batch then they might have done us all a favour and stopped this going out onto the streets but if there's a lot more of this stuff around we're likely to have a public health crisis on our hands. See you later.'

Kate and Tommy gave each other a concerned look. The thought of masses of violent young drug users running naked around the streets attacking anything that moved was truly appalling.

Dan and his sergeant, Adil Thakkar, turned up ten minutes later. Kate got them up to speed.

'So, what do you want us to do?' Kate said when she'd told Dan everything.

'Nothing, go on and get off home now. You can make a statement in the morning,' Dan said.

'But won't you need some help here?' Kate said.

Tommy gave her a look that clearly said she should leave well enough alone.

'Jo, Leigh and Chris are on their way as we speak. They'll be glad of something to do, I should think,' Dan said.

'I take it that you're still getting nowhere with the Priory Park case?' Tommy asked.

Dan gave Tommy a glum look.

'I'm just about to give up on that one. We've got one last chance, a professor up north who can put faces on dead people's skulls. It's worth a shot anyway.'

'Yes, I've seen that done on the TV. The best of luck with that,' Tommy replied.

'We'll need it. Anyway, we'll know in a couple of days when we get the results. Go on then, see you later,' Dan said before making his way over to talk to the Inspector.

Tommy gave Adil the key to the flat.

'Don't worry, I'll look after Martin's camera,' Adil promised.

'And don't forget my laptop. You can rewind the video and see what happened for yourselves. Believe me, it's well worth a look.'

'Sorry, Tommy,' Kate said as he drove her home.

'For what?'

'For volunteering you back there. I could see that you didn't think much of the idea.'

'Well, I'm late as it is and Bridget will be waiting.'

Kate wondered what it must be like to have someone to go home to, someone you loved. All she had was an empty flat that she hated being in. It wasn't home it was just somewhere to sleep. She stopped herself, it was beginning to taste like self-pity and she didn't want to go down that road.

'What's the Priory Park case?' she asked, changing the subject.

'Oh, a body was found in the lake in Priory Park in Bedford. It's a pleasure lake and right in the centre of the town. At first, they thought that it was just a drunk who'd fell in and drowned until they did the autopsy. Then they found that he'd been strangled. Dan and the team have been working flat out on the case but nothing's turned up so far. They still have no idea who the victim was.'

'So, he's going to try facial reconstruction?' Kate said. 'He must be desperate.'

'I think he is,' Tommy replied. 'I'll say one thing for Dan though, he never gives up a case without a fight.'

Kate's phone went off. Tommy heard her say 'yes' and then 'we'll be with you in less than thirty minutes.'

Tommy, hearing the 'we', gave her a look a mild annoyance.

Kate smiled at him and said nothing for a moment.

'Okay then. Where to now?' he asked with a resigned expression.

'Home, for you anyway. That was Mac and he wants to see us straight away.'

'Oh, good,' was all Tommy could think in way of a reply.

Mac had been working hard on the files that Martin had sent over. He was amazed at how much information someone could cram into a phone.

The vital evidence turned out to be the call logs and a video, in fact the very last video that Adeline ever made.

She'd left a suicide note.

Chapter Nineteen

'I don't know Mac that well but it sounds as though he's on to something,' Kate said as they turned off the motorway into Letchworth.

'I wouldn't be at all surprised,' Tommy said in a matter of fact way.

Kate glanced over and thought Tommy looked tired. She suddenly felt tired herself. She looked at the car's clock as they pulled into Mac's road. It was nearly nine. It had been a very long day indeed.

Mac, on the other hand, looked alert and quite pleased with himself.

'I'm sorry for dragging you all the way back here but I think we might have just cracked the case.'

This certainly woke Kate up.

'What have you found?' she asked urgently.

'This,' Mac said turning his laptop screen around. 'I've got it on speakers.'

The screen showed a still image of Adeline. She looked sad and desperate. Mac pressed play.

'I'm sorry but I can't go on like this, I haven't got any money or friends or even family now. I had friends but I lost them all when I got them hooked on drugs, they're just customers now. I can't even go to the police. I wish to God I could but, if I did, then I know they'd kill them, little Hadya and Hussain. Ashley said we should go to the police and look what happened to her. I don't want to die like that. We're all stuck, all of us even Doctor Eman. There's no hope, no way out except for one. Goodbye, I love you all.'

There was a moment's silence before Kate said, 'Poor girl,' with some feeling.

'Who are Hadya and whoever the other one was?' Tommy asked.

'Hadya and Hussein. They're Arabic forenames and obviously children as she said they were little. I've got an idea about that,' Mac replied.

'And who's Doctor Eman?' Kate asked.

Mac smiled widely.

'Yes, that had me puzzled too until I had another look on the Al-Faran Clinic's website where there's an article that mentions the ever-caring Dr. Eman Al-Faran.'

'Oh, it's her first name then,' Kate said feeling a little foolish.

Mac waited as he watched Kate think her way through it. Then the penny dropped.

'Oh God yes, *dre man*!' Kate finally said, 'that's her, isn't it?'

'Well done,' Mac said. 'People go on a lot about how incorrect punctuation can change the meaning of things but texting on a mobile phone and misplacing a space can achieve exactly the same result.'

'Sorry what's that?' Tommy asked.

'Remember the text that Ashley sent to her friend Trina? It mentioned that '*dre mans men were coming*'. What she really meant was 'dr emans men are coming', she just got the spacing wrong. I supposed she was scared at the time and that didn't help.'

'Yes, I see,' Tommy said excitedly. 'So, do you think that it was the doctor's guards who did this?'

'I'm not so sure. I found a security company online who claim that the Al-Faran Clinic is one of their clients. They seem reputable enough. Anyway, if that had been the case then Ashley wouldn't have had any defensive wounds, would she? No, from everything I've read I think it's likely that there was just one person involved in the attack and I'm beginning to think that person might be the doctor herself.'

'Why is that?' Kate asked.

'Well, let me take a wild guess and say that the guards were all dark skinned and possibly Middle Eastern in appearance.'

Kate and Tommy looked at each other as they thought.

'You're right but how could you possibly know that?' Kate asked.

'I've got a feeling about the doctor and, if I'm right, I've come across quite a few like her before. They think that the world revolves around them and other people are there just to be used. Anyway, Adeline certainly kept up contact with Dr. Al-Faran, she phoned her every few days. However, the day before she killed herself, she rang the doctor's number twenty-two times. The doctor never replied, she'd probably blocked Adeline's number by then I should think.'

'So, what do you think was going on?' Kate asked.

'Let me tell you my theory...'

After Mac had explained it all Kate said, 'Well, it all makes sense but we've no real evidence at the moment.'

'That's true but knowing where to look for evidence is always the first step, however, there might be another way,' Mac said. 'There's a Sherlock Holmes story where he mentions a strategy they used to use when tiger hunting in India.'

'What's that?' Tommy asked.

'They'd tether a goat under a tree and then they'd hide in the tree and wait for the tiger to come for its dinner. While it was eating the goat, they'd shoot it. I think we should tether a goat too.'

Mac explained his idea.

'Are you sure Mac? It could be dangerous,' Kate asked looking concerned.

Mac looked at Tommy who also looked worried.

'Yes, I'm sure. You two go and get yourself a coffee or something stronger while I ring Dan and Tommy. And not a word to Bridget about any of this.'

Tommy nodded but Kate could hear him mutter something about, 'A rock and a hard place.'

Bridget sat up when they walked into the living room. The TV was on and was showing a somewhat gory operation being performed.

'Oh please,' Tommy said, 'I've seen enough blood for one day.'

'Bad day, was it?' she asked.

She could tell from his expression that it had been.

'Do you want a beer and I could do you some sandwiches too, if you like?'

'Oh please, that would be great,' Tommy said with a smile.

'Can I get you anything, Kate?' Bridget asked.

'A beer and a sandwich would be more than fine.'

'Okay, two sandwiches and three beers,' Bridget said as she went into the kitchen.

She saw Tommy's eyes follow Bridget as she walked out of the room. When she'd gone he turned back towards Kate.

'What a day!' he said as he sat back.

'Yes, and to think that not all that long ago I used to feel that my job wasn't exciting enough. Of course, that was before I met Mac.'

Kate looked around the room. She'd never been in a prefab before and she found it much roomier and warmer than she'd have thought.

'These places are like the Tardis, aren't they? You know bigger on the inside. How come Mac is living here though? I'd have thought that a DCS might have lived in something a bit grander.'

'Apparently that was down to Bridget's mum Nora. This was the first house she ever had and she loved the garden and the countryside around here so much. Mac had thought they'd only be here a couple of years but she wouldn't move and that was that,' Tommy explained.

'Where is she then, this Nora?'

'She's dead,' Tommy explained lowering his voice a little. 'She died last year and I know Bridget's still grieving. It really hit Mac very hard too from what Bridget's told me.'

'Oh,' was all that Kate could say.

Her own mother came into her mind and she felt like crying, her loss was suddenly as sharp as the day she died. She was more than glad when Bridget came in carrying a tray.

The beer was crisp and cold and the sandwiches were good, made even better by a sudden hunger. Bridget sipped at her beer and smiled while she watched the two of them eat.

When they'd finished Bridget asked, 'Where do you live, Kate?'

'Oh Hatfield, I've not lived there long. Oh bloody hell!' Kate said clearly annoyed with herself.

'What is it?' Bridget asked.

'I'm forgetting the time. I'll need the catch the train soon. Will you be able to ring me a taxi?'

'I'm under instructions from on high, in other words my dad, and he says you're to stay the night. We have a guest room so there's no point in going all the way home when you have to be back here again tomorrow morning anyway. Is that alright?'

Bridget knew it was as she could see Kate visibly relax.

'Thanks Bridget, really thanks.'

'It's nothing. Just relax and we'll have a few more beers and when you're ready I'll show you to your bed.'

Kate did have a few more beers and had a surprisingly good evening. She even laughed once or twice.

She woke up some time during the night to go to the toilet and passed outside Mac's room on the way. The light was on and she could hear sounds like those an animal might make. The idea of anyone being in so much pain frightened her. She could still hear the sounds echoing in her head as she lay back down before sleep overtook her once more.

Chapter Twenty

Kate once again found herself in the windowless room in the Al-Faran Clinic waiting for the doctor to show up. She took out her phone and called Dan.

'Hi Dan, I just thought that I'd give you a quick update…

'Yes, I'm at the clinic now…'

'If I'm honest I've no idea what I'm doing here. It's a wild goose chase and I honestly feel that I'm wasting my time…'

The doctor was in another room, watching Kate on a TV screen and listening to every word she said. She was very interested to hear what Kate had to say.

'Look, we both know it's the drugs gang, especially after Leah Whyte's murder yesterday but, as you know, Mac has this bee in his bonnet about the clinic…'

Kate listened.

'Well, he's saying that he has some evidence that will implicate the clinic but, of course, he won't tell anyone else what it is until he sees you tomorrow…'

She listened again.

'Okay boss, I'll go along with it but only because you say so. God, I've got to babysit for him this evening as well. His nurse has to go early and his daughter has a late shift at the hospital…'

She listened once again.

'Well okay, if you say so then I suppose I'll have to go along with it. I'll let you know if I come up with anything. See you later,' Kate said just before she ended the call.

The doctor sensed a threat. She'd listen to the one-sided conversation again in more detail later. She looked at herself in the mirror, smiled and went to be interviewed.

'By yourself today, DS Grimsson?' the doctor asked as she entered the room.

Kate noticed that she had another black ensemble on today, a silk blouse and lace trimmed trousers. Black must be her colour.

Gucci perhaps? Kate thought with just the slightest tinge of jealousy.

'Yes, my colleague is following up another lead.'

The doctor sat down and smiled professionally at Kate.

'So, how can I help?'

'I've just got a couple of questions,' Kate said. 'We were wondering if you'd ever heard of someone called Trina Derbyshere?'

The doctor gave it some thought but her reaction, just a split second after she'd mentioned Trina's name, convinced Kate that it was a name that she'd heard before.

'I don't think so,' the doctor replied. 'Who is she?'

'She was a friend of Ashley's, someone we think that she might have confided in.'

'No, I don't remember meeting any of Ashley's friends.'

'What about Adeline Smyth-Stortford?' Kate asked.

'Oh yes, I was forgetting that she was a friend of Ashley's. That's probably because they were here at different times. I never saw them together but I do remember Ashley saying that she knew Adeline, from school I think it was.'

'One of my colleagues has asked me to ask if you're aware of anyone in the clinic who might be dealing drugs,' Kate asked.

'We don't allow drugs of any sort on the premises, not even alcohol. If we were aware of anything like that then we'd let you know immediately. The whole thrust of the treatment programme here is to totally separate the client from their usual environment for a while and to separate them from their addictions too.'

'Okay, just one more question,' Kate said.

The fact that Kate didn't pursue this surprised the doctor. In fact, she was beginning to feel that Kate was just going through the motions.

'Have you had any further thoughts about the man that Ashley met at the back gate?'

It was the first time that the doctor thought that Kate looked interested.

'No, I'm sorry,' the doctor replied.

'That's a shame. I think that finding him would help us enormously. In the footage you sent us he hands Ashley something. We've processed the video and it looks like drugs to us. Most of us think that the drugs gang might have had some sort of contact in here and that they were dealing drugs at your back gate.'

'Oh dear, I'll make sure that we keep more security out there and, if we spot anything, I'll let you know,' the doctor said.

'We'd be grateful if you could. I'm convinced that the drugs gang are behind all this especially after Leah Whyte, Ashley's sister, was murdered yesterday,' Kate said.

Although this wasn't news to the doctor, she feigned a look of surprise.

'Ashley's sister? Do you know who killed her?'

'Yes, a prominent member of the drugs gang. We're sure they're in it up their necks. Well most of us do anyway,' Kate said a little sniffily.

Kate gave the doctor a card with her mobile number on it and said her goodbyes.

Now we wait, she thought, as she was escorted from the clinic.

She waited for an hour and a half. The caller was a man who said that he had some vital information about drug dealing at the clinic. He could only see her at five o'clock and in a pub in Hemel Hempstead. Kate tried to negotiate a different time but agreed in the end to meet him.

178

'We're on!' she said when the call had ended.

Dan smiled, 'Well done Kate, you'd make a good actress.'

He turned to the team who had all been listening in to the call.

'Come on, we've got some preparations to make.'

For once Mac was totally alone in the house. It was so quiet he could hear his alarm clock ticking. Mac jumped slightly when the door to his bedroom opened.

'I can see that you're surprised to see me, Mr. Maguire.'

'Dr. Al-Faran, I take it? And yes, I am surprised. What in God's name are you doing in my house?'

'This has nothing to do with God, believe me,' the doctor said with a smile. 'I'm here to kill you.'

'I'm expecting someone any...'

'Oh yes of course, the unusual looking DS Grimsson. Well, I can confirm that right at this minute she's sitting in a pub in Hemel Hempstead waiting for someone who's never going to turn up,' the doctor said with a confident smile. 'I've also got people watching your daughter, who at this very moment has an emergency on her hands, so it would seem that she won't be coming either. Her boyfriend, DC Nugent, is also in the pub in Hemel Hempstead, keeping guard on Miss Grimsson no doubt, and your nurse is on her way to Addenbrooke's Hospital where she's just heard that her husband has had an accident. I think I've just about covered everyone.'

Mac frowned. She had indeed, well except for one perhaps.

'My daughter will have called...'

'Your good friend Mr. Timothy Teagan no doubt but unfortunately he's already in Norfolk to discuss a lucrative deal to renovate some Regency furniture. Even if he turned around straight away, we'll still have a good hour or more. It's just me and you Mr. Maguire. And this

179

of course,' she said pulling out a syringe from her pocket.

Mac looked at it but said nothing.

'You're not curious Mr. Maguire?' she asked with a complacent smile.

Mac still said nothing. The doctor noticed he was sweating.

'Yes, fear will do that to you, make you sweat,' she said.

'So, what's in it?' Mac eventually asked.

'Something you know all too well. It's Fentanyl but this is at a strength that will instantly cure all your ills, Mr. Maguire.'

'Well, at least it's not a hatchet.'

'No, it's not,' the doctor said with a smile. 'Oh, that had to be done. Miss Whyte was talking about going see you people so she had to be stopped. However, the surprising thing was how much I enjoyed it. It was like there was some mad animal spirit inside me that I just gave free rein to and it was quite exhilarating really,' she said with a smile, 'but this, now this is just business. I know you think you have something on me and right now I don't care what it is. Real or not, I believe in nipping opposition in the bud.'

'You just don't believe that you can be beaten, do you?' Mac asked.

The doctor smiled again, 'No, at least not by the likes of you. The police have always been several steps behind and they still will be when they discover your body. It will, of course, look like suicide.'

'And how do you think you'll manage that? Bad back or not, I guarantee that I'll put up a fight.'

'I don't think so,' the doctor said as she pulled out a gun. She pulled out a silencer and screwed it on. 'It's your choice, you'll either allow me to inject you and die a peaceful death or I'll shoot you and then I'll sit in the hallway and shoot the first person who comes through the front door. There's a very good chance that it will be your daughter.'

'So, if I allow you to inject me, then you'll make it look like suicide and no-one else will be hurt?' Mac asked.

'Of course. I take it that, like most people in pain, you have a stash of painkillers hidden somewhere?'

Mac involuntarily glanced at the chest of drawers.

'Oh, your sock drawer! God how unoriginal is that?' the doctor said. 'Yes, I'll take some of your patches and mix them with hot water and then leave the glass with its residue on the floor by your bed for your forensics people to find.'

'What about the injection itself, won't they notice that?' Mac asked the sweat now running down his face.

'Oh no, I'll inject you in the armpit, that will be very difficult to find but, to be honest, even if they do find it so what? They'll never be able to connect it with me,' she said confidently.

'They might if you shoot me.'

'I doubt it. A professional hit on an ex-policeman and his daughter, I'd guess that they'd start looking for people you've crossed, criminals with a grudge. With a career like yours, I'm sure that there must be lots of them.'

'You've really thought this through, haven't you?' Mac said.

'Oh yes, I always cover every eventuality. So, what's it to be then? A peaceful death or do I have to shoot you and then kill someone else too? I warn you that I always keep my word.'

Mac gave this some thought.

'Who are Hadya and Hussein?'

'Oh, you've heard about my beautiful children then. Hadya's six and Hussein is eight, they're wonderful little children,' she said with that smile again.

Mac was beginning to hate that smile.

'They don't exist, do they?' he said.

'No of course not but my little band of drug pushers don't know that. I tell them that I'm a victim too, that the nasty Islamic fundamentalists have my lovely little children and they'll kill them if they don't do exactly what I tell them to do. Throw in a few tears and you've got them.'

That explained Adeline's 'innocent victims'. She obviously believed in the doctor's theatrics.

'I expect you told them that the Islamic boogie men killed Ashley too?' Mac asked.

'Of course, I mean they do chop people's heads off you know and all these big muscled Middle Eastern types wandering around the clinic, fundamentalists all of them,' she said with a big smile.

Mac went silent again.

'There's no point in delaying anymore Mr. Maguire, the decision has to be made,' the doctor said.

She placed the gun on the chair and took the cap off the needle. She was now at least two paces away from the gun.

'Aston Villa are playing a bit better these days, don't you think?' he said.

The doctor's face showed her total puzzlement. It was not what she'd expected him to say.

'What?' was all she could get out before the bedroom door crashed open.

The doctor looked to her left and found that she was looking down the barrels of two semi-automatic rifles behind which were two police firearms officers.

'Move away from the gun and place the syringe on the chest of drawers!' one of the firearms officers shouted.

The doctor looked dazed and froze like a statue.

'MOVE NOW!'

She did as she was ordered and robotically placed the syringe on the top of the chest of drawers.

'Down on the floor, on your stomach, hands on the back of your head.'

Again, she couldn't move. It was as though she was in shock.

'On the floor NOW!' the firearms officer shouted.

She slowly lay down. The firearms officer pulled her arms down and cable tied them together at the wrists. He pulled her up on her feet and dragged her towards the door. She looked at Mac as she went out but it wasn't the look he'd expected, a look of venomous hatred, instead it was the dazed look of someone who's world had just suddenly fallen apart.

She was someone who had always taken risks and always won, until now that is. Mac wondered how she'd cope with losing. Not well, he reckoned.

Another officer came in and checked that he was okay.

'Oh, never better actually,' he replied which was only the truth.

When he'd originally had the idea, he'd thought it would be a bit of a long shot and he wasn't absolutely sure that the doctor would go for it. However, by presenting her with an immediate threat and then an immediate opportunity to deal with it, he felt that there was just a chance that she just might bite. After all, in her world she was always right and always would be, everyone else was stupid and there just to be used.

His thoughts were interrupted by a man in a white suit carrying a big black case.

'Mr. Maguire, we meet again,' Bob Yeardley said.

'Yes, we do. How are you, Bob?'

'Well, you lot are keeping me busy enough but then again that's the way I like it. So, what have we got then?'

'Just the syringe on top of the chest of drawers and the gun on the chair over there. There won't be any prints on them or in the house, she was wearing latex gloves,' Mac explained.

'A nice quick one for a change then,' he said.

He took a camera out of his case and took several photos of the room and then specifically of the syringe and the gun. He then carefully placed the syringe in one evidence bag and then placed the gun in another. He said his goodbyes to Mac.

A few minutes later Dan Carter walked in with a smile as wide as a Cheshire cat.

'Well, that worked out okay. I must admit that I was a bit surprised that she went for it but you were right.'

'I'm as surprised as you are really,' Mac said.

'I've given the go ahead for the team and the local police to raid the clinic. I've told Kate and Tommy the good news and they're going to join the team there. We'll hopefully turn up quite a bit more evidence although I'm not sure we'll really need it after this.'

'Yes, and to think that she planted cameras all over the clinic and yet she didn't think that anyone else might be smart enough to do the same,' Mac said. 'It's ironic really.'

'You know, I remember not long after I became a detective that we had a case where we had a wire on someone. We needed a van full of technology and about four people to look after it. The sound quality was rubbish too. Now all you need is Martin's little camera and a tiny microphone. We've been sitting in the car a street away watching it all happen in full colour with stereo sound on Martin's laptop. Where is the camera by the way?' Dan said as he looked around the room.

'It's there behind some boxes on top of the wardrobe,' Mac replied.

'Martin did a bloody good job of hiding it, didn't he?'

'Are you going to buy him one now you've seen it in action?'

'No,' Dan replied. 'I'm going to buy him two. We'll need one for back up.'

'That will make him a happy man.'

184

'Well, it's a really nice piece of kit and I can make a good case for it in terms of the man hours we'll save doing observation duties. If anyone questions it, I'll just play them the video of what happened here. I'm sure that will convince them. Thanks Mac, I must admit that when she pulled that gun, I was a bit worried.'

'Yes, me too if I'm honest. Thankfully, when she got the syringe out and placed the gun on the chair, it gave me an opportunity to safely say the code word.'

'Yes, Aston Villa, your favourite football team. You could see that you saying that really threw her.'

'Well, I suppose it did sound somewhat surreal,' Mac admitted with a smile. 'Oh, talking of guns,' Mac said, 'can you give me a hand?'

Mac unbuttoned his pyjama top to reveal the black bulletproof body armour underneath.

'The doctor thought I was sweating through fear. She may have been partly right but this definitely didn't help.'

Dan helped him get the body armour off and then get his pyjama top back on. They'd just finished when Martin strolled in.

'Hi Mac,' he said, his face beaming. 'That was absolutely brilliant!'

'Thanks Martin,' Mac said feeling ever so slightly embarrassed.

'Oh, sorry Mac, I was talking about the camera. Great resolution and the wide-angle lens was terrific, it caught absolutely everything. You were pretty good too though.'

Mac and Dan exchanged looks and both burst out laughing.

'I take it that you've got it all backed up?' Dan said once he'd calmed down.

'Yes, no problem with that,' Martin said as he stood on a chair and retrieved his precious camera from the top of the wardrobe. He pulled out the jack lead that ran to a small microphone.

'Great, well the doctor won't interview herself. See you later Mac and thanks again. Another win and a big one too,' Dan said as he held out his hand.

Mac shook it.

Then he was alone but not for long. Two minutes later Amrit's head appeared around the door.

'A cup of tea?' she suggested.

'Oh yes please,' Mac replied. 'Get yourself one and I'll tell you all about it.'

'Oh goody!' Amrit said with an expectant smile on her face. 'The season finale at last.'

Chapter Twenty One

Amrit brought Mac his mid-morning cup of tea. She could see that he was studying some photographs on his laptop.

'How did your weekend go, after all the excitement on Friday?' she asked as she sat down.

'It was okay, quiet really, but I suppose anything would be quiet after that. I had to make a statement of course and then Tim dropped by on Saturday to tell me at length all about his trip to Norfolk.'

'Bit of a wild goose chase for him, was it?'

'Well, I did warn him to just go along with any offers he might get that would involve him leaving the area so he was prepared for a disappointment. Anyway, while he was there, he only noticed this poster saying that there was a sale on at a country house not far from Norwich and so he decided to give it a try. He reckons he's got at least two real bargains so it all worked out for him in the end. I don't know how he does it,' Mac said with a smile.

Amrit gave Mac a thoughtful look.

'Why do you think she did it?'

'Did what?'

'That doctor. You'd have thought that she'd have made enough money with what she charged for the clinic without having to sell drugs,' Amrit asked.

'Not forgetting the blackmail from what I'm hearing. I suppose that for some people they can never have enough money, they always want more. However, with the doctor I honestly don't think it was just the money. I've come across people like her before, they like to manipulate and control others, it makes them feel superior, I suppose. She'd created an environment in which her rich clients would be at their most vulnerable, having to deal with coming off drugs, while being totally cut off from any external support. She had them at her mercy and, if you want my best guess, I think that she just couldn't help herself.'

'So, what's next now that you've solved the Whyte case?' Amrit asked.

'Well, we've still got the Bardolph case. If it really is a case that is.'

Amrit smiled at Mac's use of the word 'we'.

'Oh yes, I was nearly forgetting about that,' Amrit said. 'Any luck so far?'

Mac shook his head.

'No, nothing so far. I've decided to go through every single record and photo in the five candidate cases we've got left once again,' Mac said as he took a sip from his travel mug. 'After all, I've still got almost four weeks to go until they let me out of here so, unfortunately, there's lots of time left.'

'You make it sound like a prison. It's not that bad is it?' Amrit asked.

'No, I suppose not but it would be so nice to get out for a bit and under my own steam at that.'

'Personally, I think that you've done very well so far, Mac. I know it's difficult but you're coping, well most of the time.'

'Well, I have to admit that, if it wasn't for Dan's cases, then you'd be scraping me off the ceiling by now. By the way I'm going through the Maynard case again as well and I wondered if you'd managed to have a chat with your friend yet?' Mac asked.

'The Maynard case?' Amrit said her face crinkling in puzzlement.

'Yes, you said that you had a friend who worked at Papworth, Dr. Zaynab Teymouri I think her name was.'

'Oh, you mean Terri, the poor girl whose car broke down and who ended up with her throat cut, don't you?'

'That's right,' Mac said.

'Oh yes, I had a long chat with Zaynab on the phone not long after I mentioned her name to you.'

'And?' Mac asked.

'And not a lot really. She didn't know Terri that well but she did remember all the investigations. It seemed to go on for months she said.'

'So, in all the time since Terri's murder there've been no rumours at the hospital or fingers pointed at anyone?'

'Not from what Zaynab told me,' Amrit said. 'It still seems to be a complete mystery to everyone there.'

Mac was expecting this but still felt a little pang of disappointment. It was one case that he'd have loved to have cracked.

'By the way the answer is yes,' Amrit said as she got up to leave.

'Yes?' Mac's face showed his puzzlement.

'Bridget had a quick word with me before I started this morning and she said that you might want me permanently for a few days a week,' she explained.

'And you said yes?'

'Of course, I'm like you in that I like to keep myself busy.'

Mac felt hugely relieved. Of course, it would be great to have some help around the house and the acupuncture would be a godsend when he was in real difficulties but he had to admit that he liked the company too.

'Thanks, Amrit, really,' Mac said with feeling.

'Oh, it's nothing. I like to help and the fact that working here saves me the cost of a subscription to the True Crime channel has nothing to do with it whatsoever,' she said with a wicked grin as she went out of the door.

Mac laughed out loud.

So, the next few days were going to be spent going over the minutiae of the remaining case files once more. Mac summarised them –

Terri Maynard, car breaks down, has her throat cut after being raped

Marie Callaghan, head bashed in after leaving a nightclub, probably after refusing to be raped

Agniezka Coleman, stabbed several times on her way home from work, absolutely no clue why

Edith Dickinson, pensioner, head bashed in with a blunt instrument. Burglary?

Asma Rafiq, just seventeen years old, stabbed, possible honour killing

He then once again played back the video of the one-sided conversation that Cassandra Bardolph had with herself –

'What is it? There's blood on your hands, what's happened?'

'You killed her? Oh my God, she's dead and you're saying it's your fault? Tell me exactly what happened, every detail.'

'We need to get you away, they'll be looking for you and you could be in danger. Don't worry I know just what to do.'

The obvious implication of this was that whoever Cassandra was speaking to had admitted to killing a woman and, if 'they' were the police, then Cassandra herself seemed to be a willing accomplice after the fact.

Mac suddenly remembered his request to Martin regarding information about Cassandra Bardolph. In all the excitement of the Whyte case he'd forgotten all about it. He searched through his emails and there it was. Martin was as efficient as ever.

Mac was still thinking about what he'd learned when Amrit came in with lunch for the both of them. After making sure that Mac's tray was set up just right, she settled comfortably in the chair and started eating.

'Those samosas were quite special,' Mac said as he dabbed at his mouth with a tissue.

'Oh, they were just my everyday samosas,' she replied.

'I really find it hard to believe that they could be improved upon.'

This brought a big smile from Amrit.

'Anyway, back to business. Martin sent me some information about Cassandra Bardolph a while back and in all the fuss I forgot about it. It makes for interesting reading,' Mac said.

'Go on,' Amrit prompted.

'Okay, first of all she was an only child. Her father died when she was a young girl and her mother died when she was in her twenties. Her parents were also only children so there were no close relatives either. She received a modest amount of money regularly each month from some sort of trust fund, enough to pay her bills and other expenses. As there was no mortgage on the house, I suppose that she got by. Except for every now and then she'd buy herself a new car.'

'Well, I suppose we all need a car,' Amrit said.

'Perhaps but she always bought a top of the range BMW sports car, the last one cost her nearly a hundred thousand pounds.'

'Oh well, we all have our little treats, I suppose.'

'She obviously had some capital tucked away but it's not obvious where. She read Ancient and Mediaeval History at an Oxford University and got a first-class degree with honours. After that she appears to have done nothing really, she never worked, never even travelled.'

'How can you be sure, about her travelling I mean?' Amrit asked.

'Well, she never applied for a passport so she couldn't have travelled abroad.'

'I wonder if she might have been a little like that Emily Dickinson, a recluse,' Amrit ventured.

Mac wondered what she might have to do with a dead pensioner when he realised that she was talking about *Emily* Dickinson and not Edith.

'She was a poet, wasn't she?' Mac asked.

'Yes, that's right, she lived in America in the nineteenth century. I saw a film about her, sad it was too the way she locked herself away from everyone. Towards the end she never even left her bedroom.'

Mac could only sympathise, he felt like he was turning into a recluse too.

'Well, that's as good a guess as any I suppose.'

Mac wasn't really convinced however. It was as though Cassandra Bardolph had walked so lightly through her life that she never left a single footprint. This lack of any detail about her life only intrigued him more.

The days rolled by as Mac examined every one of the cases thoroughly. For Terri Maynard and Marie Callaghan, try as he might, he couldn't find anything at all that would give him the slightest traction. As for Edith Dickinson he remembered his earlier thought and rattled off an email to Martin.

That just left Agniezka Coleman and Asma Rafiq.

He read carefully through Agniezka's case file again. In Mac's experience this type of frenzied stabbing was either due to strong personal feelings, a jealous lover or a fierce family feud perhaps. The only other explanation was that it had been carried out by someone with a severe mental illness. He didn't like the latter as it was a rarer occurrence than most people might think. However, if it was the former it couldn't have been her husband because he was at work when his wife was murdered and it couldn't be anyone from her family because that were all back in Poland.

His initial thoughts about mistaken identity came back to him. He looked at the exact spot where she had been killed on street view. The entryway between the three storied block of flats and the house next door could be clearly seen from the street. He looked at the photos taken at the time again. Back then a large bush obscured the view of the entryway so anyone passing by on the street wouldn't have had a clear view. It looked a good place to set a trap.

He looked closely at the photos of the crime scene. He could see that there was a high brick wall on the left and a high wooden fence on the right, presumably behind which was the back garden belonging to the house. This puzzled him as, if the killer was lying in wait in the entryway itself, Agniezka should have been able to see him as soon as she entered as there was nowhere that he could hide. Walking home late at night he doubted most women would walk into an alleyway knowing that someone was already lurking there.

He looked closely at the photos once again. He was wrong, there was a place to hide. A gate almost seamlessly formed part of the wooden fence. He looked again through the statements to see if the investigators had interviewed anyone from the house. He couldn't find anything at first which he thought was a bit odd.

He eventually found a note tucked away in the file that stated that they'd tried to contact the owners of the house and had finally established that Mr. and Mrs. Everson had been just one week into a three-week Mediterranean cruise when the murder had taken place. They were eventually interviewed and they stated that they hadn't left their house keys with anyone and they always kept the gate to the back garden locked.

Mac thought about this. He considered it more than likely that the killer had waited behind the gate. It would have been the perfect hiding place and it would have given the killer the element of surprise. It would have been easy enough for most people to climb over the fence and unlock the gate and this could even have been done the night before.

Of course, the murderer would have had to have known that the Eversons were away, so that might be something that could be followed up. However, he was still puzzled. If that had been how it happened then why didn't the murderer pull Agniezka's body into the Everson's garden, lock the gate and then go? It would certainly have delayed finding the body which would surely have helped the murderer by making the exact time of death much harder to pin down.

Mac followed this tenuous thought. What if the killer didn't want any delay? What if he wanted the body to be found as soon as possible? Why might that be though? If the body is found quickly then it's much easier to be precise about the time of death but why might the murderer want this?

Of course! It was all about time. Maybe it wasn't mistaken identity after all.

He did a Google search and it produced something of great interest. A story from a local paper dated just over two and a half years after the murder announced the wedding of John Coleman and Angela Gardner. In the short article John explained how Angela had become a friend after his wife was inexplicably murdered and eventually friendship had grown into love.

Mac bet it had. He spent hours looking over all the CCTV footage and there was John clearly visible for just about every minute between nine and when he knocked off at eleven. He could see Angela working in the background too. She walked towards the toilet around five minutes to nine and didn't reappear anywhere in the store for over fifteen minutes. He looked at the map. If there was a back entrance to the supermarket then fifteen minutes would be plenty of time for her to walk to the entryway, lie in wait, then kill Agniezka and return to the store.

At the time of the investigation John Coleman had been squeaky clean with not even the slightest rumour having been heard about him having an affair or having any sort of problem with his marriage. The thought struck Mac that perhaps he might have loved his wife and been totally happy with his marriage. Maybe it was all down to Angela.

Did she harbour a secret love for her supervisor? It wasn't uncommon and, even if John had returned her love, there would have been a problem. Agniezka, like many Poles, was a devout Catholic and was well known at her local church. She would never have agreed to a divorce. So, Angela might have wanted to get rid of her but in a way that wouldn't implicate her husband. After all what would be the point of having the object of your desire banged up in prison for twenty-five years?

Mac thought it through. Angela didn't appear to have been on the investigators' radar but then why should she have been? She was just one of forty-nine people working in the supermarket that night, a lot of whom he guessed would have gone off camera for varying amounts of time around the time of the murder, especially if they were smokers. At the time there might have been nothing between John and Angela except in Angela's head.

Mac took a step back. It was all just supposition but it could be a lead and one only made possible by the passage of time. The case would have been well and truly frozen by the time John and Angela got married. The original investigators had possibly forgotten all about the murder, it was just one out of a never-ending string of cases after all. In that space of time they might even have moved on to other jobs or left the area.

Mac sighed, he had a feeling that he might be on to something but there was no evidence and it was highly unlikely that any would be uncovered after all this time. There would have been blood on the clothes of whoever killed Agniezka and a knife to be gotten rid of. Mac could see it in his mind's eye.

In a supermarket as big as that one they would prob-ably have had hundreds of knives in stock. He went back through the file. One investigator stated that they seized and checked all the knives that had been in stock but a supermarket is a big place. What about the stock they probably kept around the back? Even if they knew about that it would be easy to wash the knife put it back in its box and then place that and several other boxes of knives in a stores location that wouldn't be found on the computer system. They wouldn't exist and so no-one would ever know they were there. If they did find them then it would just look like a mistake anyway. She could have come back later, perhaps weeks later, and simply put the knives back where they belonged. Perhaps she later destroyed the knife that killed her love rival or perhaps she just allowed it to be sold. Someone might have been slicing their roast beef with a murder weapon without knowing it.

What about the clothes then? He replayed the video and, although the colour wasn't great, he could see that she was wearing a dark red track suit of some sort.

What a good colour to be wearing if you're about to knife someone, he thought.

So, what would he do? It was late in the evening and, being March, it would be dark out. Wearing the dark red track suit, he'd go and kill his victim and then return to the supermarket. He'd have a bag somewhere near the toilets with an identical track suit in its original packaging. All he needed to do was simply change into the new tracksuit and carefully insert the old suit into the packaging and place it at the back of the display rack. The next day perhaps buy the tracksuit yourself and simply walk away with the evidence.

If she was indeed the killer, the supermarket, vast and surely full of secret places only known to the staff, would be a great place to hide evidence such as knives and clothes and, perhaps best of all, you could simply hide them in plain sight on the display shelves.

Mac sighed. Yes, he'd worked out who could have done it and how they might have done it but there was just one snag – there was no evidence. He smiled as he remembered flying a kite similar to this one in a case and Peter Harper shooting it down with four words.

'Where's the proof then?' he'd asked.

He knew that there was a good chance he was right but there was also a chance that he was wrong. If Angela hadn't carried out the murder and the police started asking questions then might it plant the idea in her husband's mind? Perhaps they had children now and the mistrust created might end up breaking up a family. Mac knew he couldn't take that chance.

Unfortunately, poor Agniezka would end up in the same pile as Terri, Marie and Edith, unsolved and likely to stay that way. All he had now was the Asma Rafiq case left and he had little hope of cracking that one.

Chapter Twenty Two

It was Thursday and Mac realised that he wasn't far off being halfway through his prison sentence. Amrit had just taken away his empty plate after he'd dispatched another of her wonderful lunches. He realised that he was being spoiled. Somehow, just having a sandwich at mid-day now, would seem like something of a hardship.

He then got a call from Dan. He wanted to come and visit. Mac was more than happy to see him but, knowing Dan, he knew that there would be some point to the visit.

He was right.

'We're on a run, Mac,' Dan said. 'Our idea of using facial reconstruction actually worked!'

'Really? You found out whose body it was in the Priory Park lake?'

'We did,' Dan said with a proud smile.

'Well, don't forget that it was all your idea, I just put you in touch with the professor. Go on then, tell me how you did it.'

'Well, the professor was good enough to do us three photos with different variations in skin tone and hair-style to give us a better chance of identification. We decided to start off with those properties that were closest to the lake and then spiral outwards. We got a positive identification after just an hour from a woman who ran a corner shop two streets away from the lake. She identified our dead man as 'Ginger'. Unfortunately, she didn't know any name beyond that but she knew where he used to live. She said that he'd shared a flat above a nearby shop with another young man called Ally. Apparently, both of them used to visit the corner shop regularly, mostly for alcohol. They were both from Scotland and made a living working in the local bars.

The woman remembered that Ally had told her a while back that Ginger had gone back to Scotland.

So, we waited until this Ally was at home and then we raided the flat. Ally didn't even try to deny that he had murdered his friend, whose name was John MacGregor by the way. He said that it happened after they'd both had more than a few drinks. They'd been playing a football video game and had gotten into an argument.'

'Let me guess Messi or Ronaldo, who's the greatest?' Mac ventured.

'Spot on. So Ginger is saying Ronaldo while Ally goes for Messi. After arguing about this for quite some time and, with even more alcohol having being taken on board, Ally decided he'd had enough and strangled Ginger with the lead that connected the controller to the video game box. He then went to bed and decided to get rid of his friend's body by dragging it to the lake the next night. Imagine this, he didn't try to cover it up in any way and he managed to drag it down a couple of streets without anyone noticing.'

'It was almost as though he was hoping that he'd get caught,' Mac said.

'I think you might be right. He certainly didn't seem that upset when we knocked down his door. I think it was more a relief than anything else.'

'So, another one solved. You must be making your bosses very happy,' Mac said.

'Yes, they're more than happy with the team. So happy in fact that they signed off on Martin's cameras without a single moan.'

'How's the case against the doctor going?' Mac asked.

'Well, it's going to take some time. She was only partly right about the encryption on her computer system though. Our experts think it should be break-able without losing the data but it's going to take them a while. We're in no hurry though. She hired some high-powered barristers to try and get bail but it didn't work, so thankfully she's safely in jail for a while which gives us time to build a really good case. Once we crack the computer system, we can then start contacting all her former patients. I guess that we won't have too much trouble finding all the people she's victimised and, hopefully, there'll be at least some who will be willing to testify against her. Especially when they learn that all her threats were just smoke and mirrors. We've got one witness already.'

'Who's that?' Mac asked.

'Trina Derbyshere,' Dan replied. 'She gave herself up to the Canadian Police and they flew her back here on Wednesday. We've already taken an initial statement. It makes interesting reading. I'll send it over to you if you like.'

'That would be great, thanks Dan.'

'You know, I never knew how much I was helping myself when I sent those cold cases over to you. Thanks Mac, I'll see you later.'

It was strange, Mac thought, how easily some cases could be solved once you've got that crucial bit of evidence. All the surmising and theories in the world aren't anywhere near as good as a single hair or skin cell.

He sighed as he returned to the Rafiq case. He really wished that he could find some evidence that would tell him exactly what had happened. A Muslim girl is killed and the family close ranks. Then her brother disappears and goes and fights and dies for the religious cause in Afghanistan, a classic honour killing scenario in every respect. So, what was it about this case that grated with Mac?

In his statement a friend of Asma's brother said that, while Youssef had mentioned fighting in Afghanistan, he'd been fairly sure that it was just talk because he only ever mentioned it once he'd had a few drinks.

His family said that they were surprised too. He'd gone out one night with his friends, then came home late, packed a bag and left without saying goodbye. Mac supposed that the investigators took all this with a pinch of salt as they were probably thinking that the family were lying and had actually helped to get Youssef out of the country.

The police searched Youssef's room again after he disappeared and found the knife, still with his sister's blood on it, and a computer print-off from a Jihadi website all about how to get to Afghanistan.

But what if Youssef's family wasn't lying? Mac thought.

Does anyone really go out with friends one night and then suddenly make the decision to go abroad and do it there and then? Wouldn't it, at the very least, take some setting up?

Mac read all the statements from Youssef's friends again. He was trying to get an idea of what Youssef was like. Impulsive certainly and he also seemed to have a thing about women. One friend said that as far as Youssef was concerned all women were just whores but when another friend had mentioned that he quite fancied his sister Youssef pulled a knife on him and had to be restrained.

So that confirmed that the knife was likely to be Youssef's and that he had a thing about his sister too. Mac had to admit that it was highly probable that he had killed his sister but he couldn't help feeling that there was a lot more to it than that. Mac kept digging away, after all he didn't have anything else to do.

He noticed that there was a new email from Dan and he opened it with some anticipation. It was Trina Derbyshere's statement. Mac read it several times. It certainly made things a little clearer.

Trina said that Ashley had broken down and one night told her all about the doctor. About how she'd supplied her with heroin in the clinic and about the threats she'd made if she didn't start dealing drugs for her. Trina had advised her to go to the police and tell them everything but Ashley felt that she couldn't. Ashley too had believed in the existence of Hadya and Hussein and she told Trina that if any harm came to them because of her then she wouldn't be able to live with herself.

While Trina didn't take drugs herself, quite a lot of the clients she worked for did. Working for the public relations company involved looking after the needs of visiting clients many of which were film or rock stars. Those 'needs' often included women, drink and, of course, drugs. Trina got the drugs from Ashley to try and help her out. After Ashley was murdered Trina didn't know what to do. She could only hope that whoever killed Ashley didn't know about her and so she tried to keep a very low profile. Then one day she received a photograph in the mail. It clearly showed her and Ashley exchanging drugs and money. She had no idea who it came from but Mac guessed that it was from the doctor. He also guessed that it had the intended outcome as Trina immediately fled to Canada.

He had to admire the doctor a little. She could, of course, have killed Trina too but that would have exploded the myth of the murderer being from the drugs gang. Two close friends being murdered would constitute a pattern. He guessed that the doctor might have been unsure whether Trina knew anything any-way but she obviously decided not to take any chances and sent her the photo. It had the desired outcome too.

He reluctantly returned to the Rafiq case. He re-read everything and then re-read it again and learned nothing. He was not far from giving up on it.

Tommy was taking the chance to take Bridget out for a meal while Mac spent a quiet evening indoors with Tim who had brought around some very nice and very cold cans of lager. They spent the evening dissecting their favourite football team. Now a division lower after getting relegated, Aston Villa were definitely playing better but neither of them were sure if they were playing anywhere near well enough to get promoted again. Talking about this kept them going all night.

A sudden stabbing pain woke Mac up in the night. He wearily turned on the light. It was three fifteen. He lay back and looked at the cracks in the ceiling. He knew that there would be no sleep for a while so he fired up his laptop. After checking the latest news and football gossip he reluctantly opened the Rafiq file once more.

He decided to check all the statements once again and he started with that of Lawrence Taylor. Lawrence explained what he'd done to try and save Asma's life and how he'd been taught CPR and other life saving techniques at school. Mac had just reached the end when his hand slipped on the mouse. He thought that he'd been on the last page and was about to scroll up again but he found that he'd been wrong, there was another page. He looked again and it definitely stated '2 of 2 pages' but he could now see the top of another page below it. It said '3 of 3 pages' and Mac cursed whoever had taken the statement for their sloppiness.

The third page just had a scrawled note –

'Mr. Taylor has stated that he gave an incorrect address when we spoke to him first as he was in shock. His correct address is below...'

Mac looked at the address and his pulse started racing.

He'd found the link that he'd been looking for!

Mac checked it twice. He'd been right, it was the same address as Cassandra Bardolph's. So, Lawrence Taylor was living with Cassandra at the time that Asma Rafiq was killed.

Was it Lawrence who had blood on his hands?

Had Lawrence murdered Asma after all?

Chapter Twenty Three

Mac went straight back to Harry Jeavis' statement. He was the cyclist who had been the first to find Asma after she'd been stabbed.

He said that he took notice of the man in the dark hoodie as he nearly collided with him as he ran past. He noticed that the man had yellow trainers on and also that they were stained with something red. Then he saw Asma lying on the ground. A stream of blood was already running from her body towards the gutter. He got off his bike and went to her. He looked up and saw Lawrence Taylor come from the right and walk towards him. Lawrence broke into a run and then tried CPR while Harry phoned for an ambulance.

That's where the blood on his hands came from then, Mac thought.

He looked again at the photos of the murder scene. It was on one of the protected cycle and walk ways that ran all over Stevenage. Asma was killed near a junction where several walkways met underneath the centre of a massive traffic island. It was just a few steps away from a subway where the walkway went under the main road. Asma's killer must have been waiting in there for her.

Harry Jeavis was cycling towards the junction from the left-hand side of the subway. He'd been intending to go straight on towards the aerospace factory where he worked when the man in the hoodie nearly ran into him and he then saw Asma on the ground. She'd been stabbed several times but she was still alive when he got to her. Then Lawrence Taylor had come from the direction that Harry Jeavis had been heading towards. Mac looked it up on street view. Nothing much would have changed in twelve years. It confirmed what he'd thought.

Lawrence Taylor couldn't possibly have murdered Asma Rafiq.

Harry Jeavis would have had a clear view ahead right down the walkway that Lawrence had appeared from. If Lawrence had killed Asma he'd have had to have stabbed her then run back up the walkway and at that point Harry would surely have seen him. Yet Harry said that he saw no-one except for the hooded man.

So, if Lawrence didn't kill Asma then why would he have said that he did to Cassandra? Had he contributed to Asma's murder in some way? Mac felt that there was an unresolved mystery around this case and he desperately wanted to know what really happened.

He started looking for Lawrence Taylor. He contacted the school and asked if they could send him a copy of his school records. They said that they could send them on Monday but only once they'd received a formal request. Mac emailed Martin and asked him to send the request to the school. There was nothing else he could do until he received those records.

The weekend went slowly enough although it did have one notable event. After watching Mac and Bridget play, Tommy decided he wanted to learn how to play backgammon himself. So, Mac spent most of Sunday teaching him what he knew about the game. He must have been a good teacher because Tommy ended up winning by seven games to two.

Mac put it down to beginner's luck.

The school records didn't turn up until Monday afternoon. Mac went through them with a fine-toothed comb. Apparently, Lawrence Taylor had been a model pupil with a good attendance record, apart from a bad patch when he was fourteen, and his marks were consistently well above average. He'd ended up in the Sixth Form College and his grades were good enough to get him a place at an Oxford College. Strangely enough it was the same college that Cassandra had attended.

He picked up the phone and called the university. Once again, he needed to get Martin to send them a formal request. He rang Martin up and explained what he needed.

'It should only take me a minute or so,' Martin said.

'There's one more thing, could you see what you can find out about Lawrence Taylor's work history and anything else about him that you might be easily able to access?' Mac asked. 'I'm sorry for dumping more work on you.'

'No problem, I'm not all that busy at the moment if I'm honest.'

'Why is that? Aren't you helping with the effort to break the code on the Al-Faran Clinic's computers?' Mac asked.

'They've let me have a look at what they're doing and it's fascinating but they've got a specialist team from the Met working on it. The encryption's a bit special from what they're telling me.'

Mac thought Martin sounded a bit wistful.

'Oh, before I forget, I do have some information for you about that pensioner that was killed in her own home,' Martin continued. 'If you remember you asked me to find out about Edith Dickinson's children and whether any of them had gotten divorced.'

'Oh yes, did you come up with anything?'

'Well sort of. A few years ago, Barry, her daughter Ellen's husband, suggested to her that they should have a trial separation but Ellen didn't agree. In the end she went for something a bit more permanent.'

'A divorce, I take it?' Mac asked.

'Not quite,' Martin said, 'she killed him. A kitchen knife in the stomach while he was asleep. She rang for an ambulance but the medical people reckon that she must have waited until there was hardly any blood left in him. She got life with a minimum of twenty years.'

'Well, I wasn't expecting that. Can you do me a favour? Tell Dan that if wants to close another case then it might be worth getting someone to speak to her. There's a chance that either she or her husband or both killed Ellen's mum, Edith Dickinson. When a couple are involved in a murder it can often put a strain on the relationship over time and that's why I was asking if any of Edith's children might have been divorced. Who knows but she might confess? It's not like she's got anything to lose.'

'Okay, I'll pass the message on. See you Mac.'

It took two more days before he received the college records for Lawrence Taylor. He'd studied English Language and Literature and ended up with a two-one. Mac smiled when he read a tutor's note stating that *'Lawrence has a first-rate mind and would have gotten a first if he could have stayed away from the pub once in a while.'*

Apart from going to the pub he was also part of a drama group that seemed to have gotten something of a reputation at the time. And that was it, Mac still hadn't found what he was looking for. Of course, it would help if he knew exactly what it was.

He was still thinking about the mysterious Lawrence Taylor when he received an email from Martin. He'd searched as hard as he could and could find no work record of anyone called Lawrence Taylor who was the same age and had the same birth date. He also checked with the benefits agencies and drew a blank there as well.

This really puzzled Mac. If he didn't work and he didn't draw benefits what did he do? Had he come into money and gone abroad or just changed his name? If he had changed his name then why? Most people who change their names do it because bad things have happened to them or perhaps because they've done bad things to others.

Mac was no nearer cracking the mystery.

He sighed, perhaps there wasn't one and he was just losing his grip.

He read through the college records again. He had his epiphany when he read Lawrence's full name on the very first page of the file.

Lawrence Nathaniel Taylor.

Oh, of course! Mac mentally kicked himself.

He smiled. The reason why Lawrence had changed his name was now crystal clear. Talk about hiding in plain sight.

He looked up some information on the internet and then sent off an email. He wondered how long he'd have to wait and what he'd do in the meantime.

Chapter Twenty Four

He didn't get a reply until the Monday afterwards. Mac smiled when he read it. Lawrence Taylor was coming to see him. At last he'd find out exactly what lay behind Cassandra Bardolph's mysterious utterances.

Mac had a think and decided that the less people who knew about it the better. He'd have to tell Amrit though, after all someone would have to open the door for him. He wondered how she'd take it. He told her the news after lunch.

'Oh, by the way we're going to have a visitor tomorrow but I'm going to have to ask you to keep it a complete secret.'

'I'm surprised that you'd even ask,' Amrit replied with a little look of disappointment. 'I'd never tell anyone about who comes here. Who is it?'

'Do you remember the Rafiq case?'

'Oh yes, the poor young girl who was stabbed by her brother.'

'Yes, that's the one. Well, there are some features of the case that still puzzled me,' Mac said, 'so I've managed to track down the young student who tried to save Asma's life by giving her CPR.'

Amrit's face crinkled with thought.

'Lawrence somebody, wasn't it?'

'Yes, Lawrence Taylor. Anyway, he's coming to see me tomorrow around mid-day and I'd like to keep the visit as secret as possible.'

'Why is that? Is he someone important now?' Amrit asked.

'Well yes, I think you could say that,' Mac said. 'He no longer calls himself Lawrence Taylor though, he changed his name.'

'Why was that?' Amrit asked. 'Did he become a criminal or something?'

'No, he became an actor. His full name was Lawrence Nathaniel Taylor so he changed it to…'

Mac left the sentence hanging. He could see the wheels whir round in Amrit's mind. He could see from her expression the exact moment when the penny dropped.

'You don't mean….no you couldn't mean…' she said. 'Not Nathaniel Bardolph!'

'You've got it. Yes Mr. Bardolph is coming to see us and I need to keep it quiet as possible so please tell no-one.'

'Just let me just check first that it's not some other Nathaniel Bardolph we're talking about here. You're talking about *the* Nathaniel Bardolph, the one who's the most drop dead gorgeous human being on the planet, the one who they're all tipping to be the next James Bond, the one who not long ago got the Oscar for best leading actor. That Nathaniel Bardolph?' she asked.

'Yes, that's the one.'

Amrit screamed and jumped up and down like a little girl.

'Oh, I absolutely love him! Just wait until I tell my husband…'

Mac shook his head.

'Well, my daughter, I've got to be able to tell her…'

Mac shook his head again.

'My friends?' Amrit asked trying to the last.

'I've promised that he can come here in complete confidence and I don't want a posse from the press greeting him at the front door. Remember that he's connected to a murder case and, if that got out, it might have quite an effect on his career.'

Amrit looked a little shame-faced as she said, 'I'm sorry Mac but Nathaniel Bardolph…okay, I'll keep it a secret even if it kills me and it probably will. However, I must make just one phone call.'

'Who are you calling?'

'My hairdresser. I need to beg her for an emergency appointment first thing tomorrow morning and the problem is I can't even tell her why.'

Mac let nothing slip about the impending visit that evening to Bridget or Tommy and hoped that Amrit had done the same.

Amrit was late the next morning and had to let herself in. Bridget and Tommy had already gone to work.

'Is this one of the new range of nurse's uniforms that I've been hearing about?' Mac asked.

Amrit was dazzling, literally. She wore a saffron coloured sari that had the most exquisite details on it and it sparkled as it was encrusted in sequins and sparkly stones. Her hair had been parted down the centre and a large hair decoration consisting of pearls and saffron coloured stones hung on her forehead. She had a wide jewelled bangle on each wrist. She looked like she'd just stepped out of a Bollywood movie.

'It's just something I threw on,' she said nonchalantly.

Threw on starting at five this morning, Mac thought.

For the next few hours Mac tried to concentrate on re-reading the case. The fact that Amrit kept coming in every ten minutes and checking that her favourite actor was still coming or asking how she looked didn't really help much.

At last a knock on the door was heard.

Amrit made no move towards the door, instead she looked at Mac with something like terror.

'Amrit, open the door.'

'It might be him though,' she said.

'I hope it is. Do I have to do it myself?'

She reluctantly left the room. A minute later a tall slim man with mid-length hair and designer stubble walked in followed by an adoring Amrit. Mac thought it a wonder that she didn't melt into a puddle on the floor.

However, even he had to admit that his visitor was very handsome.

'Mr. Bardolph, I'm Mac Maguire,' he said as he held out his hand.

He received a firm handshake back.

'Please take a seat and you too Amrit, you look like you need to sit down. This is Amrit my nurse, she's been helping me with my cases as I'm stuck in bed for a while. She can be trusted to keep this visit secret.'

Nathaniel sat down and looked at the floor. Mac gave him some time to think.

'So, what do you want to know?' he eventually asked.

'While I've been confined to bed, I've been helping the Major Crime Unit with some of their cold cases, one of which was Asma Rafiq's. I'm trying to make some sense of it but there are parts that I find a little puzzling. I was just wondering if you'd like to tell us what you can remember about Asma's murder.'

Nathaniel looked straight at Mac. His eyes looked bleary and tired.

'I knew this was coming. I've not been sleeping well lately, I've been having dreams, dreams about Asma. I haven't consciously thought about her for a few years now so I knew that there must be a reason. Then, when my agent told me about your email, I knew why. Where shall I start?'

'Tell me about you and Asma,' Mac asked softly.

'I loved her, Mr. Maguire, and she loved me. It wasn't a teenaged thing, it was real. I still love her now, even all these years later, but I didn't know that until recently. At the time we had to keep it all a secret because of her family, especially her brother. She was hoping that we could go to the same university and there we could have had a life together, far away from everyone, especially her family. That was the plan anyway. And then that morning it all fell apart. I felt her life literally slipping through my fingers and there was nothing I could do about it.'

'Why didn't you tell the police about you and Asma?' Mac asked.

'I honestly don't know. I can only think that I was in shock and we'd been so used to keeping everything secret, I suppose that it was like a reflex. I was in such a state I even gave the police the wrong address.'

'What was the address you gave?'

'My mum's house in Stevenage,' Nathaniel answered. 'I lived there until I was fourteen.'

'What happened when you were fourteen?'

Mac was interested as he remembered his poor attendance record at around that time.

'My mum died.'

'Oh, I'm sorry,' Mac said.

'Yes, so was I. She was as mad as could be but she was all I had, well almost all. I never knew who my dad was but my mum did have a partner she lived with on and off for ten years or so. She and Aunt Cassie really loved each other but, unfortunately, they split up the year before mum died. The year before mum killed herself. After that I had nowhere else to go and so I turned up on Cassie's doorstep one morning and she took me in. If I'm honest, I loved her almost as much as I did my mum and she had the added advantage of being rational most of the time. She provided me with the stability I needed and we got on well. I got my life back together, well sort of.'

'What was your aunt like?' Mac asked.

'Cassie? She was lovely, she fussed a bit but she looked after me well. She always made sure that I had everything I needed, especially when she was away.'

'Away? Where did she go?' Mac asked.

'All over the place, I remember some of the little gifts she brought me back; a Yankees baseball cap from New

213

York, a Juventus football shirt from Italy and a set of those little Russian dolls that go inside each other.'

'What did she do on these trips?'

Mac was really interested in what a woman who had no passport was doing travelling abroad.

'I'm not sure but she was an expert on mediaeval manuscripts and she said that she was hired to verify that certain manuscripts were real, that type of thing. She never really spoke much about it.'

At this point Mac glanced over at Amrit who was gazing wide-eyed at his visitor with a dreamy smile on her lips.

'What happened after you gave your statement?' Mac asked.

'The police gave me a lift home. I let myself in and sat on the sofa. I'd washed my hands but I could still see blood between my fingers. I started shaking and couldn't stop. Cassie came in, saw the blood on my hands and asked me what had happened. I told her about Asma and I said that I'd killed her, I said that it was my fault that she was dead.'

Mac could see the teardrops collecting in the corner of his visitor's eyes.

'Why would you say that?'

'Because I thought it was true at the time. I had a friend called Marcus, he was my best friend, still is. Well, a few days before Asma's murder we got our hands on some cider and got pretty drunk. Marcus started telling me that I should get myself a girlfriend and he kept on and on about it. So, I told him that I already had one and I told him who it was. I swore him to secrecy but when I saw Asma that morning I thought he must have told someone and that Youssef had killed her because he'd found out she was going out with me.'

'Why were you so certain that it was Youssef?' Mac asked.

'Because Asma had told me about his yellow trainers and how much they'd cost him. She thought he was silly. I knew it was him.'

'And you told your aunt this?' Mac asked.

Nathaniel nodded.

'When I told Cassie, she was afraid that Youssef might be after me as well. She said she knew exactly what to do.'

'And what did you do?'

'Cassie told me to shower and then pack a bag with a week's worth of clothes. When we walked to the car, I asked her why she didn't have a bag too but she said she'd join me later, that she had some work to do. We drove to Stevenage Police Station where I gave a formal statement. I nearly forgot to tell them my address again.'

'But you still didn't tell them about you and Asma,' Mac stated.

'No, Cassie told me not to,' Nathaniel replied. 'She said that it would be best to keep it a secret as it would only complicate things. My whole world had just imploded and I hadn't any idea of what to do about it so I just had to trust her. After the Police Station she drove me to a house in London. I'm not sure exactly where it was except that the street it in was in was a mews so I suppose it must have been somewhere central like Kensington. The house was right at the end of the cul-de-sac, it was small but very nice. She introduced me to a man called Caspar who she said would look after me until she got back. Then she left.'

'What was Caspar like?'

'Oh, he was in his late twenties I suppose, not tall but muscular. He always wore long sleeved shirts but I did see him once when he was washing, he had scars on his arms. I remember he was very light on his feet. He'd walk around the house and you'd never hear a thing. He was good company though. He was funny and he made me laugh a lot. Looking back, I find it strange that I could laugh but I suppose that I needed some sort of release.'

'Is there anything else that you can tell me about Caspar?' Mac asked.

'Well, the windows of the house looked straight down the street,' Nathaniel replied. 'There was only one way into the street from the road so you could see everything that came and went. Caspar spent a lot of time looking out of the window. Then there was the time he disappeared.'

'Disappeared? How?' Mac asked.

He was getting totally engrossed in Nathaniel's story.

'I don't know, I just know that he wasn't in the house. I woke up early the next morning and found that he'd gone. The house wasn't that big and I looked everywhere so I knew that he must have gone out. I sat by the window looking for him as the only way in was the front door. Then suddenly Caspar appeared behind me. He made light of it and I never asked him where he'd been. It was strange.'

'Was it just Caspar who looked after you?'

'No, there was another man who sat looking out of the window at night. He hardly said a word to me. He was tall and rough-looking. He also had a gun.'

'A gun?' Mac said in surprise. 'What type of gun?'

This was getting even more mysterious.

'I've no idea I only saw the grip when he bent down once. He had it in a holster under his armpit.'

'So, what happened then?' Mac asked.

'Nothing really. Caspar and I played a lot of video games, he was really good and beat me just about every time. Then a couple of days later Cassie came and took me away. We went to a five-star hotel and spent a week there. She took me to the theatre, believe it or not I'd never been to one before. We went to the Globe and saw The Tempest with Mark Rylance and that changed everything for me. I'll never forget that play, it mirrored my life as it was at that moment. I really felt as if I was lost and in the eye of a storm too. The actors were absolutely incredible, there were just the three of them playing all the parts and, while I was sitting there, I suddenly had the thought that I could do that too. We went and saw some other plays and it was good, it gave me a little time before I had to start processing Asma's death.'

'Weren't you worried about Asma's family, her brother?'

'No, Cassie said that I shouldn't worry about that,' Nathaniel said. 'She said that Youssef had left the country and that he wouldn't be coming back. She also said that none of her family knew about me, Marcus had kept it a secret after all. She said that Youssef had killed her because she'd refused to marry a friend of her uncle's back in Pakistan.'

'How did she know all this, did she say?' Mac asked.

'She said that she knew someone in the police.'

Mac doubted that even the police could have any certainty about whether or not Youssef Rafiq would ever return at that point. So how could she possibly know that?

'Is there anything else you can add?' Mac asked.

'Not really. After we returned from London I went back to school and tried to keep things as normal as possible but it was hard. I was so glad when it was time for me to go to university, a fresh start with people who didn't know my story. I had my bad times there too I suppose and drank too much but, then again, I was a student so hopefully no-one noticed. Cassie was so good to me when I told her that I wanted to try acting. She gave me enough money to last me three years, without that I'd have never made it.'

'When did you notice that your aunt was having problems?' Mac asked.

Nathaniel frowned. It was obviously something he didn't want to think about.

'I didn't, she noticed it herself. She told me that she'd stopped working because she'd been having problems remembering. She told me that it was Alzheimer's and that she'd been almost expecting it as her mother had contracted it when she was only forty-eight. I got her the best treatment I could and it seemed to help a little at first but then she got worse, much worse. I took her over to the States for some new treatment but that didn't work either. In the end her doctor advised that the best we could do for her was to find somewhere where she'd be looked after until she died. There was no hope. The retirement home was recommended to me and, it being in Letchworth, I thought that I'd be able to visit her every now and again.'

'But you didn't,' Mac said.

'No, I didn't,' Nathaniel admitted. 'I could say that I was busy and make excuses but it wasn't that. Cassie had always been so, I don't know, full of life, her own person. I'm sorry but I'm not explaining it very well. I visited her at the hospital before she was moved to the retirement home and, while her body was there, she wasn't. Her eyes were blank and I knew that, whatever it was that had made Cassie the person she'd been, was gone. Although her body was still breathing, the Cassie I loved was dead. I just couldn't bear to see her like that.'

'I can understand that,' Mac said. 'Thank you and I'm sorry for bringing this all up for you again but you've clarified quite a number of points that have been puzzling me. I won't be writing any sort of a report about this and, as I promised, what you've told us won't leave this room.'

'Thank you, Mr. Maguire,' Nathaniel said. 'I can't help thinking that for some reason I needed reminding about Asma. The dreams I've been having have cert-ainly done that and it's been unexpectedly good to talk about her and what happened. She was lovely, beautiful yes, but there was a lot more to her than that. She had this fierce intelligence and quick mind, the discussions we used to have about religion, politics, science, books. I was nearly forgetting about all that. I realise now that, ever since I lost her, I've never been really close to a woman. Oh, I've used them I suppose, the papers will tell you that I've had a different woman every night. That's not quite true but it's not that far off, I suppose. Then, not long ago, I met this girl. She's not one of the film crowd, she's a writer. She was brought in at short notice when our regular script doctor fell ill. She's just like Asma. I mean she doesn't look much like her but she has the same sparky intellect and fearlessness that Asma had. She didn't care in the slightest about me being a film star, all that meant nothing to her. We were close for a while before I pushed her away just as I had all the others. I know why now. It was fear. I was afraid of investing too much in one person because that person can always die. You shouldn't live in fear though, should you Mr. Maguire?'

'No, no you shouldn't,' Mac said.

'Thank you. I think it's done me good to talk about it after all this time. It's given me a lot to think about.'

With that Nathaniel Bardolph shook Mac's hand and then followed Amrit out into the hall.

Amrit came back a minute later beaming from ear to ear, 'He kissed me on the hand, Nathaniel Bardolph kissed me on the hand. I shall never wash it again.'

Mac thought she was taking it a bit far until she winked at him.

'Cup of tea?' she asked.

'Most definitely.'

Chapter Twenty Five

Mac whiled away some of his time by going through the remaining cold cases but made no headway with any of them. As his pain slowly started to recede, he actually started reading some of the books that Bridget had bought him.

However, there was an event that broke the monotony. He had another visit from Dan Carter and he looked very pleased with himself.

'Two more wins Mac! The only problem I'm going to have is that my boss might start expecting this all the time,' Dan said with a big smile.

Mac was puzzled.

'Let me explain, Mac. I did as you suggested and I went over to the prison and interviewed Ellen Dickinson personally. I eventually pried out of her the reason that she killed her husband. He'd lied about his wife being with him when her mother had died and Ellen was afraid that, once he was out of her control, he might spill the beans. Apparently, she and her mother had a blazing row, not unusual so she said, but this one went a bit too far. She picked up a statuette, it was solid metal so quite weighty, and bashed her mother's skull in with it. She then took the statuette home, washed it and put it on her mantelpiece if you can believe that.'

Mac gave this some thought.

'Her brother and sister, Robert and Eloise, knew too, didn't they? Neither of them mentioned that the statuette had gone.'

'Well, Eloise is saying nothing but Robert admitted as much,' Dan said. 'They'd all painted a rosy picture of a happy family but from what Robert told us his mother was not a nice person. She took delight in playing her children off against each other and had been quite cruel to them when they were young.'

'What was the statuette of?' Mac asked out of curiosity.

'Elvis, Edith was mad about him apparently.'

Mac could only smile and shake his head.

'You said you had two wins?'

Dan's smile returned.

'Yes, and it was thanks to all that ringing around you did a while back. Well, a couple of days ago, just outside Edinburgh, a young woman's car broke down on a country road. Unfortunately, her mobile phone's battery was dead so she tried to flag down a passing car for help. Does this sound familiar?'

'Terri Maynard!' Mac said feeling suddenly excited. 'Go on.'

'Well, someone stopped to help her, a courier van for a firm that worked out of Edinburgh airport. The young woman, Danielle Goldfisch, stated that the man seemed helpful enough at first but then pulled a box cutter from his pocket and held it to her throat. He said that he was going to rape her.'

'She lived to tell the tale then!' Mac said with surprise.

'Better than that, just listen. So, he had the box cutter at her throat and, luckily for her, it caused a small cut. Unluckily for him Miss Goldfisch happens to be a Tae Kwon Do champion, in fact she's been trying to get into the national Olympics team so she must be pretty good. Anyway, a few seconds later the man, a Mr. John Oldson, is in a heap on the ground with a broken wrist and a shattered kneecap. She used his phone to call the police and when they turned up Mr. Oldson started screaming blue murder about how she'd attacked him. However, the injury to Miss Goldfish's neck and her blood being on Mr. Oldson's box cutter confirmed her story. They were going to charge him with attempted GBH when one of the officers remembered your phone call. So, they got a sample of Oldson's DNA and sent it to us for comparison. I just heard an hour ago that we've got a match for Terri Maynard's murderer and so I thought I'd come and tell you.'

Mac's smile couldn't have been wider.

'That's great news. I was so sure that he would do it again. It was just bad luck that led to Terri Maynard's murder in the first place but it looks like it was the murderer's turn to have bad luck this time. A Tae Kwon Do champion! What's the odds on that?'

Dan's news kept Mac's spirits up for quite some time. However, the days still passed too slowly but 'Freedom Day', as Mac was beginning to think of it, eventually came.

Surrounded by an audience consisting of his doctor, Bridget, Tim and Tommy he sat up and then tried to stand. It felt strange and thankfully not as painful as he'd expected. The doctor told him to take it easy as he'd need to build up his muscle strength again. It was unexpectedly wonderful to just sit in the garden and look around him, the grass was an incredibly luxurious green and the flowers were in bright technicolour. It was as though he was seeing it all for the first time.

One morning Kate joined him in the garden. She'd popped by to say goodbye as her attachment had ended with the Whyte case and she was going back to work at Hatfield station. Although she brightened up when they discussed the case, Mac couldn't help feeling her sadness and he wished he could do something to help her. She seemed totally adrift at the moment and Mac made sure to get a promise from her to keep in touch.

He still found it incredibly hard to walk more than a few steps at first but he gradually got better and, while he had spikes of pain every now and again, it was never quite as bad as it had been.

Just over a week after this he received an excited phone call from Amrit.

'I can't believe it Mac! I'm walking on clouds but what shall I tell Prem?'

'I'm sorry Amrit but what on earth are you talking about?'

'My invite, haven't you had one?' she asked.

Mac asked her to hang on while he had a look at the post. There was a fancy looking envelope which he opened up. It contained an invite to the premiere in London of Nathaniel Bardolph's latest blockbuster film. Not only that but it was an invite to the VIP area so they'd get to meet all the stars of the film too. Mac could see Amrit's problem, how could she possibly explain this without letting the cat out of the bag?

'What about a competition? Can we say that we were bored and jointly entered a competition in the paper? What do you think?' Mac asked.

'Yes, that could work. Oh, Mac it was so nice of him to remember us, wasn't it? Who are you going to ~~bring~~? take' she asked excitedly.

'No-one.'

There followed a few seconds of silence.

'No-one, you're not going then?'

He could hear the disappointment in her voice.

'No, I'm going to give it to Bridget and Tommy, it's the least I can do. They'll enjoy a night out in London.'

'Ah, that's such a nice thing to do. We can all go together then. Tell her to ring me and I'll book the hotel. Oh Mac, I can't wait!'

Bridget and Tommy were so happy when Mac gave them the invite. It made him happy just seeing their excitement. They thankfully didn't ask for too many details about the fictitious competition so he didn't have to lie too much.

It was more than three weeks before Mac was allowed to drive by himself. The first place he went to was the retirement home. He rang Mrs. Collins and made an appointment to see Cassandra Bardolph. He was curious and wanted to see her for himself.

She was much smaller than he'd expected, only five feet five or so, and he wondered if she'd shrunk. Her face was still smooth and unwrinkled and she didn't look her age. She sat in a chair blank eyed and unmoving. He spoke to her but it got no reaction whatsoever. He sat and looked at her and wondered. What he'd been thinking seemed impossible and yet he couldn't get the notion out of his mind. She was a conundrum.

This small woman, an expert in mediaeval documents by all accounts, had at very short notice been able to get her adopted nephew into a safe house and provide what sounded like professional guards around the clock. Guards with guns come to that. The house was situated at the very end of a mews, a street with one entrance so anyone coming in and out could be seen. From what he'd learned it looked like the house also had a secret back entrance, a means of escape possibly? A safe house then. It sounded like a very professional set up indeed.

She had no apparent means of income yet she could afford to buy top of the range sports cars and find enough money to fund Nathaniel for three years. She also travelled a lot yet she had no passport. How was that possible?

What had she been doing when Lawrence was in the safe house in London? And how could she be so certain that Youssef Rafiq would no longer be a problem?

Mac had all these questions rattling around his head yet he knew that they were never going to be answered and this annoyed him. The answers were somewhere in her head, locked away for good.

He sat back and sighed as he realised that they might not even be there anymore, that they might have all been swept away by the dementia that was slowly dissolving her brain. He could fully understand why Nathaniel hadn't wanted to visit his aunt. She was alive, breathing and eating but there really was no-one there.

He popped in and saw Emily on his way out. She was doing well on her computer programming course and had started writing little games. She showed him one and Mac was very impressed. She also bemoaned the fact that her beloved Brentford hadn't made the play-offs last season. However, she brightened up somewhat when she pointed out to Mac that they had finished above Aston Villa.

Mac stood on the pavement outside the retirement home and wondered what to do next. Remembering his favourite saying, 'If in doubt go to the pub' he rang Tim, who was all for an early session, and then Eileen his favourite taxi driver. By the time he got home she was waiting there for him.

She dropped him outside the Magnets. Then he saw Nathaniel Bardolph's face in the window of the newsagent's opposite so he went over to have a look. It was one of those popular women's magazines that specialised in film and TV stars, their diets, homes and so on. The headline read –

'Nat gets engaged and breaks all our hearts.'

He went in and bought a copy. Apparently, Nathaniel had proposed to a girl called Julie Planter who was a writer and they were now engaged. It explained how they'd met on set after she'd replaced a scriptwriter who'd fallen ill.

It appeared that Nathaniel Bardolph had conquered his fear after all. Mac smiled and wished him and his fiancée all the luck in the world.

Tim had managed to occupy their favourite table, number thirteen next to the window, and Mac had the sudden feeling of slipping back into a warm and comfortable rut. He told Tim all about the case and his theories and how frustrated he was at not being able to know what had really happened.

'Oh well,' Tim said with a grave expression. 'We should just be grateful for the things that we do know, the deep truths that form the very bedrock of our lives.'

Tim's unexpected seriousness intrigued Mac.

'Such as?' he asked.

'Knowing when it's your round,' Tim said holding up his empty glass.

Mac laughed out loud and went to the bar.

Thank God for Tim, he thought.

Twelve years earlier

Cass felt that she'd been more than lucky to have been at home that morning and not away on a job. She'd been in the kitchen when she heard the front door open. She grabbed a knife and held it behind her back as she tip-toed into the living room.

It was only Lawry though but something was really wrong. He just sat there shaking and looking at the back of his hands. She looked and could clearly see blood in between his fingers. He was in a terrible state and it took her a while to find out what had happened to him. As soon as she fully grasped the situation, she started thinking about what to do.

While Lawry was in the shower, she made a few phone calls and called in a few favours. She'd leave him with Caspar and Mikel for a day or two in the London house while she worked on a solution. He'd be safe there.

She realised how much his safety mattered to her. She'd loved his mother more than anyone in her life and had only split up with her when she knew that she'd go down with her too if she stayed any longer. Her happiest moment was when Lawry had turned up at her door looking for somewhere to stay. She'd never thought of having children, it wasn't part of her game plan, but Lawry was like a gift. She would protect him, whatever it cost.

She made sure that Lawry made a formal statement to the police and gave them her mobile number explaining they were going away for a few days. The policeman was very sympathetic. After she dropped Lawry off in London, she returned home and started planning. She found out where the Rafiqs lived and started watching the house. Youssef went out around eight to the pub and met up with six or seven of his friends. Some of them commiserated with him about his sister but one or two looked at him very strangely.

They know, she thought.

They all decided to go to a nightclub that evening and Cass knew that this was her chance. She went home and put her make up on and a dress which showed off her cleavage to advantage. She was over forty now but she knew that she'd pass for much younger. She'd have no problems there especially when he had his beer goggles on. She hid in a corner of the club and watched him intently.

It was past one and Youssef was weaving towards the door when she intercepted him. She asked him if he wanted a ride and made it clear that there might be much more than that involved.

He didn't say no. She told him to meet her around the corner in a few minutes. She didn't want them to be seen together as there were CCTV cameras covering the entrance to the club. She'd worked out on her way into the club that there was a blind spot in the camera coverage and she made sure she left taking the same path.

She saw his eyes go wide when he saw her car.

'Wow, is this really yours?'

'Of course,' she said as she unlocked the BMW.

'Can I drive?' he asked. 'I've always wanted to try one of these.'

She smiled indulgently at him.

'Not now, you've had a drink, but, if you're nice to me, tomorrow perhaps.'

Another inducement for him to go with her. He didn't hesitate and climbed in the passenger seat. She didn't drive fast but she made sure that her hand rubbed his leg when she changed gear. He smiled at her and grabbed her crotch.

A subtle lover then. She managed to smile back while he did this.

She turned off her headlights when she drove into her street. She didn't want the neighbours knowing more than they should. She pressed a finger to her lips before she got out telling him that he should keep quiet. He smiled and did the same back to her.

She opened one half of the garage doors and ushered him inside. She shut and locked the door behind her and then turned on the light. Youssef could see that the garage was empty and that the floor was covered with a plastic sheet. He briefly wondered why. He then saw the door that led into the house.

'I take it the bedroom's this way?' he said smiling as he pointed towards the door.

'I'm afraid that this is as far as you go, Mr. Rafiq,' she said flatly.

He watched her as she threw her bag into a corner. Then she took her shoes off and threw them into the same corner. Drunk as he was it took him quite a while to realise that she knew his name even though he'd never told her what it was.

'Oh, come on, don't change your mind now. We could have such fun,' he said.

'Oh, I'll have fun Mr. Rafiq but I'll guarantee that you won't like it.'

He couldn't make out what was happening. She'd totally changed, her face looked different as did the way she walked.

'What's going on here?' he asked somewhat belatedly getting that a night of sex might not be why he was brought here.

'You killed your sister and I'd like to know why,' she said in a matter-of-fact way.

He looked surprised at this.

'No, I didn't,' he said. 'And anyway, what's it to you?'

He had no idea what was happening. He looked around half expecting to see someone else.

'There's just you and me here, Mr. Rafiq, and you haven't answered my question.'

'Go to hell,' he shouted and made towards the garage door.

Cass blocked his way.

'Oh, the evening isn't over yet although I forecast that it will be a very short one for you,' she said.

It sounded like a threat but this just confused him more, she was a woman and almost a dwarf at that without her heels.

'Let me tell you something then,' Cassie said. 'I have a nephew, he's more like a son to me really, and he's really upset.'

'And what's that to me?' he shouted at her.

'It was you that upset him. He loved your sister and she loved him. They were going to go to university and then live a life together. You ended the dream for him and, because of that, I'm now going to end you.'

That was definitely a threat. He looked around again but they were still alone.

'And how are you going to do that? Have you got some six foot gorilla hidden away somewhere?'

'Why is it that you men always think that women can't do anything without having to have a man around. Haven't you heard, Mr. Rafiq, that sisters are doing it for themselves these days?'

He made to go but she blocked him again.

'So, why did you kill her then?' she asked. 'Did you know about my nephew?'

'No, I didn't but I do now and he'll be next. He can join that whore in hell.'

It disconcerted him when she only smiled at his threats. She knew that it would help if she could get him angry.

'So, if it wasn't him what was it? Was it the arranged marriage or was it really because you fancied her yourself?'

She'd only thrown that out to rile him but she could see from his face that she'd hit the jackpot.

'Yes, that was it, wasn't it? You wanted to shag your own sister and when she wouldn't you killed her and then you call it an 'honour killing'. My God, you men can be such hypocritical bastards.'

'Bitch,' he shouted as he took a swing at her.

She evaded it easily. She needed to get him as angry as possible so she hit him in the face. He shot her a look of pure hatred as he pulled a sling knife from his pocket. He locked the blade and started slashing out at her.

She was amazed at his stupidity. He actually had the knife with him. She smiled as she had already thought of a very good use for it.

He wasn't all that good with a blade and she easily ducked out of the way. All he was slashing was fresh air and it made him even angrier. He was ready for her now.

After one wild lunge she ducked under his arm and grabbed his wrist with her right hand as she did so. She swivelled around and then pulled his arm straight so the elbow joint was fully locked. She then brought the heel of her left hand down on the locked out joint with all the force she had which was considerable. With some satisfaction she heard the elbow joint shatter just before he let out a scream of pain. The knife fell to the floor and she kicked it towards the wall.

While he was still screaming, she went behind him and caught hold of his left wrist, pulled the arm straight and shattered that elbow joint too. He turned pale and stopped screaming, the pain was just too great.

She kicked out at the back of his legs causing him to collapse into a kneeling position. She quickly wrapped her legs around his waist and her arms around his neck before throwing her weight backwards. Their combined weight had now trapped his legs and his arms were useless.

'Now, listen Mr. Rafiq because this is important. This is called a choke hold and it's called that because I'm going to use it to choke you to death. However, before you go, I just wanted to tell you one thing. You may not believe it but God is a woman. However, this is something that you'll be able to confirm for yourself very soon. I'd also like to tell you that she has a special room in hell for men like you. Goodbye, Mr. Rafiq.'

She increased the pressure and held on for longer than she probably needed to. She then let go of her hold a little, just enough to check with her finger for a pulse in his neck. There wasn't one. She released her hold and got out from underneath him. She checked his wrist for a pulse. He was dead. She straightened his legs and moved his arms by his side.

She looked down and smiled at a job well done before going over to the corner and retrieving her handbag and shoes. She took her car keys out and put them in a plastic bag. She sealed the bag and placed it near the wall. She put the handbag and the shoes on top of Mr. Rafiq. She then stripped completely and put her clothes and underwear on top of the corpse.

She folded the plastic sheet on the floor around the body and wrapped it tightly. She got a roll of duct tape from the rear of the garage and folded the ends of the plastic over until it resembled a spring roll. She secured the plastic sheeting with the duct tape. She then wrapped the plastic in the old carpet that lay beneath and sealed that too with the tape. She cut off the last piece and placed the roll of tape inside the flap before sealing the package with the final piece of tape.

She dragged the carpet towards the wall and then placed tins of paint and odds and ends in front of it. It just looked like an old roll of carpet.

Naked, she opened the door to the house and put some flip flops on that were by the door. She made straight to the shower and scrubbed herself, making sure that every little trace of him was gone. She dried herself and then changed into a black track suit and black trainers. She still had work to do.

She drove back to the Rafiq's house. It was now nearly three o'clock in the morning. She climbed over the back fence. There were no lights on. She noiselessly walked towards the back door. It was just a standard lock and she had it open in seconds. Using a small but powerful torch she found the stairs and went up. All the doors were shut except for one. She put an ear to the shut doors and listened. She could hear the sound of people sleeping.

She opened the other door slowly and peeked inside. It was empty. This was obviously Youssef's room. She started looking around when she heard a noise. She rolled herself under the bed and waited. A few seconds later the door opened and she heard a woman's voice say something that she couldn't understand. The door closed again.

Probably his loving mother wondering where he was, she thought. She wondered if this particular mother had loved her daughter too.

She waited until she was sure that the woman would have gone back to sleep. From her vantage point she could see that there was a loose floor board just under the bed. She rolled herself out and had a look. Under the floor board there was a stash of porn magazines. Cass smiled as she pulled out the knife. She opened the plastic bag and dropped the knife into the hidey hole. She then replaced the floor board leaving it slightly askew so that it would be easier to notice if there was a search.

She found a sports bag in the wardrobe and started filling it with clothes. While she was putting in some socks she came across his passport.

Perfect, she thought as she threw it in the bag. He had a wash bag containing shaving gear and deodorant and that went in too. She zipped the bag up and attached a clip to the handles. The clip was attached to a long roll of thin rope. She opened the window and carefully lowered the bag to the ground then dropped the rope too. She shut the window and, before she went, she placed some print-offs from a Jihadi website in the back of his sock drawer.

She tip-toed back down the stairs and then locked the kitchen door behind her. She retrieved the bag and the rope and went back over the garden fence.

She smiled. Yet another flawless job.

There was just one more thing to do before she could get some well-earned sleep. Turning the lights off again she rolled the car noiselessly into her driveway and waited for a while. She got out, locked the car and then kicked it before running into the house.

She could hear the alarm squawking as she ran up the stairs. She put on her bedroom light and opened the curtains. She then put a white dressing gown on over the black track suit and slowly made her way down-stairs. She wanted to give it some time and make sure that the neighbours were well awake.

She walked outside and turned off the alarm. She looked up at the Ballard's bedroom next door to see Mrs. Ballard looking out at her. She smiled and waved at her before going back inside.

Perfect.

She slept well and woke when the alarm went off at nine. She knew that Mrs. Ballard liked to be in her garden early in the morning. She put on her 'librarian' outfit, a flowery dress with a cardigan that didn't quite match, and walked outside. There she was pulling weeds. She came over as soon as she saw her.

'What was all that about last night, the alarm and everything?' Mrs. Ballard asked with some concern.

'Oh, I'm not sure. I didn't sleep all that well last night and I thought I heard noises outside. I opened the curtains and looked outside and there were two men, young men I think, both dressed in those black hoodie things. They were looking at my car. I turned on the bedroom light and they ran off but they must have touched the car as they went and that set off the alarm,' she explained.

'Oh, my dear,' Mrs. Ballard said in horror, 'aren't we even safe in Letchworth? You should tell the police.'

'Well, there's no damage so perhaps they were just looking.'

She left it at that.

She made a few calls and then went back to bed. She'd need the sleep as it would be another busy night.

A soon as it was dark, she drove the car into the garage and placed Mr. Rafiq in the boot along with his sports bag. She then placed two plastic covered items inside the car in the back passenger well. She drove to an industrial area in North London, to a scrapyard where they melted down waste metals. She'd been here before.

'Miss Green,' a man in a soiled boiler suit said, 'it's been a while. How are you?'

'I'm very well thank you. As this is a special job there's a little bonus in there for you,' she said as she handed him a thick envelope.

'As generous as always,' he said as he tucked the envelope into an inside pocket. 'Well, I need a cigarette so I'll see you later.'

The man walked off. She knew where everything was. She got the pallet truck and raised it up to the height of the boot and rolled the carpet onto it. She then placed the sports bag on it too. She rolled it towards the conveyor belt that ran into a furnace. The furnace was white hot and she could feel the heat energy on her skin as she rolled the carpet containing Mr. Rafiq onto the belt. She placed the bag on it too and stood and watched as they both disappeared into the fire. In a few minutes she knew that Mr. Rafiq would be reduced to a scum on the surface of the metal pool. She thought that this was highly appropriate considering the kind of man he'd been.

She returned the pallet truck to where it had been and waved goodbye to the man on her way out.

She drove back home and sat in the car and waited. It was eleven thirty when she went over to the house and smashed one of the little windows in the porch. She went back to the car and drove off at speed with no lights on.

The tyres squealed as she took the corner. Someone was driving towards her so she seized the opportunity and flicked the car towards them causing them to swerve.

They won't forget that in a hurry, she thought.

She then turned on the headlights and made for the motorway. She smiled. She was really going to enjoy this.

She'd picked her route carefully. She wanted a good stretch of fast road with cameras towards the end. She wanted to finally see how fast she could get the car to go. She hit eighty going on to the motorway and was well over a hundred a few seconds later. She got up as high as she could and whooped out loud as the speed-ometer reached one hundred and fifty. A succession of speed cameras flashed at her.

She reluctantly left at the next exit and made her way down increasingly narrow country roads to the spot she'd selected. It was a sort of layby and she'd selected it because it had been used before for the same purpose. She took the two plastic packages and placed them behind a bush further up the road. She opened up the bonnet and got two plastic bottles from the boot. They contained liquid fuel for barbecues. She was following a previous MO to the letter.

She sprayed most of the first bottle in the boot and the rest inside the car on the seats. The second bottle she sprayed on the hot engine, it immediately burst into flames. She threw the bottle into the fire and walked away. She took a fresh purple track suit out of one of plastic bags and changed. She put the old tracksuit into the bag and waited. It only took a minute or so before there was a loud 'Crump' as the fuel tank exploded. She knew that there was little chance of anyone coming immediately as the spot was so remote so she went back to the car and threw the plastic bag into the flames.

She had now removed all traces of Youssef Rafiq.

She unzipped the other bag and opened up the foldable cycle. She then cycled away from the burning car. About a half a mile away there was a bus shelter. She sat there in the darkness until it was light enough then she mounted the bike and started back towards home. She arrived not long after six and went in through the back garden.

She was hungry so she ate a leisurely breakfast and then got changed into her librarian outfit again. Just before nine she went outside and started crying. Mrs. Ballard came straight over.

'What is it dear?'

'My car, it's gone!' Cass exclaimed. 'They've broken my window too.'

Mrs. Ballard phoned the police and they were very nice when they arrived. It all sounded very familiar to them. They asked Cass if she kept her car keys in the porch.

She nodded, 'Yes but I always keep it locked.'

'What they do is smash a window and then use a probe with a magnet on the end to snag your keys, like fishing really. Once they've got the keys they're away. If it's who we think it is then I'm afraid that you might find that your car has been burnt out,' the policeman said with mournful expression.

He was of course right and her car was found a few hours later just where they expected it to be.

Cass wondered what she could do in London to make Lawry feel a bit better. She thought about this as she drove to the city in the hire car that had been provided by the insurance company.

The cinema perhaps? No, he could always go to the cinema in Letchworth, it had to be something special. The theatre maybe?

Yes, that sounded good, she thought.

She wondered if he'd like it.

THE END

I hope you enjoyed this story. If you have please
leave a review and let me know what you think. *PCW*

Also in the Mac Maguire series

The Body in the Boot

The Dead Squirrel

The Weeping Women

The Blackness

Two Dogs

The Match of the Day Murders

The Chancer

The Tiger's Back

The Eight Bench Walk

You can find out more about me and my books by
visiting my website –
https://patrickcwalshauthor.wordpress.com/

Printed by Amazon Italia Logistica S.r.l.
Torrazza Piemonte (TO), Italy